It was supposed to be a milk run . . .

The autocannon rounds struck her weary 'Mech everywhere at once. She reeled backwards under the impact, almost losing her footing. Warning lights flared, indicating lost weapons and internal damage. Her *Quickdraw* was dying all around her, and Hawke knew it. She fired what she had left, a barrage of lasers and short-range missiles that miraculously found their mark on the Jager-*Mech*, killing its forward charge like a stone wall.

"Heimdall, what's your twenty?"

"Three minutes twenty-seven seconds out, Lantern One. Hang on."

Hawke concentrated on her breathing, mopping sweat from her forehead. Droplets of blood still stained the inside of her blastshield. It no longer mattered.

She knew she'd be dead soon anyway.

MechWarrior

By Blood
Betrayed

Blaine Lee Pardoe
and Mel Odom

A ROC BOOK

ROC
Published by New American Library, a division of
Penguin Putnam Inc., 375 Hudson Street,
New York, New York 10014, U.S.A.
Penguin Books Ltd, 27 Wrights Lane, London W8 5TZ, England
Penguin Books Australia Ltd, Ringwood, Victoria, Australia
Penguin Books Canada Ltd, 10 Alcorn Avenue,
Toronto, Ontario, Canada M4V 3B2
Penguin Books (N.Z.) Ltd, 182–190 Wairau Road,
Auckland 10, New Zealand

Penguin Books Ltd, Registered Offices:
Harmondsworth, Middlesex, England

First published by Roc, an imprint of New American Library, a division of Penguin
Putnam Inc.

First Printing, November 1999
10   9   8   7   6   5   4   3   2

Series Editor: Donna Ippolito
Cover Art: Chris Moore
Mechanical Drawings: FASA Art Department

 REGISTERED TRADEMARK—MARCA REGISTRADA

Special thanks go out to my agent, Ethan Ellenberg, and also Bryan Nystul, Mel Odom, and Donna Ippolito. Thanks to Annalise Raziq for her patience when having to send each file to me, one at a time.

I want to acknowledge the contributions of the real-life Gary Hershorin and Mary Sutcliffe, whose names I blatantly stole and used. Gary is not a bad guy, really. And it was just a lucky guess about the mustache. My cousin Bill Gilbert is the source of Davis Gilbert. My nephew Jeremy Lewis is the grizzled sergeant. Jody Glancy is, well, Glancy.

Dan Plunkett and Cullen Tilman—we are gods!

Also thanks to all of my friends who put up with me while I worked on "the chair" during the writing of this book. The last pass was written from my new writer's perch—a refinished and restored B-52 downward-firing ejection seat, now converted for office use. Despite the constant ribbing from everyone about every aspect of this project—this seat rocks! Writing about 'Mech combat from a real-life command console was awesome. If I could only get that PPC wired in. . . .

—B. L. Pardoe

This book is dedicated to my wife Cyndi, my children, Alexander and Victoria, Sandy (arf!) Maroo the Wonderdog, and, as always, my alma mater, Central Michigan University. It is also dedicated to the fans of BattleTech out there who enjoy the fiction, the fights, and the intrigue.

Also, to the other authors who write BattleTech. Is this fun or what?

—B. L. Pardoe

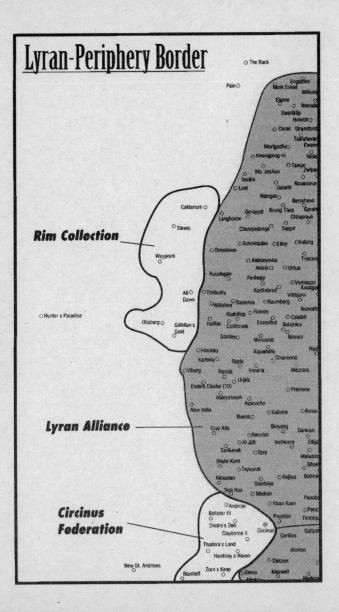

Lyran-Periphery Border

The Rack○

Pain○

Engadine○
Main Street○ Willkung○
Elume○ Neeraba○
Swartklip○
Howick○
Canal○ Strandtront○
Tsalhanavar○
Ewann○
Moriguchic○ Müller○
Kwangeong-ni○
Tainjin○
Zwipeo○
Ma'anshan○
Issaba○ Houasseur○
Lost○ Qanatir○
Niangol○
Baryshevo○
Qurayyat○ Krung Thep○ Garahr○
Langhorne○ Chhaprauli○
Champadanga○ Sappir○
Ammindav○ Ettler○ ○Kelang
Ormstown○
Triestin○
Alekseyevka○
Aklala○ ○Virtue
Ferihegy○
Pucologan○ ○Vermezzo
Kostinbrod○ Kvistgaa○
Vintijarvi○
Timbuktu○ Sapienza○ Kaumberg○ Ixuneato○
Wiltshire○ Firenze○ Calafell○
Kladnitca○ Enzesfeld○ Balajnica○
Halifax○ Coldbrook○ Novara○
Stanley○ Mercades○
Aiguebelle○ Rigil○
Hinckley○ Chiaverina○
Karksila○ Rapta○ Venaria○ Mezzana○
Viborg○ Floridit○
Ender's Cluster (10)○ Urjala○ Premana○
Aberystwyth○
Ayacucho○
New India○ Valloire○ Aorux○
Buera○
Binyang○ Daroian○
Revivim○ Inchicore○ Ettija○
Al Jafr○
Sankavak○ Ilzra○ Maisons○
Shahr Kord○ Bilces○
Teyvarob○ Rajkot○ Bobruf○
Althastan○
Song Hoa○ Stantsiya○
Madirun○ Penobs○
Andiron○ Khon Kaen○ Pence○
Baltazar III○ Poulsbo○ Timbiqu○
Diedre's Den○ ⊙Circinus Galisin○
Clayborne II○ Cerillos○
Thadora's Land○ Alorton○
Hardisey's Haven○ Dalcour○
New St. Andrews○ Blantleff○ Zorn's Keep○ Sierra○ Maxwell○ Madera○

Rim Collection —
Caldarium○
Slewis○
Waypoint○
All○ Dawn
Hunter's Paradise○
Otisberg○ Gilfillan's○ Gold

Lyran Alliance —
Cruz Alta○

Circinus Federation —

1

Birdsong Ridge
Caldarium, Rim Collection
The Periphery
15 January 3059

"Owlflight One, this is Lantern One," said Lieutenant Livia Hawke, but Billy Wallace didn't answer. That was worrisome. She checked her *Quickdraw*'s primary and secondary displays once more. Sensors picked up no enemy movement in the area, but the other two BattleMechs of her command lance lit up clearly on her head's up display. Ditto the infrared scans and the magnetic resonance checks that usually sniffed out fusion reactor signatures of nearby 'Mechs. The terrain was just too damn difficult for accurate readings.

Her company was advancing under radio silence while Billy Wallace in his *Jenner* scouted up into the hills for some sign of the pirates. He was supposed to signal via a burst-transmission blip.

Just a friendly knock to let her know he was still ambulatory. But he hadn't.

Where was he?

The long wait ate at her nerves like ants crawling on her skin. Hawke glanced up from the secondary display and out into the night through her cockpit's polycarbonate viewport. She tried, but couldn't shake the uneasiness that gripped her. She and the rest of First Company continued forward slowly, hoping Wallace would signal any real trouble before the rest of them stumbled into it.

The terrain of Birdsong Ridge, with its steep cliffs and rugged hills covered with tall trees and dense undergrowth, was deadly to 'Mechs. Battle-Mechs could climb, but it took a lot of skill to keep one upright under these conditions. Not to mention that visibility was almost nil. The pale moonlight rendered the landscape in near 2-D to the unaided eye. Even the *Quickdraw*'s IR scanners struggled to keep up with the changing geoforms. Some of that was the terrain, some of it was that Hawke's 'Mech was an older model. Out here, among the far-flung planets of the Periphery, there wasn't much of the newer tech.

Old tech, new tech, to Hawke it didn't make much difference. A 'Mech was only as good as the MechWarrior at its controls. Besides, the locals reported only three to five pirate 'Mechs in the raid on Porth some weeks ago. The odds were with her. She and First Company would roust them with ease. Able's Aces had been protecting the struggling worlds of the Rim Collection for the last dozen years. It was what they got paid for.

Major Able himself would have been at the

head of this pirate hunt, except that Hopper Morrison's band hit a munitions plant on Waypoint shortly before the major's departure for Caldarium. He had reassigned the mission to Livia Hawke, and took off for Waypoint instead.

Pirate raids were a fact of life in the Periphery, but Morrison's Extractors were notorious for being as merciless as they were greedy. "King" Hopper Morrison and his band had been making a name for themselves lately, and they now claimed two worlds in nearby space. Morrison had christened them Pain and The Rack, and had dug in so fiercely no one could blast him out.

The Aces had been keeping them at bay, but their three battalions were spread dangerously thin over the six worlds they defended. Morrison and his band had only grown bolder, brazenly proclaiming their identity before hitting Waypoint and destroying two 'Mechs and killing sixteen personnel. The attack was so in your face Major Able was sure its real aim was to cast doubt on the Aces' ability to protect the Rim planets.

Hawke had fought them herself on Otisberg, and had a souvenir scar ten centimeters long and four centimeters across at its widest point from a recent skirmish. Each time Morrison struck, he drove more of a wedge between Able's Aces and the Council of Planets that ruled the Rim Collection.

Hawke stabbed the key to open the commline. Her blood was up thinking about Morrison's band and she was out of patience. "Lantern Two, this is One."

"Go, One," Benjamin Rassor said in his calm voice.

Despite the tension, Hawke smiled even as she scanned the night. Benjamin was ever the professional. Aggressive and quick, he was always eager for the chance to get into the cockpit of a bigger and better 'Mech. His ambition and drive were among the reasons she'd taken him as a sometimes lover. He could be passionate by night, but never blur the lines of command that separated them in the outside world.

"Stand ready, Two," Hawke said, taking the control joysticks. "We're going to recce the area and try to find out what happened to Owlflight. If things turn sour, we're going to need the back door."

"Affirmative, One," Benjamin replied. "We're standing hard here. Good hunting."

Hawke rocked against the cockpit's restraint straps as the leg and hip actuators pushed the sixty tons of 'Mech into a walk. The *Quickdraw*'s cruising speed was fifty-four kph, too fast for the terrain under existing conditions.

"Raptor One, this is Lantern One," she called.

"Acknowledged, Lantern One, you have Raptor One," returned Lieutenant Jon Jamison, commander of the company's aerofighter lance. Its two SPR-H5 *Sparrowhawk*s were equipped with medium and small lasers and speeds that made them choice first-response attack craft.

"I want a fly-by, Raptor One," Hawke said. "A full sensor array over a five-klick spread from my mark. Do not engage unless fired upon and you can identify the target. We've got a unit down somewhere out there."

"Not to worry, Lantern One," Jamison said. He

was a careful, capable pilot, and as brave as they came. "Raptor One is the angel on your shoulder."

Hawke swept the terrain again with her sensors, more uneasy by the minute. With the 'Mech's onboard programming and vids, she got a full 360-degree view on her head's up display, but the HUD compressed it into a 120-degree arc. Learning to maneuver using the compressed full-scan had been one of the hardest things to master in her training.

She did a quick check of her target interlock circuits and her weapons. The *Quickdraw* carried two medium Omicron 4000 lasers at the end of each arm and two more on its back. A Delta Dart long-range missile ten-rack was mounted on its left torso, and a Hovertec short-range missile quad occupied the 'Mech's chest cavity. She knew the *Quickdraw* and its weapons like the back of her hand and felt much better as the pre-heat and load lights on her tactical display showed her armed and ready.

She opened the commline to her command lance. "Crosby."

"Here, Lieutenant," Crosby replied.

"We're moving in. I've got point and Amos is walking slack. That leaves you the middle."

"Affirmative, Lieut. Waiting around like this was about to drive me out of my gourd. Kicking butt's what I signed on for."

Hawke watched Leonid Crosby's *Dervish* step out from the copse of trees he'd been using as cover. Crosby was impulsive and quick-tempered. If he weren't such a damn good MechWarrior who knew how to deliver fire-support in the heat of the battle, Major Able would surely have busted him down through the ranks and put him out on the street by now. As it was, Crosby usually ended up pulling extra duty as punishment for infractions, or fined. Or both.

Behind him, Derrick Amos moved his *Orion* into position. "Ready," he said in that whispery, soft voice of his. Amos was something of an enigma around the barracks. No one knew much about where he was from or what he'd done before joining on, nor did he seem inclined to tell. That was all right with Hawke, because the one thing she knew about Amos was the only thing she cared about. She could always count on him in a fight.

"Move out," she commanded, working her own joystick and foot pedal controls, pushing the *Quickdraw* up to cruise speed. Right now she had to find out what had happened to Billy Wallace and his *Jenner,* even if it meant she and her command were walking into the jaws of a trap.

She glanced up and saw Raptor Lance's two *Sparrowhawk*s sweep in on her right flank. At the same instant there was a brilliant double flash in the air. To a civilian, it might have looked like a bolt of bright blue lightning. To Hawke, it was something much more sinister—particle projection cannon, and more than one of them. Bad news, very bad news.

She reached for the communications controls but too late. Swarms of missiles arced up at the already-damaged aerofighters as they reeled under the PPC attacks. She heard Jamison scream in her neurohelmet's ear piece, then a long, extended hiss abruptly cut off his death wail. The missiles slammed into his fighter, which exploded in a ball of fire.

The other *Sparrowhawk* attempted to bank, trying to evade the attack. Bright amber laser lights lanced upward, slicing into its wing. Neither pilot had time to eject. Hawke was sure neither had survived. In a matter of seconds her company had suddenly lost one-sixth of its firepower.

"Lantern One to all personnel," she called over the commline. "They knew we were coming. Fall back to your perimeter markers immediately!"

Hawke's voice boomed into her neurohelmet's microphone, but all she heard back was the irritating hiss of static. Jamming. The pirates had let the Aces wander into the rocky crags of Birdsong Ridge, then had cut them off from the rest of the universe.

They'd walked straight into a trap.

2

Birdsong Ridge
Caldarium, Rim Collection
The Periphery
15 January 3059

The plan had been for Livia Hawke and her force to climb up to Birdsong Ridge, which extended some two hundred kilometers east to west, from the east. Ben Rassor and his lance of four 'Mechs would approach from nearly twenty kilometers to the south, then would cut west and climb to the ridgetop along a narrow defile. The two forces would reach the top of the ridge from opposite sides at the same time. Ben's lance would draw the raiders' attention to the flank while Hawke swept down from the high ground with the bulk of their force.

It was supposed to be a milk run, but the plan had gone up in smoke along with Raptor's fighters.

Hawke continued to sweep the area with her sensors. Tailing mounds, tall piles of earth and rejected ore fragments left over from the planet's heavy mining days, stood in twenty-meter cones throughout the area. Low scrub and stubborn weeds grew among them. Her heart pounded in her ears as she frantically moved forward, searching for an enemy, any enemy.

"Lantern One!" Crosby bawled in warning, cutting through the static. Her tactical display lit up with the target at the same time she heard his cry. The computer identified the KTO-20 *Kintaro* coming at Hawke a nanosecond after she recognized it herself. It stood more man-shaped than many, with a wide-legged stance and broad feet.

The *Kintaro* had taken cover behind a tailing mound, with its left-arm SRM launcher extended and locked from less than two hundred meters out.

Still moving, knowing she didn't have time to get the other 'Mech into her field of fire, Hawke pushed the *Quickdraw* forward. A short-range missile streaked from the *Kintaro*'s arm, the burning propellant flaring out in a dazzle of fire that blotted out the 'Mech. The missile whooshed by Hawke, missing her by centimeters, then impacted against the tailing mound behind her.

The warhead detonated on impact, blowing free tons of rock and debris. A huge boulder bounced off the *Quickdraw*, straining the 'Mech's gyro system and Hawke's skills to keep it upright. The impact battered the 'Mech's armor plating, its force ripping some of the plates completely off. Dust filled the air, obscuring the viewscreen and choking down the 'Mech's filtration units, which whined loudly as they compensated. BattleMechs were designed to work in any kind of environment, from the vacuum of space to underwater, but that did not mean they were indestructible.

Then the second wave of debris and rock struck as the mass blown into the air began to rain down.

Hawke worked her 'Mech's foot pedals furiously, scrambling for footing, cursing loudly inside her neurohelmet as she fought the lateral control joystick. Smelling blood, the *Kintaro* pounded after her, its slimmer design giving it an advantage in maneuvering between the tailing mounds. She saw the markings on its torso in the distance.

Morrison's Extractors.

Hawke twisted the *Quickdraw*'s hand lasers to the side and switched her target interlock circuits to bring all four lasers on-line with the same trigger. She swept the area, searching for a lock as the *Kintaro* skidded around a tailing mound. It brought its right arm up, leveling both lasers as well as its left-arm SRM. The puffs of smoke from the missile rack flared as she hit the trigger.

Hawke fired all four lasers, hoping she had enough of a lock. The *Kintaro* returned fire, its heavy laser stitching across her vulnerable rear armor. Heat rushed over Hawke, and the warning klaxon screamed as her 'Mech pushed closer to overheating. The *Kintaro*'s SRM salvo buried itself into her right leg and hip, grinding metal and shredding armor plating in a massive blast.

The concussive wave slammed over the *Quickdraw* and knocked it off balance. The gyro whined as her neurohelmet tried to use Hawke's own sense of balance to compensate. Despite her skill, the hip and leg actuators couldn't overcome gravity. She went down.

Knowing she couldn't stop the fall, she stretched out the *Quickdraw*'s arms to lessen the impact. They tore into the earth, digging a trench a meter deep and nearly ten meters long before she could stop. The impact threw Hawke against the restraint straps in the cockpit, promising bruises in the days to come—assuming she lived that long. She was thrown forward, and her neurohelmet thudded against the Mech's viewscreen. Blood from her split lip smeared the inside of the helmet's shield when she sat back.

She grabbed the joystick again and rocked it hard side to side, clawing her way to a standing position. Checking the HUD's compressed view, she saw the *Kintaro* standing behind her. Her 'Mech's stats rolled beneath the screen, letting her know that the combined laser blast and near-miss from the SRM had peeled sixty-two percent of her rear armor away. Light on armor to begin with, she couldn't take another direct hit from behind. She turned quickly, hoping the *Quickdraw*'s ankle actuators still held together.

The *Kintaro* had staggered back. The pilot had backed off the attack, probably surprised at the four lasers lashing out at him. Enough of Hawke's laser fire had hit his left arm to set off its SRM ammunition supply. As she watched, the missiles reached critical heat and blew, rupturing the arm and blowing it free of the *Kintaro*'s torso.

In the distance, she saw three of her fellow Acers engaging enemies hidden by rocks and debris. Lasers and autocannon rounds that missed lit up the shadows of Birdsong Ridge as she struggled to survive. The tactical display was flashing, telling her an even worse story. Her people were starting to drop, their 'Mechs destroyed or crippled.

Hawke didn't let up, operating on pure reflex and survival instinct. She brought the forward lasers on target again and fired an SRM from her chest the instant she heard the audible tone of a target lock. The missile punched into the *Kintaro*'s center mass. The armor kept it from actually penetrating, but as off-balance as the *Kintaro* already was, the explosion knocked it off its feet. Hawke brought the lasers on-line as the pirate 'Mech fell backward. She struggled to keep it in her targeting reticle, waiting for that perfect shot that would finish her foe.

Burn lines lit up across the *Kintaro* as she sprayed her ruby lasers over it; the ferro-fibrous armor had fragmented. The pilot flailed the 'Mech's one remaining arm and tried to get up. Suddenly the hissing in her ear stopped. Somehow the jamming had been silenced. Instead she heard the screams and shouts and curses of her company. This was a trap, and her people were getting pounded.

"Livia!" Ben called over the din of the battle on the commline. "We're under fire and outgunned. I've lost Rivenburg, Nelson, and Fuller. I'm pulling back." Hawke had never heard this panic in Ben's voice.

"Benjamin, extract your lance. Fall back to the second perimeter waypoint," she ordered. Then she opened a wide-beam channel to the rest of her company. "Aces, we're booking out of here. Lantern Lance, take the rear guard. Owlflight on the right flank, Raptor on the left. Fall back to the staging area. Withdraw and provide cover fire."

There were usually two ways out of any trap. One was to try to punch through it, the other was the way you came in. Hawke had ordered the latter, but with the high ground of the ridge above them, she knew it wasn't going to be easy.

Just then, the *Kintaro* slowed enough to give her a target. Blasting away with her lasers, she wasn't sure if this would be enough to tear the 'Mech's head off, but it was sufficient to activate the cockpit ejection system. She saw the pirate 'Mech's huge head come apart as the cockpit blew out. Reacting quickly, she tried to bring the forward lasers on-line with the cockpit, almost achieving a lock before the cockpit and pilot hit the tailing mound behind him. Off-balance as the cockpit was, it ejected into the mound instead of into the air the way it was supposed to.

Cockpit and pilot broke and came apart.

Hawke turned from the downed 'Mech immediately, knowing it no longer presented a threat. She checked her *Quickdraw*'s systems reports. The cockpit heat levels had spiked, thanks to her running and use of the SRMs and the lasers so close together. The air inside the cockpit felt thick as a swamp in the summer. Hawke knew it would have been even worse if she hadn't stripped down to the shorts and tank top most MechWarriors adopted to deal with heat even their cooling vests couldn't vent away.

"Ben, what's your twenty?" she asked, then saw Crosby's 'Mech lose its right arm to a laser salvo. She darted her *Quickdraw* back to get a firing angle on his foe.

"There's too many of them. Oh my God—th—" Ben's voice broke off.

Her eyes cut to the tactical display and saw that his 'Mech was down and flashing on the overlaid map. She had no time to absorb the information. The man she loved was either dead or near death. She moved to assist Crosby, but as his burned and battered *Dervish* turned, a PPC blast devoured him in a ball of fire. Her whole body tensed in the explosion, and she continued to fall back.

"Heimdall, this is Lantern One," she called through gritted teeth.

"Lantern One, Heimdall reads you five by five."

Heimdall was the lead *Leopard* Class DropShip that had brought The Hawke's Talons to Caldarium. Hawke's mind raced, sorting through the possibilities. She kept the *Quickdraw* moving backward over the uneven terrain that tossed her around in the cockpit. "Heimdall, execute emergency exfiltration Alpha-Alpha-Seven."

"Heimdall copies, Lantern One. We're on our way."

Hawke wondered if the DropShip would arrive in time or whether it would simply fly over and see the dead remains of her command sprawled among the rocks of the ridge.

An Extractor *JagerMech* locked onto her at the same time Hawke spotted it. It was built like a man hunched over, with high-riding shoulders and head sunken into its chest. Both arms ended in the blunt snouts of General Motors Nova-5 autocannons that belched a rapid series of muzzle flashes. The pulse lasers mounted on either side of its torso flared to life as well, getting ready to spit crimson death.

Hawke triggered the *Quickdraw*'s jump jets, venting compressed super-heated air through its legs. The 'Mech rose to vacate a space that was suddenly filled with pulse-laser beams and an autocannon salvo of high-explosive armor-piercing rounds. Several rounds slammed into her already battered legs, taking with them the tiny bits of remaining armor and mauling her 'Mech's myomer muscles. Another ripple of heat rose in the cockpit as the jets did their work.

Propelled fifty meters into the air, Hawke searched frantically for a safe place to come down. She'd feathered the jets, setting herself up to land behind a tailing mound to buy herself some more time. For a few moments it almost worked, but her 'Mech's left leg seemed to drag, cutting her speed.

Damn, she thought. Actuator damage. She saw another Acer 'Mech move behind her cover mound, dropping back as well. The black and gray *Orion* bore pockmarks from missiles and worse damage to its torso from laser scarring.

"Amos," she called. "Cover the right. I'll take the left."

A barrage of missiles from a nearby pirate *Trebuchet* cut off her order from ever happening. The missiles enveloped Amos' *Orion* in a ball of orange and crimson flames, and it crashed near her. The vibration of its impact shook her in her seat. And then she heard the warning signal of the *Jager-Mech*'s weapons locking onto her.

The autocannon rounds struck her battered 'Mech everywhere at once. The *Quickdraw* reeled backward under the impact, almost losing its footing. Warning lights flared, indicating lost weapons and internal damage. The *Quickdraw* was dying all around her, and Hawke knew it. She fired what she had left, a barrage of lasers and short-range missiles that miraculously found their mark on the *JagerMech*, stopping its charge forward like a stone wall.

"Heimdall, what's your twenty?"

"Three minutes twenty-seven seconds out, Lantern One. Hang on."

Hawke concentrated on her breathing, mopping sweat from her forehead. Droplets of blood still stained the inside of her blast shield. It no longer mattered. She knew she'd be dead soon anyway.

Fire away, you bastard, Hawke thought. She'd lost everything she cared about anyway. First Benjamin, now her command. The time for retreat was over. She changed direction and began to charge forward, bringing every ounce of firepower and energy her mangled *Quickdraw* could muster against the *JagerMech*.

There was an eerie silence in her mind as she moved. She charged into the *JagerMech* at a trot, which was the most the *Quickdraw* could manage right now. The two 'Mechs collided, and she felt a wave of heat and heard the rumble of explosions. She didn't remember hitting the ejection seat control, but she knew she must have. There was a ripple of cool air, a ringing in her ears, a feeling of weightlessness, and the roar of explosions.

She hit hard. After that, she didn't know anything at all.

3

Outside Thorpe
Slewis, Rim Collection
The Periphery
26 February 3059

From the journal of Harley Rassor:

I'm not much of a writer. But with all that happened tonight and early this morning, I think it's best to start putting the words down. Maybe it will help me understand, or at least sort it all out.

At eighteen, I'm tall, with Da's height and broad shoulders, and built lean. But I knew from the holos Da kept of her that I had Ma's black hair, green eyes, and darker complexion. Ma died shortly after the birth of Jolee, my youngest sister. Of us all, Ben was the only one who truly remembered much of Ma. He was six years older than me, but he talked less of her than Da.

What happened tonight made me wonder what Ma would think of me now.

The plan, the killing, was Da's. He and I are not murderers, nor are our neighbors. He's got a temper, though. I've felt Da's back hand and black wrath when on occasion I came dragging home too late to properly tend my chores. Usually I'd been with Ben, my older brother, who'd already stepped out from under Da's wing. Da had come down on me the harder for it when Ben decided to join up with Able's Aces. I think he worried I might go too. I was seventeen then and of an age to do what I wanted. I stayed because I knew Da needed me, and I wasn't sure I wanted a bigger world than Thorpe, or even Slewis.

Some nights, though, I felt those stars calling out to me.

I wish they'd called me before tonight.

I was hidden up in the branches of a cathbaal tree when one of the trader reps walked under it to relieve himself. He never got out of sight of his friends, and I knew he feared what might be waiting in the forest around him.

I didn't know if he'd spotted me, so I drew my hunting knife from the sheath on my hip just in case. The sheath had been crafted by my brother Ben from ultethian leather, supple as silk and quiet as a whisper. The trader rep never heard it come free. If I had to, I knew I would kill him and then vanish into the forest. But that was not the plan.

I felt my heart thumping in my chest, the quicker rhythm telling me my body was ready for any sudden demands on it. I clenched the hunting blade in my fist and breathed quietly through my teeth as I watched him.

He was a big man, standing nearly two meters

tall, with a beard-stubbled face and hard eyes the color of off-worlder steel. He wore russet and gold DropShip coveralls, stained and patched, showing the emblem of the independent trading combine he repped. I guessed him at his early forties, probably about the age of my Da, but the trader rep was a harsh man and I knew Phelyn must have feared him.

Anger raced through me as I thought about what he and his companions had done to her and the other two girls in the village, and how afraid those girls must have been then. And how afraid they still were. I'd seen them, and I didn't think I'd get the sound of their pain-wracked voices from my mind.

I banked my anger, pushing it aside so I could concentrate on why I was here. Da had taught me that. I'd gotten my temper from him, he said, so he felt responsible. The trader reps deserved what they were going to get and I had no mercy for them. It really wasn't murder, it was justice—that's what Da and the others said. They said it a lot during the planning. I believed it too. When taking another life, you have to believe such things.

The rep kept the automatic rifle gripped in one hand while he tended his business, glancing over his shoulder to where the other five men waited nervously. They all carried rifles as well, which was why we stayed back while following them. They knew something was up, but they had no idea what was in store for them.

By choice of its people, Thorpe was a low-tech community. Once there'd been mines and high-tech processing plants, with tunnels blasted through the hard rock, snaking deep into the earth. The ore was dug out, then shipped by rail down the mountains to the processing plants in the foothills. Factories had turned the ore into metals, and then pressed and shaped the metals into components to be shipped off-world on DropShip transports. When the ore petered out, the factories and the combines that owned them had gone too.

Those left behind had to rebuild their way of life. Now we're an agri-based community, and nothing means more to us than our family and farms. Farms can be replanted. Families are forever.

Lately, in the years since the formation of the Council of Planets, Thorpe and a few of the other communities had become efficient enough to produce enough wheat and soy beans to do some limited bartering with the trader DropShips that moved through the Rim Collection. Most of them, like the one these reps worked for, were licensed by the Council of Planets and countersigned by Able's Aces. Even then, not all of them were good men.

"C'mon, Hackett," one of the other reps called out. "We ain't got all night. Those rubes in Thorpe ain't goin' to just let us walk out of here if they can help it."

"I'm coming, I'm coming," Hackett said. He tabbed up the front of his coverall, then trotted back to his friends. "Damn native beer, goes right through a man."

"Better hope it's the beer," another one said as they started moving again, "and not some quick-acting STD you got from those whores back at Thorpe." His harsh laughter echoed through the forest.

I also drew my bow then and put an arrow

through the man who'd said that. Phelyn was a friend, and I knew the other two girls as well. They weren't whores, just girls who'd been drawn too close to wild and savage men by the stories they told and the C-bills they flashed. It had happened before to girls in Thorpe, but it had been a long time since. I let out my breath and stayed my hand, remembering Da's words that it was better to get them all than to let any of them escape.

"If you'd kept the damn Packrat guarded," Hackett complained, "we wouldn't be walking out here in the middle of this frigging forest."

"We never needed to guard it before," the other man replied. He walked into an open space under the canopy of trees, and the moonlight slanted across him for the briefest moment. I recognized him by the ridge of hard scar tissue over his eyes. He was Jenkins, the rep in command of the team. He hadn't led the men in their attack on the girls, but he'd joined in.

I was the one who'd disabled their vehicle. It was an old Packrat LRPV—Long Range Patrol Vehicle—but the trading combine had retooled this one as a cargo transport. It was nothing compared to the way Ben and I had managed to get that old *Commando* stored on our property up and running. We'd worked on it together, and then he taught me how to pilot it. It was a pile of junk that wouldn't have lasted ten minutes in a battle, but it was ours and I learned how to handle it as well as anything.

Da never said a word about it to us. I understand why now, and I'd disabled the reactor in less than two minutes. Now the reps had a long walk back to town, on trails where we were posted, where we planned to carry out their deaths.

I wore my hunting leathers of soft black ter-rig hide that I'd made myself and sewn into a sleeveless tunic and breeches. Jolee had helped with the stitching. She'd been trained by Dama Elaine, Thorpe's finest seamstress, whose handi-crafts were always the first to be picked up by the trader reps.

My leathers might not have been much to look at by conventional standards, but they served my purpose well, blending me into the night. The sneak suits I'd seen while training in the militia were much better, but my hunting leathers and my knowledge of the terrain put me almost as close to that level of invisibility.

The crashing of the trader reps through the brush took a turn I hadn't expected. The game trail forked, and I'd thought they would stay with the more traveled off-shoot. I altered my own course, mirroring theirs on a lower parallel. They weren't totally stupid. The secondary trail provided a straighter path to Clowster's Crossing and the ferry Belloq maintained there.

I ran, leaping over boulders and fallen trees, not-ing ones I could harvest later for winter. Slewis' wintering pattern was going to be harsh this year. Then I focused my thoughts on the hunt again.

Da was always after me about my wandering mind, but he knew the worth of it too. Sometimes I thought of things others hadn't seen, details oth-ers had missed. I had a curious mind, which he said wasn't all that much worth to a farmer. Ben had always been more focused on getting what he wanted. The Drive—that's what Da called it. That was one of the reasons Da hadn't tried hard to talk him out of joining Able's Aces when the opportunity had come.

I didn't worry about the noise I made; it was slight against the racket of the trader reps, and I knew they'd never hear me. I followed the line of the hill up, avoiding the snare of dead branches clustered in a pile near the ridge. At the ridge line, I peered through the gloomy shadows and spotted the silhouettes of the trader reps going down into the next dip. They passed single-file, pressed closer together than they had been before.

A vetchin broke ground cover, its four wings beating the air furiously as it fled in fear from its roosting spot. It had a meter-wide wingspread that made plenty of noise. All the reps but one, a man named Brewster, hit the ground. I'd met Brewster before, and remembered his shape and gait. I watched him, seeing him move smooth as whipped butter as he brought his automatic rifle up and around.

The vetchin exploded into a mass of feathers and blood a heartbeat later. There were no sounds of shots, which told me Brewster had outfitted his weapon with a silencer. With that advantage, he could fade into the forest's shadows and pick off the farmers and herdsmen who were trailing him in search of vengeance for Phelyn and the other girls.

The familiar chill of fear touched the back of my neck and slid down my spine when I thought of the men who had volunteered for this. All of them were known to me, and most were friends.

The other five reps got to their feet warily, the air foul with their language. One laughed.

I started to shift, then I felt a gust of wind settle in behind and beside me. Gazing back over my shoulder, I saw my sister Jolee sitting behind me, hiding in the brush as I was.

She was fair-haired, like my brother Ben, who is so like our father. Her face was heart-shaped, and her clear, bright blue eyes were usually full of mischief.

"What?" I asked her.

"They've veered from the path," she whispered.

"I know."

"Da wants them turned back or slowed. He needs a few more minutes."

Exasperation filled me. "Did he offer any suggestions about how I'm supposed to do that?"

She shrugged, as only Jolee could. I'd seen her break the hearts of young men with that shrug. "He said you should use your own judgment. They're waiting in the clearing. We've got to slow them until he's ready, keep them in the open."

" 'We?' " I asked.

"Da told me to stay with you. Once you turn them, he doesn't want to take the chance they'll overrun me in the forest."

It made sense, but I knew the risks too. And I was sure Da had considered them. Me taking care of Jolee like that and him trusting me meant a lot. Da is a miser when it comes to praise, but when you got it from him, it carried a lot of weight.

"Okay," I said, "but you're going to do what I say when I say."

"Sure."

She agreed so quickly it surprised me. "Look, Harley," she added softly, "being opinionated doesn't always equal stupidity."

"Right," I said, knowing from the sound of the reps crashing through the brush that time was moving against me. "Four meters back of me, and if we start running, stay to the brush and head for Thorpe. I'll be at your heels, so don't make any sudden stops."

She nodded, and those blond curls bounced. I nodded back, then I broke into a run, stretching my legs out, eating up ground. I listened for Jolee, heard her following at the agreed upon distance.

Then I slid my compound bow from my shoulder, drew three arrows from the quiver on my right thigh, locked two in my left hand with the bow, and nocked the third. I held the bowstring and the fletchings of the arrow easily in three fingers once the break-over was achieved.

I took aim, let out half a breath, and loosed the first shaft. I was pretty sure this would slow them down until Da and the others were ready.

4

From the journal of Harley Rassor:

I wouldn't want to die by an arrow wound. You bleed to death slowly and painfully. It's not quick.

I wasn't aiming to kill, simply to get their attention. For the man I hit in the hip, however, that must have been of little consequence. He howled like a wounded dog. Then he pulled out the shaft. I could make out even from a distance that he'd ripped more of his hide in the process. I almost felt sorry for him, then I remembered what they did to those girls. My friends.

Brewster and the others were already in motion when I loosed the second shaft. He went low, taking a moment to examine the arrow and assess the direction from which the attack had come. They fired. Lots of bullets at first, but Brewster stopped them. He suspected something more than just my sniping attack.

I was in motion, staying low to the ground, breaking away beyond the ridge and seeing Jolee in motion too. She kept a tree between her and the trader reps the whole time. Bark ripped from the tree where I'd taken cover, scattering splinters over my head, back, and shoulders. Their shots were getting more deliberate.

I changed tacks again, charging up another incline. I fitted the third arrow to the bowstring. They followed me, which is just what I wanted. Da had said to slow them down. I was doing just that.

The angry and frightened hollers of the trader reps filled the air just before the harsh crash of their automatic rifles blasted the quiet. The diurnal creatures sleeping in the nearby surroundings woke suddenly and, in a cacophony of noisy fear, erupted into motion, increasing the confusion surrounding them.

"Hold your fire, dammit!" another of the men ordered roughly. I think it was Hackett. It doesn't matter now after what happened to them a few minutes later.

"To hell with that!" one of the others shouted. "They've got us surrounded!"

"Run out of bullets," Brewster barked back, "and you might as well send them an engraved invitation to come get your ass!"

That sobered them up for a moment, and they started to listen to him.

"Those rubes don't have rifles like these," Brewster said. "We've got enough ammo to hold them back until we get to the DropShip."

They were trying to take control of the initiative. My militia training and gut feelings told me that I couldn't allow that. So I loosed the shaft. It flew straight and true, burying deep into the backpack worn by the man called Hackett. I put it in from the side, not wanting to chance it passing straight through whatever items he might be carrying. The arrow struck something hard enough to yank the backpack and make Hackett stumble for a moment.

The sight of another arrow was enough to throw them into a panic. The fear had them now, running them like animals. There was safety in numbers, and they'd all been around enough to know that.

Knowing what lay ahead of them, I felt a twinge of sympathy, but I only had to think of Phelyn, remember her shattered face, to make myself go numb again to any sympathy I might feel for the men. I rose, beckoning to Jolee.

"I hope Da is ready. We have to move quietly," I whispered when she reached my side. "One of them might hang back to cover them."

"I know, Harley." Her tone was a little sarcastic.

I ignored it, remembering how I'd been at her age. She'd joined the militia last year when she was fifteen too.

After giving the trader reps a good head start, I took out three more arrows and fisted them with the bow so they'd be ready. Then I went after them, cutting through the forest and running parallel to their heading, staying closer to the river in case they decided to head back that way.

Two hundred meters further on, I was breathing easily, a fine layer of sweat building under my hunting leathers. The trader reps were running on adrenaline-laced fear; they wouldn't stop until it burned out of their systems.

I caught a few glimpses of them, but they didn't see me, I made sure of it. Seventy meters after that, they reached Crysto's clearing, a wide, empty spot in the forest where the rocky underpinnings shoved up through the soil and left a hard stone surface where nothing could grow.

Waving Jolee to shelter behind me, I broke across their backtrail, shouldered the compound bow, and grabbed the lower branches of the trees just as I heard hard bone striking the stone floor of the clearing. I peered through the tangles of branches and leaves, watching as the herd of ulteth suddenly shouldered through the low branches of the trees in front of the trader reps.

Da and the others had herded the flock together, fed them wildweed, which made them meaner. Now they were drunk, mad, and hungry . . . for flesh.

I didn't know if the men had seen ulteth before. But I knew the effect seeing them the first time had on a person. I've read that ulteth resemble Terran deer in appearance, only much larger and possessing a predatory meat-eater's diet instead of a herbivore's. If ulteth caught a man or woman all alone out in the wild, they'd run him or her down, then strip the flesh from their bones and eat it. Experienced men like Da and those with him knew how to handle the beasts, keep them at bay, until the time was right.

The ulteths knew no mercy, and Da had judged them as part of the penance the trader reps would pay. The wildweed would only make them fiercer.

There must have been three dozen ulteth breaking cover, erupting across the hard stone on their keen-edged hooves. They stood two meters tall at the shoulder, with a short, wiry-haired hide the color of antique silver that had been powder-blacked. Their treacherous horns ·were black as coal and twisted in a wreath of points. Moonlight kissed their eyes, igniting green fires. Their breath gushed out in gray fog.

Filled with blood rage, the ulteth raced at the trader reps. Hackett stood his ground stupidly, raising the automatic rifle to his shoulder. He managed one short burst that ripped bloody blossoms across the chest of the lead animal, probably penetrating the lungs.

The ulteth never even stumbled even though now it was trying to outrun death. It lowered its thick, muscled neck and caught Hackett with the cruel horns, pushing deeply into the man's flesh. A keening howl of pain tore free of Hackett's lips as the ulteth lifted him off his feet. The animal carried him forward easily, a metric ton of hide-covered fury that wouldn't be denied.

Four of the trader reps tried to run, but they got no further than a few steps. The ulteth's hooves flashed, cutting them down where they were. Dark blood spilled across the grass and underbrush, easily seen by a hunter's trained eye.

I gave the men a brief glance, knowing at once that they wouldn't be getting back up. The line of men with Da came out of the woods behind now, blades and bows in their hands. There shouldn't have been any survivors.

"Harley," Jolee called.

But I'd already seen what she was pointing out

as the ulteth ran under the tree I'd climbed. One of the men broke ranks and jumped into the brush. He had thrown himself to the side, burrowing deep into the thorny havil plants to escape the ulteth. There's no way he could have known how much the beasts despised the rash they got from contact with havil. That's what Da and the others had used to contain the herd. Then he was through the other side, running and falling down the hillside toward the river.

I dropped from the branches and launched myself after him, not thinking at all that I might be rushing to my own death.

The survivor was Brewster, and he ran like his life depended on it, moving through the trees and brush rapidly, a shadow flitting among the others. He was good, much better than the other reps had been. But he was still not a true part of the forest around him.

I was.

I shucked my bow and the quiver of arrows, marking the spot where I left them. The bow was a gift from my Da, given to me five years ago to acknowledge my ability to help stock the family larder.

The arrows were mine. I'd earned them hunting, and splitting wood, and whatever other task I could work at. Alloy shafts are expensive; always imported from off-planet, and usually not one of the mainstays of a trader's manifest. I had to pay nine or ten times their real cost to own them, but wooden shafts were hard to lathe and never lasted.

I kept Brewster in sight with difficulty, using peripheral vision to track his movement. Stare at a man in the moonlight and he'll disappear, lost in the trick of light and shadows.

Sweat coated the inside of my leathers, and they were starting to stick to my skin. I felt hot, my body heat trapped inside the waterproof garments.

I ducked, leapt, and sprinted through the trees and underbrush. I kept my elbows pumping and lifted my knees high, concentrating on breathing out rather than breathing in. I drove my boots hard against the ground, automatically feeling when the ground was soft and making adjustments. Being a good shot with the bow didn't always guarantee an instant kill. Sometimes I had to run an animal to ground, hurrying because the blood spots left behind would dry and disappear. Part of it was because I didn't like the idea of anything suffering, but neither did I want to lose my prize.

Brewster's silhouette stumbled and recovered quickly. But I knew I had him. Despite his skill and his speed, he didn't have the endurance to make it to the river before I overtook him. I knew it wouldn't take long for him to realize that, and when he did, his focus would change.

Less than a hundred meters further on, Brewster stopped in a clearing. He spun quickly and brought his automatic rifle to his shoulder, creating an unnaturally hard line of shadow that identified the movement for me.

I threw myself forward instead of sliding. I knew from my militia training that a corpsman was taught to begin shooting at the feet of a target, then ride the recoil upward. Divots exploded out of the ground behind me as the bullets dug into the dark earth.

I stayed in motion, hugging the ground and shoving my elbows against it to drive myself forward. A swath of bullets cut the leaves and branches from the brush over my head. I didn't think about dying; I never do. If I did, I'd have put my bow up for sale and stayed home. Every time I went into the forest for game, it was all or nothing. Ben had crafted the knife sheath I carried, but I'd taken down the ulteth it was made from.

The darkness masked my approach and I moved carefully, not making a sound. I breathed in through my nose and out through my mouth, focusing on the breath. Da had trained me to be calm. A breathing man was a thinking man, and a thinking man was steps ahead of one who didn't think.

The trader stopped firing and shifted in the clearing, taking advantage of the cover offered by the trees. He kept moving, peering into the darkness, because he didn't know where I was.

"Who the hell are you?" he demanded in a breathy voice. He was scared and winded.

I didn't answer. I slid my knife free of the sheath and took another cautious step toward him. My hunting leathers weighed heavily across my shoulders, wet with sweat, but they remained supple. The bone hilt of my knife lay hot and hard against my palm.

And I remembered Phelyn's face, remembered the racking sobs of her mother as she tried to comfort her only daughter. There was no softness in my heart. Phelyn was next to family, and he was an off-worlder, trash to boot.

"I know I didn't kill you," Brewster roared.

I took another step, edging ever closer.

"Those girls," Brewster said, "maybe they got a little more than they bargained for, but they made themselves available." He kept shifting, trying to read my shadow out of all those surrounding him.

Then I was six meters from him and closing, coming in on his left. Brewster was turned profile to me, and I knew that with his peripheral vision he had a better chance of seeing me than if looking at me head on.

I knew when he sensed I was there. His head froze, cocked to one side. I knew he hadn't heard me, that it was some animal sense triggering his self-preservation. He spun, bringing the automatic rifle up.

Before it rose into position, I reached out and caught the barrel, then threw a kick against his hands. The rifle came free at once, but I tossed it away, knowing he'd have gutted me before I could have reversed the rifle and used it.

Brewster was five or six centimeters shorter than me, at least ten kilos lighter. His dark brown hair had receded, only deepening his widow's peak. A mustache curled over his thin-lipped mouth like a tourquit snake-worm.

Moonlight ran along the edge of the broad blade in his hand. The blade was nearly forty centimeters long, curving into a razor-sharp point at the end. It had been vetted in the center so blood could flow out along the blade while it was embedded. The weapon was a killer's tool, not a hunter's.

"Who're you?" he demanded. His eyes narrowed as he unconsciously stepped into a circling pattern toward my left, keeping the knife between us.

"Harley Rassor," I told him quietly.

"You're hardly more than a boy."

"Maybe so," I said, "but I'm going to stand between you and that river."

He smiled, a thin, mirthless grin. "What's your stake in this, Harley Rassor?"

"I'm standing in for my friends," I said, circling with him.

"You're willing to die for them?" he taunted.

"If it came down to that, I would. But it won't."

"You're so sure?"

I wasn't, but I wasn't about to let him see that in my eyes. "You have a choice. You can give your-self up."

"And go back to stand trial in Thorpe?"

"Yes."

"If I'm found guilty of assaulting those girls, what would happen to me?" His right foot grazed a loose branch, and he immediately shifted so he wouldn't put weight on it.

"You'll get twenty or thirty years of hard labor," I said. "But you'll live."

He cursed with a smile. "No way, kid. When I get on that DropShip, all bets are off. I'll just never come this way again."

I didn't say anything.

"You're alone kid," he said. "You got the other guys. Maybe you should give some thought to be-ing satisfied with that."

"No." I didn't know if Phelyn would feel better knowing all of the men who'd been responsible for hurting her had paid for it, but at least there would be some kind of resolution.

Without warning, Brewster slashed at my stomach. I made sure I was gone by the time he got there. Holding my knife point-down in my hand, I slashed at his face, reminding him I was armed as well.

Brewster easily ducked away, but he was surprised by my speed and my willingness to take the fight to him. He backed off two steps. I stood my ground. There was nowhere for him to go.

Then he came at me, shoving his knife at my face. I slapped his arm away with my empty hand, slashed at his midsection, and caught an overhand blow on my chin that I didn't even see coming. Pain lanced through my jaw, and I tasted salty blood in my mouth. I kept focused, dodging the sweep with his knife again. He kicked me in the center of my chest with bone-breaking force.

He came at me as I stumbled and tried to recover. His blade flicked at me like a serpent's tongue, darting, seemingly everywhere at once. I used my own blade to block his, steel rasping against steel, shedding sparks in the night in brief, bright bursts. I slapped his knife arm away again, then stepped inside his guard and brought my empty hand back around in a short arc that caught him full in the face.

Brewster's nose erupted in a scarlet rush. His head popped back, but he got his weight settled again and came back for another attack, whipping the blade in overhand. Steel shrieked as our blades locked. I held him off, withdrawing as soon as he moved back.

The fight became a quick darting of knives and fists. I attacked and blocked, and the blades clashed with a ringing sound, underscored by the heavy thump of flesh on flesh. He stabbed at my left shoulder, coming out in a straight lunge. I dodged easily, pulling my shoulder back, thinking to move in and take advantage of his commitment. I was caught off-guard, moving too late to evade the swing of his blade, and felt the serrated edge slice across my forehead. Hot, burning pain was followed by a rush of blood that filled my left eye.

Half-blind, I knew he'd be expecting me to pull back, try to assess the damage, and check to see if I was all right. I didn't. I knew from experience that he couldn't get a knife blade through my skull and that a head wound bled worse than anything other than arterial flow. The eyes and the mouth are a head's weak spots, and the soft throat beneath.

He followed his attack, thinking to slash my throat before I could defend myself. I brought my knife up and whipped it around. The point grated for a moment on his ribs, then sliced between the third and fourth, plunging into the heart beyond. Pressed chest to chest and linked by the steel I'd sunk deeply into his flesh, I felt the shudder course through him.

"Damn you to hell, Harley Rassor," Brewster gasped with his last breath. He tried to kick me, but I twisted and evaded the blow.

I stared at him through my good eye, feeling the hot blood clogging the other one and running down my face. Death came to him slow, draining the strength from his limbs till soon I was holding him up. It's like that. People who watch the holovids at the theater in Thorpe see heroes shoot and the villains go down. Battle's a quick process, but death often comes so slow. Da taught me that.

I stared at Brewster and saw the light dim in his eyes, the moonlight around us suddenly not going quite as deep. I held him a couple moments longer, to be sure he wasn't faking just to get a last blow at me. His head lolled to the side and I put my face close to his, testing for his breath on my cheek to make sure. There was none.

When the threat was gone, I suddenly felt the whole weight of him in my arms. I yanked my knife free and dropped him, watching the body spill loosely across the ground.

I looked down at him, sucking in air and getting the post-adrenaline shakes the way I always did. The slight breeze felt cool against my skin, and my hunting leathers felt clammy. I didn't try to think about how I felt. I just let it all wash over me.

"Harley," Jolee called.

Peering back into the brush, I saw her balanced on the thick branch of a tree, her bow in her hands. "It's over," I said.

"I couldn't get a shot off," she said. "You were too close to him."

I nodded, trying to get my breath back.

She slung the bow over her shoulder and dropped to the ground. Drawing her knife, she approached Brewster's body and cut two lengths of cloth from his coverall without hesitation.

I waited till my breath was back to normal and the shakes had left. Jolee wiped the blood from my eye as best she could with the smaller piece of cloth, and made sure the head wound had clotted before binding it with the second piece.

Then I cleaned my knife and picked Brewster

up, slinging his corpse across my shoulders. Even if I hadn't known Da would want the body back, I wouldn't have left him there for the animals to get at. I took up the automatic rifle, too, in case any of the ulteth in the area picked up the blood spoor and came after us.

5

Outside Thorpe
Slewis, Rim Collection
The Periphery
25 February 3059

The *Leopard* Class DropShip sat like a hunkered warbird along the ridgeline above Clowster's Crossing. Harley had learned all about DropShips in his militia training and knew that the ship was old, centuries old, maybe even dating back to the days of the Star League.

The ship had been designed to carry men and 'Mechs to a battleground or fortified area, but the trader reps had cleaned out the rigging and converted it to cargo space. Some seasons, when the rain was good and the sun didn't burn the grain to the ground, the goods the people of Slewis shipped off-planet almost filled the holds.

The men standing watch around the DropShip held their stance as Harley and his father and the other Thorpe men crossed the Kinnit River on Belloq's ferry. Da had field-dressed Harley's knife wounds, saying very little even by Da's standards. Perhaps it was the vigilante justice they had invoked, but Harley thought it was something more. His father seemed to avoid his eyes, and there was no reason for him to do that.

The trader reps around the ship began to move cautiously as the party approached, taking up defensive positions as if they knew what the locals were bringing them.

Reaching the shore, Harley, Da, and his men started the climb up from the riverbank, but the trader reps didn't come down to meet them. They remained by their ship, protected by the PPCs, LRMs, and lasers that were its armament. They may have changed the cargo bays around, but it looked to Harley as if they hadn't touched the weapons.

Da kept the men moving despite the weight of the carcasses tied to the dragging sticks they carried. He held a rifle resting on his off arm, canted butt-back and up so he could get a hand around it quick enough.

Lights flared out on the DropShip as the group approached, cutting through the darkness and attracting swarms of moths and other night insects. Da halted the group at the edge of it. Somebody on the ship played a light over the bodies the men had dragged with them. With a menacing sound, the weapons array churned around to face them. Reacting instinctively Harley nocked an arrow to his bowstring and held them at the ready. It was absurd to think he could fight DropShip weapons with a bow and arrow, but it was all he had.

"I'd like to speak to Commander Gossamon," Da said, his voice loud in the stillness.

One of the trader reps moved forward, out of the shadow clinging to the *Leopard*'s underbelly. He was young, maybe ten years older than Harley, but he was smooth-shaven and wore his dark hair squared off.

"I'm Gossamon," he announced soberly, looking past the men at the loads they carried. "You want to tell me what's going on?" His right fist rested just above the holstered auto-pistol sheathed to his thigh. It was a gesture almost as comical as Harley's loading of his bow, given the firepower of the DropShip towering behind him.

"We brought your men back," Da stated. "They attacked three town girls in Thorpe while they were there. Hurt them pretty bad. They did things that people, humans, simply don't tolerate. You know what I mean."

Harley watched Gossamon as he took in the tale. He knew how the reps handled themselves. They were fine when under the lead of their commander, but get them by themselves and who knew what trouble they could get themselves into.

Gossamon kept his face blank, a skill trader reps needed if they were going to stay in business. He didn't try to play the fool; some of his men were already dead.

"I have your word on this?" he asked Da.

"Yes," Da said, his voice as solemn as a minister's.

"There'll be an investigation," Gossamon warned.

"Of course there will be," Da returned curtly.

"We'd be fools not to check into your hiring practices and review your trade permit after this."

That wasn't what Gossamon had expected after his threat. The trader combines couldn't afford to lose the business of the planets they visited.

"And if your corporation is found lacking," Da warned, "you'll be penalized by the Council of Planets. Because this won't end here."

"That isn't what I meant," Gossamon replied, trying to gain control of the conversation again. "I meant that we'd be investigating—"

"If you don't find those men as guilty as we did," Da told him, "you won't be trading here anymore. And if Thorpe goes against you, so will Slewis. Without Slewis, the Council of Planets will cancel your permit. You make sure your superiors know that."

Before Gossamon could say anything else, Da turned and just left him standing there.

Gossamon shifted his weight from foot to foot, then looked over his shoulder at his men while Da's men laid the corpses at the trader's feet. Harley watched him, wondering if Gossamon would seek his own justice for the murders. It was a deed unlike anything that had ever happened. None of the trader reps moved, silent around the hulking DropShip.

Harley and Da and his men returned to Belloq's ferry, which took them back to Clowster's Crossing. As they went, Harley stood at the railing. He stared into the dark water, thinking deep about all he had seen and done since last night.

Jolee came over to stand beside him, and when he looked up at her, he saw the moonlight turn the tears on her cheeks to diamonds. At first he thought maybe it was a delayed reaction to all that had happened with the trader reps, but something told him there was more to it.

Without words Jolee put her arms around him. She wasn't one to make a show of her feelings, more likely to laugh and make light of things than to openly display her distress. Now Harley was sure something was truly amiss.

"What's wrong?" he asked.

Jolee wiped at her eyes. "Captain Able sent a message," she said in a halting voice. "He said Ben's dead."

Cold shock seized Harley's mind and soul. The family hadn't heard from Ben in a while, but Ben had never been one to write much. He would send a few holos from time to time, with little notes written on them to tell where he was or what they were doing.

Stunned, Harley looked at his father, wanting Da to tell him it wasn't true.

Da nodded sadly. "I found out just after you set out to Thorpe to disable the trader reps' Packrat," he said, sounding like a man speaking in a dream. "I feared to say anything just then. I didn't want to take your mind off what you had to do while tracking those men. You could have gotten hurt bad too if your mind wasn't where you needed it. By then, there was nothing any of us could do about it anyway."

Mutely, Harley nodded, accepting that. "When?" he finally asked.

"Last month."

News still traveled slowly through the Rim Collection due to the distances between the worlds and the lack of communications equipment. Thorpe had a receiving system, but it took time to track down whoever the message was for. News of losses in military operations were always given high priority, but the delay this time was almost as shocking as the news. His brother had been dead for a month.

"Why did they wait so long to tell us?" he stammered. Part of him was angry at Major Able for his coldness of heart. That helped take his mind off the aching void he felt at the thought of Ben dead.

"I don't know," Da said in that quiet, forceful way he had when he'd made up his mind about something he knew wasn't going to set well with others. "But I mean to find out."

6

"I don't think you're going to find anything there that you haven't seen already." Livia Hawke looked up quickly from the holo display glowing in the air in front of her and snapped to attention. The voice was unmistakably that of Jerry Able, commander of Able's Aces.

Her right forefinger rested just above her eyebrow as she saluted smartly. "Sir, I didn't hear you come in, sir."

"At ease, Lieutenant." Major Able strode into the small room. He was an intense, compact man just slightly more than average height, but he walked tall. Once, during a hellish fire in the command center, with all the junior COs near panic,

Hawke had seen him come in and take command of the entire room with just his steely gaze.

"Thank you, sir." She dropped into parade rest, glad she'd pulled on a fresh-pressed uniform before coming to the base's IntLib. In the field, uniform dress was lax and no officer insignia was worn. But on base Major Able ran a tight ship.

Able's Aces, consisting of three battalions, was technically a regiment in strength. The Aces even had their own JumpShip, albeit a centuries-old vessel that worked most of the time. The unit's ranking system, however, had not kept up with its growth as it evolved into the standing army of the Rim Collection. Typically, a regiment was commanded by a Colonel, yet Jerry Able had never claimed the rank. Likewise, Livia Hawke, as commander of First Company, would normally have worn the rank of captain, but she was still a lieutenant. She was never sure if it was a mere technicality that the ranks hadn't been bumped up in the last few years, or if Major Able was doing it to avoid giving raises. Funds had been tight for some time, especially with the recent surge of pirate raids.

Able stared at the holovid projection hanging in the air over the viewer table. Hawke watched his face, marked by scars and by character, but could read nothing from his expression or the way he gazed at the projection.

The Intel Library kept a complete record of the Aces' activities, as well as training software and other resources. It was part of the command post that served as the Aces HQ. For the last two days, she had spent more time here than anywhere else, including her quarters.

"The footage from Birdsong Ridge," Able said softly, his eyes running across the projection.

"Yes sir," Hawke said. It came from the battle-roms the recovery teams had retrieved from Birdsong Ridge. Battleroms recorded detailed technical data as well as small gun-camera shots. For Hawke it was a chance to dissect what had happened, to try to somehow make sense of it.

"Do you really think you're going to see anything you don't already know?"

Hawke was hesitant. "I was hoping this might help me remember something. The medtech said trauma often induces partial amnesia and—"

Able faced her squarely, his posture ramrod-straight despite the long hours she knew he'd been putting in. There were rumors that the Major had once managed to stay awake for fifty hours at a stretch, wearing down the local politicians during contract negotiations.

"Your memory is very complete, Lieutenant. I know because I read the report. And I viewed the fire zone myself, not just vid footage."

"Yes, sir."

"Your company moved in against raiders, pirates from Morrison's band, and was ambushed. They held the high ground and staged several fields of fire that broke down your unit in a matter of a minute. It was an ambush, Hawke. Well-staged, well-planned, and well-executed. No matter how you slice it, though, you lost—*we* lost." Able spoke matter-of-factly, without any trace of condemnation. "In truth, you were fortunate to survive, especially with the injuries you suffered."

It was true. Her left forearm had been broken,

and she had a numerous burns, bruises, and abrasions that had required medical attention. She didn't know how many cuts had been patched together.

"The others didn't."

"No, but it's not your fault. Given what you knew at the time, would you have done anything differently?"

Major Able was right; she'd have made all the same decisions even if she could rewind the tapes of history. Her company had taken out four of the raider 'Mechs, but every one of them had given their lives to do it.

"No, sir," she said finally. "I would likely have made the same decisions, but that doesn't mean I want whoever did this thing to get away with it."

Hawke knew that the investigation and recovery team had found the battlefield picked over. Four raider 'Mechs had gone down, but at the cost of an entire Ace company. . . . Morrison's Extractors had stripped the 'Mechs of any precious salvage, and had buried the Aces' dead in a mass grave. The bodies were unidentifiable in some cases. Benjamin's was so badly burned and charred that it was only recognizable as human because of a few remaining tatters of uniform and his dog tag.

Major Able turned back to the moving figures on the holovid projection. "They won't get away with it, Lieutenant—not against this unit and not against the people we've signed on to protect."

"Sir, I didn't mean to infer that—"

"I know what you meant, Lieutenant. And I also know the effect this whole thing has had on you." He paused for a moment, seeming to consider his next words. "You were close to Benjamin Rassor, weren't you? I think the word the unit grapevine used was 'intimate.' "

Hawke was stunned. Protocol among the Aces was that a CO never commented on intimate relations between enlisted unless it showed up negatively in the field. Relationships with the local populations they served often caused more problems than those within the unit.

"Sir, I don't see how—"

"No," Able said, "you don't. That's why I'm mentioning it now. Believe it or not, Hawke, I know most of what's going on among my people. I've got a full regiment under my command. You can't manage that without having some intel on your own staff. Your relationship with Rassor wasn't general knowledge, nor will it be when we're finished here."

Hawke's face flamed, and she deliberately kept her eyes locked forward in true military fashion, staring at a spot only a few centimeters over Able's own gaze. "Yes, sir. Thank you, sir." She made her voice toneless, professional.

"Can the attitude, Lieutenant. I'm well aware of how tough this is on you. I can assure you it's not much easier from this side. I've known you for a long time, as the military goes, and I've never pried into your private business before."

Hawke knew that was true. Reluctantly, still feeling embarrassed, she returned the major's gaze.

"I wouldn't mention that relationship now," Able said as he moved to the other side of the holovid table. He leaned forward, resting his knuckles on the table, gazing at her through the silenced images of the battling 'Mechs. The ruby spears of laser beams tracked across his face, followed by the roiling orange and black of the explosions in the treeline. "Except that I think we're facing a bigger problem, the one you mentioned in your report."

Hawke nodded sadly. "They knew we were coming and they knew our plan of battle. They knew the location of Benjamin's lance—out of the dozen or so defiles we could have used, they had that one covered."

"We've got a traitor," Able said quietly.

"It's the only explanation, sir."

Jerry Able rose to his full height and rubbed his chin in thought. "Our intel boys came to the same conclusion in the final report they turned in yesterday. Since you are the sole survivor of the ambush and led that operation, all fingers will point to you."

Hawke went hot with anger. "Sir, I did not—"

Able waved his hand and cut her off. "I know you didn't. But our intel folks and I are going to let people think what they want until we can flush out the real traitor. For a while, a lot of Acers are going to focus their suspicions on you. I'm going to add to it by assigning you only light garrison and training duty here on Gillfillan's Gold. Let people talk, Lieutenant. Sooner or later we'll flush out who was behind this."

"They will pay for it, sir," she said. "I swear it."

Able nodded. "You have my word that when the time comes, you'll get first crack at the bastards. In the meantime, Lieutenant, you've got some work ahead of you. In a few days, a trading

contingent will leave Slewis and make for Gillfillan's Gold on their quarterly trade run. I'm
putting you on escort duty. To keep up the cha-
rade that I think you're the possible traitor, you'll
have only a battalion of militia infantry and a
lance of Acer 'Mechs under your direct command.
I've booked commercial JumpShip passage from
Slewis, and you'll come back on the traders'
JumpShip.

"We're also mustering in three dozen Rim-
worlders, most of them from Porth, and a few
from Slewis because Rassor was the only native
we lost in the Birdsong engagement. I'm mustering them on Slewis right now. You'll take charge of
them there, as well as doing any necessary PR
work with the trader officials.

"Simply put, you go, land, secure the LZ, get the
traders to the JumpShip, and bring them here. I'm
planning on a few surprises while you're gone,
some intel ploys to see if I can get our back-stabber
to surface. In the meantime, you play the role of
the downcast and bitter officer. Can you handle
that?"

Hawke didn't think she could, but that wasn't
the answer he wanted to hear. "Yes, sir," she said,
knowing he was only asking this of necessity. The
loss on Caldarium gave the whole Aces regiment a
black eye, and the Council of Planets wouldn't
forget it when it came time to negotiate a new
contract.

"I don't need to remind you," Able said, "that
part of the Aces' fees come from a percentage of
what the Rim Collection worlds earn each year,
but I will. If they lose product, we lose profit. And
if we lose profit, we lose the potential to get new

'Mech units and supply parts for ones that get damaged or simply wear out."

"I know, sir."

"Good will equals C-bills in this man's army," Able said. "Bottom line."

"Yes, sir."

Major Able reached out and shut off the holovid projector, killing the images of the battle that had cost both of them so much. "The base counselor hasn't heard from you, Lieutenant. Go and meet with him; that's why I pay his bills. As far as I'm concerned, what happened at Birdsong Ridge is in the past. Leave it there, or you won't be able to see the future."

Before Hawke could answer that, Jerry Able turned and left her alone in the dimly lit room, to bury the past, and face her future.

7

Outside Thorpe
Slewis, Rim Collection
The Periphery
26 February 3059

From the journal of Harley Rassor:

Ben is dead.

I still find it hard to write the words.

During the trip home, Da told me that Major Able's message said Ben had died fighting pirates on Caldarium. The message had come in the form of a field report and a letter of regret. Able had sent it via HPG, which was expensive and was a gesture of kindness on his part.

The problem was that the Rim Collection's hyperpulse generator network is an older model that batch-processes messages, and then only sends them after some time has passed. A message might almost have arrived faster coming on a cargo transport.

What they told us was that Ben was killed almost immediately, as were the rest of First Company. The bodies of three of them, including Ben's, had been burned almost past recognition.

And in the tiny bedroom where I'd listened to Ben dream about all the things he wanted to see and do, I sit now writing. Some nights mark a person's life, change it. Da had always told me so. Now I understood. I had killed a man tonight, and I had learned that my own brother was dead.

Ben was the adventurer, not me. I've always loved the outdoors, but Ben had lived for another kind of out—away from Thorpe and maybe even off-planet. I've thought about such things, but never in the same way. The forest around Thorpe has always been big enough for me, packed with plenty of adventure.

Not for Ben, though.

For all that the room seemed empty since he'd joined the Aces, it never seemed emptier than now. It took forever to clean up, wash the blood off of me. Not just my blood, but that of the man I'd killed. My leathers were caked with it in some spots, already turning a dull brown. None of that mattered. All that mattered was that Ben was gone. I would have stayed in my room all night if Da hadn't called me to the kitchen.

"You're going to need some stitches to close that wound up," he said.

"I'd guessed."

"Sit down." Da pulled out a chair next to him.

I sat.

Da went through his sewing kit. Actually it was a medkit, containing a few surgical instruments. The original medicaments had long since been used up, replaced by salves and ointments made in and around Thorpe, home-grown recipes used for generations. Jolee had called it a sewing kit when she was little, and the name had stuck.

"Are you ready to do this, boy?" he asked.

"Waiting's not going to make it any better," I replied.

"We'll take time," Da said. "Let you rest as you need it."

"Yes." I sat as comfortably as I could.

Da threaded the curved surgical needle with the thinnest thread he had. "If I sew this big, you're going to have a bad scar. With the wound being on your face, I don't want that."

"It's more at my hairline," I said.

"There's going to be a scar anyway," he told me. "We don't need to make it any bigger than it will be." For a big man, Da moved careful when he wanted to. "We'll put these in, then take them out again in about five days if everything goes well."

I closed my eyes and breathed out, relaxing. I concentrated on the smell of the baking biscuits, let my thoughts take me away from the pain. Jolee always baked when upset. Da said Ma used to be the same way.

While he worked on me, I built the kitchen in my mind, picturing the knickknacks Jolee and Ben had made to decorate it. Jolee made collages, creating pictures out of things she pasted together. Ben did carvings, capturing images deftly. Jolee had also hung pressed and dried flowers on the wall, starting about three years ago. The flowers brought gentle colors to the room.

The needle bit into my flesh and despite the trauma to the area, I felt the thread slithering through. Da pierced the other side, then used a small scissors to tie the knot when he pulled the two pieces of the wound together. Even though the bleeding had stopped earlier, a small trickle started again as he worked.

"Your brother's death leaves me with many questions," Da said finally. I must confess, I was glad he said something about it.

"Yes," I said, keeping my neck relaxed so my head hung back and he could keep tying stitches.

"I thought about sending Able an HPG to get the answers I want," Da said, tying another stitch. "But I don't know how truthful his answers will be."

"Major Able has the reputation as a fair man."

"Yes," Da agreed almost too quickly, "but I know military personnel take care of their own. Losses are losses, and some of them have to be written off as acceptable. I don't view Ben's death as anywhere near an acceptable loss. I also know that Able's dealings with the Council of Planets have turned him into a politician as much as a military man these days. He's going to be looking out for himself and his unit. He's got to deal with both a political and military version of the truth, and right now I'm not sure which one we've been handed."

Jolee sat across from us, her eyes wet with pain.

The hurt in my chest was more than what I felt in my wound.

"The way those 'Mechs were taken on Birdsong Ridge," Da went on, his hands as steady as ever, "tells me they were set up. It was an ambush pure and simple."

I was a little surprised at this. Da had never

seemed to know anything remotely connected to the military. Now, he spoke like a man with experience.

I'd lost track of how many stitches he'd put in, but he kept right on stitching. "When a military operation falls so short of its objective, it's because they didn't know everything. Someone set them up, or deliberately withheld intel they needed."

He paused, setting another stitch. "I think there's someone inside Able's Aces who betrayed the unit and let those men die in an ambush. Unless I miss my guess, Jerry Able's probably thinking the same thing." He spoke as if he knew the Major personally, but I know that's not possible. Da's a farmer, a hunter, not a warrior.

I ran Da's thinking through my mind, not liking the turns it took, but recognizing the worth all the same.

"There was one person who survived the attack," Da said. "I've had Chilton send a message to Porth to a 'friend' from my youth, from the old days."

My ears perked up. Da had never talked before about any old days, and he didn't this time either.

"There's not much data out there other than the news reports, and usually those are doctored or slanted. Chilton was able to get one piece of information I didn't have, though. There was a survivor of what happened up on this Birdsong Ridge. A Lieutenant Livia Hawke."

"You think she had something to do with it?" I asked.

"I think it's noticeable that she did," Da said.

"Able won't let this go," I said. "There'll be

more pressure on him and the President to bring in other mercenary units to beef up our defenses."

"I didn't think Able would," Da replied. "But whoever planned this is also going to be planning for him to investigate. He and his people."

"You think the lies will continue?" I asked.

"Maybe. I know I don't want to entirely rely on what Able is willing to tell the Council of Planets. And what they're willing, in turn, to pass on to us. I trust Jerry Able. I just don't trust those who might filter his messages to us. That's why I want Ben represented, our family represented, in this matter. I want to know—" Da's voice broke just a little, but his hands never faltered in their stitching.

I opened my eyes and looked up at him. I couldn't remember him crying when my mother died, though knowing the kind of man he was, I was sure he did so in his own privacy. He'd never remarried, saying there would never be another woman for him.

"I want to know what happened to Ben," Da went on. "And I want his ashes brought home. They cremated him on Caldarium."

My throat tightened and got dry. I hadn't even thought about what they'd do with Ben's body. It was so hard thinking about that, about there being a body.

"How can we do any of that, Da?" I asked.

"I want you to join up with the Aces and find out what you can," he said, calmly starting another stitch.

I sat quietly and flicked a glance over at Jolee, who looked as surprised as I felt. "Are you that sure they'll take me?"

Da nodded, but didn't take his eyes off his work. "Yes. Your scores are high enough, and your militia service here on Slewis hasn't gone unnoticed. You've got some experience in that bucket-of-bolts 'Mech out on the back of our property.

"They'll take you. I'll make sure of it. Like I said, I've a friend from the old days, someone who owes me and who can make sure it happens. In fact, I've already sent him a message."

Da had always teased Ben and I for working on that old 'Mech. Odd that it was one of the things that was now going to change my whole life.

I didn't ask him any more about how he would get Major Able to accept me as a member of the Aces. One thing I'd learned about Da, he didn't promise anything he couldn't deliver.

Da stitched for another few minutes, then declared he was done. He cleaned the needles and put the medkit away. By then Jolee's biscuits were done, too.

We ate in silence, each one lost in our thoughts. I'm sure Da and Jolee were as aware as I was of the chair sitting empty at one end of the table Da had polished enough that you could see your reflection in it. The churned butter, honey, and jam were good, but we hadn't much appetite.

"Able's rebuilding the company he lost, and I hear some of the new recruits have arrived on one of the trader ships. Word is he's sending transport for them back to Gillfillan's Gold in a few days' time. You should be well enough to travel by then."

I nodded, regretting the movement as the headache sloshed around between my temples.

"How do you feel about going, boy?" Da asked.

I knew I had a choice; I always had. "It needs to be done," I told him. "And I'm the best one to do it."

"That's how I see it."

"It's scary, though."

"Being away from home?"

I thought of the night sky, with all those stars sparkling bright and hard. "Being up there. Out there in so much—*openness*."

"Inside a ship or a 'Mech," Da said, "you don't notice it so much."

I hoped not. Somehow space had seemed a lot more friendly listening to Ben tell about it.

"The men and women you're going to meet," Da said, "the ones making up Able's core army, they're not all good."

"I didn't think they were," I said.

"They've got their own way of doing things, their own way of looking at things. Sometimes, they're not much different than the trader reps. It depends on the man leading them." He got up after that and went to his room.

After an hour or so, I gave up trying to sleep. I went barefoot to the window facing east and opened it. Da had put us here on purpose so the sun would wake us every morning—on days we got to sleep even that late.

I climbed through the window and grabbed the eaves. Lying still for so long, my muscles had tightened up. Movement also seemed to increase my pounding headache.

I pulled myself up on the eaves and crawled up the slanted roof. Da had built it with enough angle that snow had a hard time staying, but it was rough enough that Ben and I had often lain on it with no problem. We'd talked about so many things over the years, not agreeing on everything, but talking about them all the same.

I missed him so much then, knowing I'd never have the chance to just lie back and look up at the stars and talk to my brother about anything that came to mind. After awhile, I slept, but I was troubled by nightmares of Ben and the trader reps and bright, hot blood.

8

DropShip **General Gordon**
Inbound Slewis, Rim Collection
The Periphery
16 March 3059

Livia Hawke braced for the attack, setting most of her weight back onto her right leg. She adjusted her right foot, turning it perpendicular to her left, which was forward.

Gunnery Sergeant Harry Coombs, "Gunney" to his peers and subordinates, came at her without hesitation. He stood a head taller than she did, his body blocky with muscle. His gray hair was buzzed short, and he wore gray sweats, which showed sweaty at the neck, chest, and armpits. Both of them were dressed in full-contact protective headgear and gloves and padded boots.

Coombs' hands flashed to the attack, darting toward her face. He moved with lightning speed, far faster than anyone might guess for someone of his size.

Hawke gave ground to the attack, meeting it with her own chopping hands. The sound of flesh striking flesh echoed across *General Gordon*'s deck. The DropShip was currently burning insystem, which gave them some gravity for working out. Not much, but enough.

The *General Gordon* was an older *Union* Class model, outfitted to carry up to a full company of a dozen BattleMechs or vehicles into battle. A Jump-Ship, on the other hand, traveled between star systems, moving from the nadir or zenith point above the gravity well of one to another. A JumpShip was up to a kilometer long, but not designed for use inside the gravity of a solar system. That was what DropShips were for. Docked to the hull of a JumpShip, they would ride along between stars. Unlike their starship cousins, they could travel from the jump point to a planet and land on its surface.

The dozen or so off-duty personnel in the area had gathered around the exercise mat when Coombs and Hawke had squared off after moving through martial arts kata warm-ups. Neither she nor the sergeant had spoken to the other at any time prior to or during the encounter.

The walls of the muster deck were lusterless, the green and gray military paint now chipped. As Hawke fended off a chop of his right arm, using her cast to painfully deflect the blow, she caught the smell of sweat that hung in the air. The *General Gordon* had been commissioned centuries ago. Fights and combat-sims had been run on this same deck over all that time. This was not the first, nor would it be the last.

Hawke had chosen her time for a combat-sim, and Coombs had readily agreed. As occasional sparring partners who relished a challenge, they had a history within the Aces. She'd even noticed C-Bills changing hands on the sidelines. There was something magical about a non-com taking on an officer.

Coombs pressed his attack, coming straight at her. He caught her with a glancing blow, but one that told her he wasn't giving her room for error. She tried to sweep his legs, but he artfully jumped to dodge the attack. His fists flew at her like a hurricane of pain, and most of the blows she was able to block, but her defensive stance seemed to drain her ability to take the offense. The sweat stinging her eyes only served to remind her that he was asking and giving no quarter—per her own orders.

She countered, deflecting his blows. Over the years of their association, she knew Coombs depended on his size and height and reach to give him an advantage. In most cases, it did. Hawke was able to hold her own in spite of it.

Hawke moved smoothly, but the movements didn't feel smooth to her. Her injuries twinged and pulled, reminding her that her convalescence wasn't completely over. The workout was helping. The medtech had used a special bonding cast that let her move the arm even while knitting the damage from her break. The lingering pain helped purge some of her hurt over what had happened on Birdsong Ridge.

Coombs shifted his weight and began to advance, hitting her firm stomach with a powerful blow, knocking her back a step. Hawke did not waver long, swinging her leg again under his, this time catching his heel. Coombs went down and rolled, when a sudden, cackling hiss boomed over the loudspeaker, followed by a voice echoing across the bay. "Lieutenant Hawke, incoming priority data dump from Slewis."

Suddenly the fight stopped. Livia Hawke drew a deep breath, straightened up, and looked at the Gunnery Sergeant. Coombs slapped the mat in frustration and rolled up to his feet. He raised his hands, looking at her expectantly.

"Enough," Hawke said. Breathing hard, she shook her head. "Enough," she repeated. "I push any further and I'm going to drop." Her face was covered with sweat, and her heart hammered.

Coombs hesitated for just a moment, then let his own guard drop. "Yes, sir."

They bowed to each other, left palms covering clenched right fists. Hawke glanced up and caught the towel one of the privates tossed to her. She nodded thanks, then mopped her face.

"Catch you later, Gunney," she told Coombs wearily as she made her way to the communications terminal on one of the support beams. Her noteputer was docked into it and was flashing that it had received the data transmitted from Slewis.

She'd been expecting it. Major Able had told her he would be sending files on the new recruits and any intel updates via HPG to Slewis so that she'd have the latest information. Hyperpulse generators were the only way to send interstellar communications that you wanted to arrive in your lifetime. The Rim Collection's HPG stations were old class C-stations, a low priority for transmissions. This one had arrived a mere few days before her arrival. Such was life in the Periphery. In the Inner Sphere, such a transmission would have arrived long before.

Her arm ached in the cast as she pulled the noteputer from its docking port and pulled up the data. She and her lance were scheduled to arrive on Slewis on March 19. There, she would link up with the local militia and one of the Aces groundpounder lances of armor and infantry.

The traders were already on Slewis and were scheduled to depart on March 25. They were most vulnerable when on the ground during the final stages of trading, when cargoes were being loaded for transport. That was when pirates and raiders usually struck; hitting empty transports made little sense.

Reading the HPG message, Hawke saw that Major Able was changing the schedule. He had stepped up the traders' departure to March 23. Her eyes darted through the classified data dump and she understood the reason instantly. Moving up the dates would throw off any pirate attack. Moreover, if there was a traitor in the ranks of the Aces, it would limit the number of possible suspects as well as provide very little time for such a traitor to relay the change in plan.

Taking off two days earlier meant landing on Gillfillan's Gold two days earlier as well. If the pirates attacked the traders, the only way they could know the timetable was from someone in the ranks of the Aces. And, most likely, the intel staff was carefully monitoring contacts and communications for hints of such covert contact.

For Hawke, it meant she had a lot of work to do in a short time. The trader party would have to be briefed on the new timetable, and deployment plans would be much tighter. None of it was impossible, but it added a new element of urgency she hadn't counted on.

The rest of the data dump was routine messages, information on the replacement troops that had been rallied on Slewis to replenish those she'd lost on Birdsong Ridge. She pulled the list of the eleven new troopers and scanned it quickly. As a native of the Rim Collection, she always wondered whether she might spot a familiar family name or even that of an old friend. It was rare, but it did happen.

This time, one name stood out. *Pvt. Rassor, Harley Dain.* Rassor. Memories of Benjamin swept over her. She recalled him speaking fondly about his younger brother and that the brother's name was Harley. She told herself it could be someone else, but her heart pounded as she clicked on the private's name and pulled up his service record in detail.

There it was. The entry hadn't even been updated yet, still listing Benjamin Rassor as his only brother. Hawke stared at the data. She was just beginning to work through her feelings about Ben's death. She didn't need someone around who would be a continual reminder of her failure at Birdsong Ridge.

Not if she could help it. Major Able upheld some fairly rigid procedures regarding personnel. Family members of Aces killed in action were not allowed to serve for several years. He had implemented that rule when the Aces began rotating in the local Rim Collection militias. Its intention was to prevent having kin joining on with revenge motives or other ideas about remedying past failures or losses.

Livia Hawke quickly re-docked her noteputer and accessed the communications system. This was one problem she could solve here and now. Private Harley Rassor would not be joining Able's Aces—she would make sure of that.

9

DropShip **General Gordon**
Inbound Slewis, Rim Collection
The Periphery
16 March 3059

Secured Transmission Data-Send:
Security Level Emerald
Eyes Only
To: Major Jerry Able
20: Command Post, Gillfillan's Gold
From: Lieutenant Livia Hawke
20: Dropship *General Gordon,* Inbound Slewis
COMSTAR ENCODING SEQUENCE
    AC_RIM004.322
ACCOUNT AA210102301.L

Subject: Rassor, Harley Dain
Private, Slewis Militia

Sir:

It has just come to my attention that a recent conscript from the Slewis Militia has been added to the Aces corps. I don't know how this addition has escaped your notice, but I want to bring it to your attention.

Private Harley Rassor shows up on the roster of new recruits, but I believe he should not be moved into active service among the Aces, because of the death of Benjamin Rassor, his brother. The Rassor family were only notified of Ben's death a matter of weeks ago. As you've pointed out to me, emotional fall-out must be dealt with before a soldier can take the field.

My concern is that Private Rassor has not had ample time to do that. Pursuant to standing Aces General Order #143, I would recommend postponing his induction till an exploratory intake can be performed.

Sincerely,

Lieutenant Livia Hawke
1st Battalion, Able's Hammers
1st Company, The Hawke's Talons

Livia Hawke typed the message into the communications console and prepared it for transmission. It would be sent via traditional radio to Slewis, and would then be relayed via HPG back to Gillfillan's Gold in the next set of data dumps to be routed there. It would be slow, but she should have a response before she had to depart Slewis, a

departure she planned to make without Harley
Rassor.

As she keyed the final command, she heard her
noteputer activate. At first Hawke paid no notice,
but then she saw that her transmission wasn't
showing the usual "File Transmitted Successfully"
message. She was about to contact the bridge, to
make sure that the *General Gordon*'s communications or computer system were not on fritz, when a
message played across her screen, a message that
made her face hot with anger.

KEY WORD SEARCH AUTOLOAD
FILE RASSOR.2.COUNTERMAND
    ACTIVATED VIA
TRANSMITTER HAWKE, LIVIA,
    LIEUTENANT
KEYWORDS: Rassor, Harley, General Order,
    143, Benjamin
PROBABILITY OF HIT: 92.2%
PRECODED TEXT AS FOLLOWS:

Lieutenant Hawke,
    You are seeing this message because I
encoded a search in your most recent data
dump. It is possible that by now you have just
tried to send me a message regarding the
addition of Harley Rassor to your company
replacements. Rest assured that your message
will not reach me. Part of this automatic
procedure will delete your transmission so
that neither of us is embarrassed.
    Though I have not seen your arguments, I'm
sure you are presenting them in only the most
professional manner. However, I am, in this

case, revoking General Order #143 and allowing Private Rassor to join our ranks.

Before you send off a long list of rebuttals, you should know that I appreciate your situation, but this is not a matter you can reverse with me.

David Rassor, Benjamin and Harley's father, is an old friend of mine. We served together back in the days when we were both in the Lyran Commonwealth military. David Rassor saved my life once in a raid by House Marik. He damn near got himself killed in the process, but he was too loyal and stubborn to leave me behind. He was a wild boy then. We both were. War changed him, though. He turned his back on our way of life and came to the Rim Collection to raise a family. Knowing him, I doubt he ever told them he was one hell of a MechWarrior.

David sent me a message asking for a favor, not the sort of thing he would usually do. He's very proud. He has the idea that he hasn't gotten the whole truth about Benjamin's death and that he wants Harley to serve in our ranks until he learns all the facts. I assume he didn't ask me for the details he seeks because he either knows that I don't have them, or he fears I've become too political to tell him everything. Either way, if he wants Harley to serve in my command, the man who saved my life will get his wish.

I fully understand your concerns, both personal and professional. As such, I am attaching to this message Harley Rassor's file from the Slewis Militia.

I appreciate your professional discretion in maintaining this information as private. I look forward to your returning to Gillfillan's Gold along with your charge.

Sincerely,

Major Jerry Able
Commanding Officer, Able's Aces

FILE ATTACHMENT HRASS001.322.DOC
Name: Rassor, Harley Dain
Rank: Private, Thorpe, Slewis Militia
Field transfer to Private, 1st Battalion, Able's Hammers, 1st Company, The Hawke's Talons. Approved, JA, CO.
Posting: Gillfillan's Gold command post
Specialist MOS: BattleMech Piloting and Gunnery
Primary Training: Demolitions and Security Systems
Secondary Training: Reconnaissance

Combat Competency Ratings:
Rifle, Zeus: sharpshooter.
Rifle, Federated: sharpshooter
Pistol, any: expert
Grenade launcher: expert
Unarmed combat: superior (note: no recognized system of defense; inclusive of a number of forms)
Jump Pack: adequate
Medtech: adequate
Navigation: expert

BattleMech Experience:
Commando (Private training unverified by
   militia officers)
Assassin
Jenner

Leadership Provide Rating: 82.9% (Officer
   Potential)

Remarks:
   Rassor has strong survival skills. He also
shows leadership potential, though it does not
seem to attract him. Subject prefers taking
responsibility for himself and working alone.
Well-disciplined, but parameters of activity
must agree with subject's own periphery of
responsibility. Has competency in 'Mech
combat as well as field repairs.
Special Note: Private Rassor is skilled in native
weaponry and bows.

10

There were three DropShips on the makeshift landing area, which was nothing more than a cleared field marked with burns from the takeoffs and landings of previous DropShip transports. One was the *Leopard* Class ship Harley remembered distinctly from the night he and the others had avenged the young women of Thorpe. The other two were spheroid *Union* Class ships, towering over the field. The ships showed their age; the hulls were pockmarked with burns, scars, and meteor damage, and showed several old turrets still bristling with weapons. One of the *Union*s was marked with the insignia of Able's Aces—the *General Gordon*. The other two were commercial traders.

The sheer size of the ships made them stand out, but even as Harley and his family approached, he could make out the crowds of people at the base of the ships, and the nearly three-story forms of the BattleMechs patrolling the perimeter of the area.

The sight of the 'Mechs almost entranced him as he walked. They were mammoths, though dwarfed by the huge DropShips nearby. Walking with an almost human gait, the 'Mechs seemed oblivious to the citizens and the traders they were there to protect.

Harley adjusted his pack as he went, shifting its weight. He knew from his training that the Aces typically assigned an enlisted man armament and armor, but he'd brought along his knife anyway, as well as his hunting leathers. Uniforms would be issued, too, but Harley knew there'd be times when he'd want out of a uniform—it had been that way during his stints with the Slewis militia. Also inside the pack were a few other personal articles of clothing and an extra pair of handmade moccasin boots that snugged up just under his knees. Jolee had made him the boots, and he knew that no matter where he was, they'd remind him of her.

Poking at his shoulder blade from inside his pack was a tattered edition of the collected poems of Byron, Shelley, and Keats that Da had given him on his thirteenth birthday. Thirteen was a special age to his father, an age when he said a boy took his first steps on his way to manhood. Harley had been shocked into silence by the gift of the book. He'd figured on getting a new knife perhaps, or maybe some traps because he had started making a little extra money trapping by then. Ben, at the same age, had received a noteputer. Harley had tried to hide his disappointment, but his father saw through the false front. Da had clapped Harley on the shoulder and given him a small smile. "This isn't a gift you'll understand all at one time boy," he'd said. "This is one you'll grow into, and one that will grow into you. You're all hands and eyes right now, but it's because you're trying to find things to fill your heart."

Da was right. And during the long days that followed the death of Ben, Harley had found solace in his beloved book, and that helped get him through it.

Da spoke slowly as they approached the landing field, making sure that his only surviving son was listening carefully. "You've been on Slewis most of your life, boy. Like I said before, once you're out there, you're going to meet a lot of people. Some will be good people, others won't share your values. Pick and choose your friends carefully. A man is measured by the company he keeps and the words he speaks."

Harley nodded slowly, his eyes still transfixed by the sight of the 'Mechs patrolling the area. "Don't worry, Da. I can take care of myself."

His father was not convinced. He stopped and put his hands on Harley's shoulders to get his attention, and looked him straight in the eyes. "Don't get too lost in the moment, Harley. I know about military life. I know what it means to be in a battle. This is not a game, and unlike what we did to those scum traders, this will not always be a fight on your terms and conditions. You have to be sharper, faster, and smarter or you might end up dead. I've already lost Benjamin. I don't want to lose you too."

His words caught Harley off guard. He had never heard his father even hint of any knowledge of things military. "Da, you know I can handle myself both on and off the field, if it even comes to that. I'll find out what happened to Ben and make it right." He wanted to ask his father what he knew of battle and a soldier's life, but Da had already walked on ahead toward the ship.

It was Jolee who broke the silence. "That's a *Black Knight*," she said pointing to one of the 'Mechs. "I think the other one is a *Hussar*." Three more Battle-Mechs were visible on the far side of the Drop-Ships, which somewhat obscured their view.

Harley shook his head. Jolee had been in militia training just as he had, but her knowledge of BattleMechs was somewhat limited. "Nice try, but I think that your *'Hussar'* is really a *Sentinel*," he said.

"Are you sure?" Jolee asked.

"If it's a *Hussar*, where's the laser that is supposed to be on top of the cockpit?"

She looked and then gave Harley a frown. "Fine, it's a *Sentinel*. What kind of 'Mech do you think you'll get assigned?"

Harley shrugged. "For all I know, Major Able may post me to the infantry. It doesn't matter to me. As long as I'm in the Aces, I can find out what happened to Ben."

About two hundred meters from the landing area, the Slewis militia patrol advanced on them. Armed with Federated or Zeus heavy rifles and pistols, they didn't seem menacing compared to the size of the ships and the lance of 'Mechs in the

area. Three of the men carried pump-action shot-
guns, and the sergeant heading up the small patrol had an Imperator submachine gun canted
across the inside of his left arm.

The sergeant was not a stranger. His name was
Grant, someone Harley knew from school and
from his time in the militia.

"Good day, Rassor family," Grant said in greet-
ing. "The traders are just starting their loading
process. Access is by orders or permission only."

Harley handed a small chip over to Grant, who
took it and inserted it into his small wristcomp,
then stabbed at the buttons. Grant looked back
at his friend and smiled. "Harley Rassor is joining Able's Aces, eh? You're cleared for boarding
the DropShip *General Gordon*. At the gangway, report to Gunnery Sergeant Coombs. He'll get you
settled."

Harley knew that this was the end of the walk
with his father and sister. He turned to them, about
to say goodbye, when Grant muttered, "That's
odd." He was looking at his wristcomp. "When
your orders came through, I got a flagged file, from
Major Able himself. It says here that he wants to
personally welcome you into Able's Aces."

Grant cocked his head and studied Harley in-
quisitively. "You must have some pull in pretty
high places, Private Rassor. Nobody else got a personal invite from the old man." Grant handed
back the small chip to Harley, who slid it into his
pants pocket.

Harley cast a glance at Grant, then at his father.
Da gave Harley a knowing wink and a smile. "I
wasn't always a farmer, boy. Major Able and I go
way back, even before there was a Rim Collection.

Did you think that old *Commando* out on the back property had been abandoned there by the former owner of the land?"

Harley was too stunned to form words, but Jolee acted like she didn't even hear what Da said. She hugged Harley tightly, and he returned the hug just as strong. His father held out his callused hand and gave his son's a firm shake. There were no words for a few minutes as Harley realized he was leaving not just his home, but his former life.

"Don't worry, Da. I'll find out what happened to Ben. I'll find a way to make it right."

"Aye," his father said. "Take care of yourself as well, boy." With that, Da released Harley's hand, and he and Jolee turned and began retracing their steps toward the river in the distance.

Harley Rassor turned away from them and back toward the DropShip that towered nearby. Shifting his pack slightly, he held himself straighter and began the rest of the way toward it.

Harley was standing at the ramp that ran up and into the belly of the *General Gordon*, when a rough voice startled him. "Who are you and what are you doing here?" the voice demanded.

Harley spun about and nearly bumped into a man who was a mountain of living muscle, with close-cropped salt and pepper hair. On the sleeves of his uniform was a sergeant's insignia just under the patch for Able's Aces.

Harley's instinct told him to salute, but then he thought better of it. It was a lesson he'd learned in the militia. Someone saluting a sergeant is either kissing butt or just plain stupid. He didn't want to be in either camp to start with. Instead he snapped to attention. "Private Harley Rassor reporting for duty."

"Orders?" the sergeant demanded.

Harley pulled out his chip and handed it over. The sergeant slipped the chip into his noteputer and gave Harley a cock-eyed look. "Welcome to Able's Aces. You're Benjamin Rassor's brother, aren't you?" His voice no longer had its harsh edge.

Harley nodded. "Yes, Sergeant."

"That's Gunnery Sergeant, for the record, Private. I knew your brother pretty well. Good man. Tough loss."

Harley was about to speak when the ground quaked beneath his feet. He turned and saw, standing only a few meters away, the hulking form of an *Orion* BattleMech. Despite its patchwork of replacement armor plating, it still looked every ton as menacing as the day it came off the production line. His eyes traveled up the 'Mech from the feet to the cockpit, where the Mech-Warrior sat behind polarized glass.

A voice boomed from the 'Mech over an externally mounted speaker. "Gunnery Sergeant Coombs, we are dusting off in thirty minutes. Start running through the prep cycle ASAP. I have the militia clearing out the civilians in five." The voice was female but every ounce as commanding as the big sergeant's.

"Who was that?" Harley asked, still staring up at the 'Mech as it turned and lumbered away.

"That was Lieutenant Hawke, CO of First Battalion, First Company. You're going to be under her command, Private."

Hawke. Harley remembered the name. She was

the lone survivor of the battle of Birdsong Ridge. She had lived while his brother Ben had died—under her command. And now he would be reporting to her . . .

"What's she like?" Harley asked.

The Gunnery Sergeant waved the question aside like it was so much smoke. "You'll find out soon enough, Private. Right now, I've just been handed a shitload of work to do and not much time to do it. Haul your carcass up inside and wait in the briefing room with the other fresh meat."

"Fresh meat?" Harley turned his gaze from the *Orion* and back to the Gunnery Sergeant.

Coombs gave him a toothy grin. "Fresh meat, Rassor—replacement troops. In other words, you."

With that, Gunnery Sergeant Coombs walked away and started bellowing orders at the others. Harley turned and started the long walk up the gangway into the bowels of the DropShip that would take him from the only home he'd ever known.

11

DropShip General Gordon
Outbound Slewis, Rim Collection
The Periphery
23 March 3059

Harley felt his stomach pitch one more time as the gravity aboard the DropShip continued to slacken. He glanced at the other recruits strapped into the high-G jump seats and wondered if any of them felt as sick as he did. Some were trying to fake grins, but one of the faces was green enough that Harley knew he wasn't the only one with a queasy stomach.

A corporal had herded him and the other new additions to the Aces to their seats and helped strap them in. Harley had never been aboard a DropShip before, had never been in space. And now that he was here, after a lifetime of wondering about the sensation, he felt like throwing up. The only thing that kept his breakfast in place was the fact that he didn't want to take the verbal abuse his peers would unleash if he tossed his meal.

The DropShip was accelerating toward the JumpShip that was holding station above the gravity well of the Slewis star. The ship would continue to speed up until it was halfway there, at which point it would begin to decelerate. Harley and the others on the ship would have only slight gravity during the outbound trip, which would take some getting used to. All of this was fine on paper and in theory, but the reality of the situation was much more than Harley had bargained for. He grappled with the release mechanism on his restraint harness as did the others in the berth, swallowing back the taste of bile in his mouth.

The door to the room opened with a squeak from a hinge that seemed long overdue for maintenance. The massive frame of Gunnery Sergeant Coombs filled the doorway. "All right, boys and girls, you're in the Aces now and in the Aces we don't sit on our butts taking in the view. I want you to muster on the main deck on the double so we can go over the basics. Now move, move, move!"

Harley and the other militia recruits had been trained by Able's Aces, and he knew that orders had to be obeyed on the double. Suppressing his queasy stomach, he rose quickly and then found himself hovering above the floor for an instant in the light gravity. He didn't savor the moment at all, but instead just moved.

The main deck of the *General Gordon* also served as the 'Mech bay. Strapped into their individual bays were the four BattleMechs of the Aces escort.

Technicians worked on them, moving effortlessly in the light gravity, performing the necessary preventive maintenance. The air stung with the sticky-sweet odor of the coolant and the metallic, coppery taste of lubricants. There was also a hint of ozone in the air. Echoes of metal clanging and tools snapping rang in his ears.

As Harley and the other recruits moved into the yellow light of the bay, he stared in awe at the 'Mechs and wondered if he would be assigned one or be posted to the Aces infantry.

Gunnery Sergeant Coombs entered the bay and took his place in front of the recruits. "Ten, hut!" he barked, and they quickly dressed their line, staring straight ahead. They were twelve in all, two rows of six each.

Coombs walked slowly along the front row, staring at the recruits as if they were still in boot camp. "I'm not here to give you a grand old welcome to Able's Aces. You were all militia so you know all about the Aces and have already gone through training. Well, let me tell you, you've just left the ranks of weekend warriors to become one of those who do this for a living. We expect a lot from you, and if we don't get it, you and a lot of other people could end up dead, starting with yourselves."

Harley did not waver from his forward stare, as he'd been taught to do in the militia. It suddenly hit him that this course he'd embarked on was going to be a lot more than simply investigating the death of his brother.

"Most of you are being pressed into First Battalion," Coombs went on. "The First is known as Able's Hammers, and with damn good reason.

When there's a fight, the Hammers are usually in the thick of it. You will be serving under more experienced lance leaders in First Company, which we call the Hawke's Talons. The company's CO is Lieutenant Livia Hawke."

Harley felt his heart begin to pound slightly at hearing the name. Livia Hawke, the first link to learning what had happened to Ben. And now he might end up serving under her, a person who might very well be a traitor.

"The rest of you will be rotated into other slots in First Battalion. Duty assignments will be posted on the databoard. When we're done here, you will check them. From this point forward consider yourself on full active duty, with full gear assignment. You will each muster to the quartermaster's cage to pick up your gear. You will go to your quarters, which are also posted on the databoard, change into your uniforms and then shag your chubby little butts down here for a full briefing and workout. In thirty minutes you had all better be present and accounted for or you'll be doing more pushups than you ever dreamed were possible."

Coombs put his hands on his hips, and let his gaze move from one end of the recruit ranks to the other. He obviously wasn't finished with them yet.

"Now, you listen to me. You greenies are no longer in the militia, but part of the front line in defending the Rim Collection from every pirate, low-life raider, and mercenary wannabe. You're in the closest thing to a standing military the Rim Collection has, and your mommies and daddies, brothers and sisters, aunts and uncles are all counting on you to do your job and your duty. You might not be fighting on your home planet, but if you blow it, if you lose the fight in one spot, the raiders or pirates might strike at your homeworld next."

Harley thought back to his Da and Jolee, somewhere out there, far beyond the hull of the ship that was hurtling him and everyone else on this ship through space.

"Now then, move it, move it, move it!" Coombs barked. And in rapid succession, the new members of the Aces broke rank and raced to obey his orders.

The thirty minutes turned out to be cutting it close. The quartermaster's cage was just that, and the uniforms issued were significantly better quality than anything ever seen in the planetary militia, but still too loose for Harley's taste. He liked the tight feel of his hunting leathers, and knew this was going to take some getting used to.

Finding the quarters he shared with another recruit named Davis Gilbert took ten minutes all on its own. In the tight space the two of them managed to change and then rush back to the 'Mech bay with just two minutes to spare. The assignment sheet had not been posted yet, leaving him and the others waiting with some anticipation about where they would be posted.

Gunnery Sergeant Coombs came over and lined them up again to give them further orientation to Able's Aces. He told it to them straight, without any flowery motivational stuff. The Aces' three battalions were spread out over all six of the Rim Collection worlds, and constantly rotating to keep the pirates and other raiders off guard. Some of the senior Aces stood listening nearby, sizing up the green recruits. Occasionally Harley allowed himself a quick glance at them, hoping Coombs wouldn't spot him.

After two hours of briefing, the sergeant finally stood at parade rest and asked the standard are-there-any-questions. There was a slight shifting among the recruits, but no one spoke at first. Then a tough-looking woman from Caldarium named Jill Sutcliffe asked a question that struck at Harley's own heart. "Gunnery Sergeant, what happened to First Company that requires this kind of complete replacement?"

A lieutenant, judging by her rank bars, left the sidelines where she'd stood watching and came toward them. "I'd like to answer that, sergeant," she said.

She looked hard and lean, with her dark red hair pulled back and shaved at the temples for better contact with her neurohelmet. One arm was in a metallic cast with augmentation to allow flexible movement. Scars still fresh enough to be pink showed on her hand and on one side of her face.

The recruits snapped to attention at the presence of an officer. They had been standing for the entire time, but Harley had barely noticed. The stress was so much less in the light G environment. The lieutenant returned the salute and then gave them a crisp, "at ease," and they all dropped to parade rest.

"I am Lieutenant Livia Hawke, commanding officer of First Company. For most of you, I will end up as your CO. Who asked that question?"

Sutcliffe spoke up loud and clear. "I did, sir, Private Jill Sutcliffe."

Lieutenant Hawke nodded in acknowledgment. "Your question deserves an answer, Private. Two months ago I led my company to Caldarium to hunt down the pirates who'd attacked that planet. We tracked them to a place called Birdsong Ridge, where they staged an ambush that took out my entire command. Those pirates were members of 'King' Hopper Morrison's Extractors." She spoke slowly, gravely.

Harley almost jumped at the mention of Birdsong Ridge. Like Hawke, the scars of his hurt were still fresh.

"I was the only survivor," she went on finally, "and that was more by luck than anything else. So that's why we're rebuilding the unit from the ground up. Experienced officers from other units will serve as the lance commanders, and the rest of you will learn from them.

"I'm sure Gunney here has told you all about the Aces and how we're run. Right now we're on a mission, and we've got to get you up to speed quickly in case you're needed. We're escorting the two trader DropShips to the jump point and will be traveling with them back to Gillfillan's Gold. Once there we will also provide security at the spaceport."

She stretched her arm in the cast slightly, flexing her fingers just enough that the move was noticeable. "Morrison's Extractors have been hammering us with raids of late. They still haven't tried to attack our command base on Gillfillan's Gold, but we can't let our guard down for a minute. A planet is a large place, with lots of room for a pirate like Hopper Morrison to sneak in a raiding party. That's why I've ordered Gunney here to get any of you with 'Mech experience into the simulators and up to speed with our configurations and resources. You'll be worked out, put in shape if you aren't already, or made stronger if you are.

"Bottom line, people, we're fighting a running war with the Extractors. They caught me off guard once, and I won't let it happen again."

In other circumstances Harley might have been impressed by her conviction, but a part of him couldn't help but hate her. She was the one who had cost him his brother's life. She had lived, and Ben had died. No matter what spin she put on it, that was how he saw it.

Only time would tell about Livia Hawke. Maybe she was more than pretty words, maybe not. But one thing Harley knew for sure. He would get the full truth of what happened on Birdsong Ridge if he had to pay with his own life to do so.

12

Harley feathered the right foot pedal of the *Assassin* BattleMech, making it jog to the right slightly as he pulled the throttle back, killing some of his speed. The dull gray hill cut off his field of vision, but he could tell from his secondary tactical display that the enemy 'Mech was on the other side, obviously waiting for him. According to the magnetic anomaly readings he was getting off his foe's reactor, it was a single 'Mech, most likely the same weight class as his forty-ton *Assassin*.

He considered the situation carefully. Going over the top of the hill would give him the high ground, an advantage in a charge. Then again, he could sweep the flank of the hill, taking on the enemy from the side. But he knew from his training that if he could detect the enemy, the enemy could detect him.

Every BattleMech was different, varying in the amount of armor and weapon configurations it carried. Those found in the Periphery tended to be older-class models like the *Assassin*, some dating back to the days of the Star League. But that didn't make the huge war machines any less deadly. Powered with fusion reactors and armed with enough firepower to level a city block, the three-story machines were fearsome.

Activating his com system, he coded in the frequency of his counterpart 'Mech, a fifty-ton *Centurion* piloted by an experienced Acer, Corporal Jord MacAuld. Jord was nearly three kilometers behind Harley. They had already encountered a heavier *Quickdraw*, and Jord's machine had suffered some damage to its hip actuator, which was slowing him down.

The *Quickdraw*'s MechWarrior was good and very fast. He'd managed to shred a big chunk of the armor off Harley's torso and right arm, and had done considerable damage to Jord's *Centurion* before buying the farm. Jord had told Harley to scout ahead and report back, and the reactor reading on his sensors told Harley it was time to call his backup.

"Alpha Leader, this is Alpha One," he said, cutting the throttle back to bring his 'Mech to walking pace toward the hill that seemed to loom in the distance. "I have a single-contact MAD reading at coordinates three-niner-two-point-two-one. Target is stationary. Request permission to engage."

"Confirming coordinates at three-niner-two-point-two-one. Permission denied, Alpha One. Hold off for a few minutes, Rassor," came back Jord. "You don't know what you're up against yet. Wait until I'm in range and can provide some support."

Harley licked the salty taste from his upper lip. He didn't want to wait. He wanted to fight. That was what the training was for, to test battle skills. He'd taken some damage, but he was running at almost ninety percent full efficiency. Given the damage Jord had already taken, it would be several minutes before he'd be close enough to provide any real assistance.

Harley came to a stop, and the moment he did, his secondary display began to tell a different story. The stationary reading was moving, traveling up the far side of the hill, closing the distance between them. His heart began to pound as he watched the image approach. Though it still was not in line of sight, he knew it would be only minutes before his *Assassin* and the other 'Mech would be able to see and shoot at each other.

Almost fidgety, Harley reached over and checked his target interlock circuits. On the primary trigger he had his medium laser and short-range missile rack. The secondary trigger controlled his five-pack of long-range missiles. Harley's fingers almost caressed the trigger controls on the joystick as he waited.

"Alpha Leader, this is Alpha One," he said into his neurohelmet mike. "Bogey is closing on my position. Request permission to engage."

"Negative, Alpha One," came back Jord's voice.

"Do not engage. Keep the bogey distanced and fall back until I can provide you support."

Harley shook his head, thinking this was a bad call. Ben had once told him that any plan ceased to have meaning once the enemy was engaged. Harley finally understood that. Jord's plan was already outdated in his mind. He had a lone target of the same weight class. He should be able to hold his own against it long enough for Jord to catch up to him. Either he would already have taken out the enemy 'Mech or Jord would arrive in time to assist, if necessary.

Ramming the throttle forward, Harley started toward the hill, racing up the steep sides to face the enemy. "Alpha Leader, this is Alpha One. I am engaging the enemy." The cockpit bounced slightly as he moved, and it felt warmer, more humid.

He spotted the *Spider* about the same time it spotted him. At thirty tons, the slightly smaller 'Mech was armed with a pair of medium lasers and its speed. The *Spider*'s MechWarrior didn't hesitate, opening up with a well-placed shot that slammed into Harley's center torso like a javelin. One of the lasers missed, but the other quaked Harley's cockpit forward and backward as the damage display showed a staggering loss of armor.

The impact shook Harley's senses enough to make him react. Triggering his second target interlock, he sent a salvo of five long-range missiles racing up the gray hillside. Two went wide and into nothingness, while three peppered the arm and right torso of the *Spider*. The shot seemed to stop the advance of the enemy 'Mech, which turned and began to race back toward the top of the hill.

"Alpha One, this is Alpha Leader. Break off your attack," Jord said, his anger just barely controlled. But Harley knew that the *Spider* was on the run, outgunned and outmassed. It was making a break to survive. If he didn't pursue now, its superior speed would put it out of his range. This was his first combat sim run with the Aces, and he wasn't going to botch it. He pressed the throttle full forward and felt a wave of hot air around his feet, which began to spike the temperature in the small cockpit.

"No can do, Alpha Leader. Am engaged and almost done here. When I'm finished with this guy, we can talk about it."

As the *Spider* reached the crest of the hill, Harley heard the tone in his ear indicating weapons lock. He thumbed his primary trigger and let go with the laser and short-range missiles. The laser missed, sweeping the air to the right of the *Spider* by a good eight meters. The missiles, however, found their mark. More powerful than their long-range brethren, the short-range missiles plowed into the right leg of the *Spider*, shredding most of the armor there. The enemy 'Mech seemed to stumble down the other side of the hill, out of sight but far from out of mind.

Harley was charging to the top of the hill to engage his foe when his secondary display flared a warning light. His eyes scanned down the dull gray hill and saw the *Spider* as well as a menacing, eighty-ton *Zeus*. Instantly, Harley understood what had happened. The huge assault class 'Mech had been behind the hill the whole time, its fusion reactor either shut down or in low-power mode. It had been waiting while the enemy *Spider* lured him in.

Too late, Harley realized he'd been led into an ambush.

The *Zeus* fired the moment Harley appeared, letting go with its autocannon and long-range missiles. Fifteen of the missiles were in flight by the time Harley worked his joystick to bring the targeting reticle to bear on the monster 'Mech. The missiles slashed across his torso and arm, splaying armor wildly. Harley wasn't sure how many of the salvo had hit, but judging by the warning lights on the cockpit display, it was a significant number.

Now the *Zeus* fired its autocannon, shooting a stream of sabot rounds into the *Assassin*'s left leg at the knee joint. The *Assassin* pitched wildly, and Harley experienced the vibrations of his cockpit like being inside a giant blender. His 'Mech staggered back, and he lost his balance.

Harley slammed down on both of the foot pedals and attempted to twist the joystick in an effort to compensate for the damage and the balance change, but he had no luck. The *Assassin* fell heavily onto its back, mangling armor plating as it did and throwing Harley violently against his seat's restraining straps.

"Alpha Leader, I've got a *Zeus* up here on the other side of the hill. I'm down," he said, while struggling to rock the BattleMech back to standing. It was slow going, but he rose just in time to meet a laser blast from the once-again-advancing *Spider*. The laserfire dug in where he'd already lost armor, finishing the job. Harley's damage display readings told that one of his heat sinks was now no more than a worthless hunk of dead weight. One thing was for sure, his 'Mech was going to be running a lot hotter if he lived through this.

He still had weapons and determination. More on instinct than by the targeting and tracking system, Harley swung his medium laser around and fired down at the spindly *Spider*, which was much closer than the looming *Zeus*. The crimson beam scarred the armor plating on the *Spider*'s torso, digging deep. A flare shot out, telling Harley he'd hit the fusion reactor shielding. The *Spider* toppled backward, but Harley didn't wait to see the fall. Instead, he backed down the hill to be spared the assault from the *Spider*'s partner.

But where in the hell was Jord? Harley didn't wait for the arrival of the *Zeus*. He turned around and made a break down the hillside at a full run. Hot, wet air filled the cockpit from the loss of the heat sink and the exertion of his 'Mech. He glanced at his secondary display and saw that he'd lost his long-range missile rack and ammo.

Luck had been on his side, however; the ammo in his torso hadn't detonated. He wondered just how long his luck would hold out.

"Alpha Leader, now would be a good time for you to show up with that fire support," he said to Jord over his neurohelmet mike.

Out of the corner of his eye, through his cockpit viewscreen, he finally saw Jord's *Centurion*. It was not alone. Another 'Mech was shooting at it, a *Grasshopper*, cutting it to shreds with its deadly array of medium lasers. Jord was too far away for Harley to give him any help. Besides, he would have signaled if his com system was still on line.

Harley saw his choice, with not much time to make it. He could attempt to flee, but there was too much enemy activity in the area to hope to get out. He could try and link up with Jord, but the distance was too far for him to hope to arrive in time. He could also turn and attack, but that was suicide.

Attacking, however, was the last thing the enemy would expect. He checked his jump jet controls and verified that they were on-line just as the *Zeus'* autocannon sent a volley of shells rippling past his cockpit window.

Thumbing the control, he brought the jump jets to full blast. The powerful thrusters were designed to provide 'Mechs with a limited jumping capability. He planned to use it to turn his 'Mech into a weapon. He rose into the air and angled the *Assassin* back up the slope to where the *Zeus* was still rushing downward, firing at Harley wildly as he rose in the air.

The heat in the cockpit reached a new zenith, but Harley ignored it. The cooling vest he wore over his bare torso pumped coolant fluid around his body to pull some of the heat away, but it was a losing proposition. His focus was on the larger 'Mech as he closed the gap with the running *Zeus*. Just before the assault 'Mech passed under him, Harley did what every MechWarrior dreams and fears. He cut off the jump jets.

The *Assassin* dropped with such force that as he hit the *Zeus* its feet dug deeply into the shoulders and cockpit of the rushing 'Mech. Everything happened so fast that Harley could barely keep up with the string of events. The *Zeus* tumbled under him, and he lost control of his *Assassin,* its leg armor and support struts breaking as the two 'Mechs collided. The *Zeus* spilled down the hill while Harley's 'Mech fell face first, again throwing him hard against the restraining straps. His neurohelmet banged against the cockpit controls, and a hiss of steam or coolant spewed into the air in front of him, blocking his view of the hillside.

His ears were ringing slightly as he tried to make some sense out of the data his displays were giving him. The fall had cost him dearly. The number of red and yellow warning lights on his damage display alone painted a grim picture. If the sensors were accurate, his right arm and the medium laser housed there were nothing more than worthless scrap. His jump jets and legs were badly damaged, and he had apparently lost his right knee actuator and his gyro. He still had power, but there was no way for him to move, no way to stand up, and no way to fight. The battle was done, over, for him at least.

He'd lost his first 'Mech in a combat environ. How he handled the defeat was important if he didn't want to get posted to the infantry.

Checking his short-range sensors, he saw that the *Zeus* was only a few meters away, shut down, not moving. Apparently Harley's attack had had the desired effect, taking down the enemy 'Mech at the cost of his own.

There was some satisfaction, however. He was still alive, and he had prevailed against superior numbers. His long-range sensors, damaged either in the fall or from the heat in the cockpit, were off-line. Harley knew that somewhere out there was the *Spider*, and hopefully Jord was having better luck than he was with his own enemy.

There was a loud knock on the cockpit "hatch." Reaching up in the dimly lit confines, Harley opened it and stepped out onto the flight deck of the *General Gordon*. The cooler air of the ship's deck made goose bumps pop out on his arms and legs as he moved. He removed the neurohelmet and tucked it under one arm. His arms and neck ached as he moved; he hadn't realized how much he'd tensed up during the simulated combat.

Turning back to glance at the simulator pod, he saw that already the fake steam and smoke had been shut off and that the system was resetting itself. The rocking pistons that had simulated the impact damage leveled and reset to a horizontal position. From four nearby simulator pods, other veteran Aces MechWarriors as well as green recruits emerged. All were drenched in sweat like him. Some frowned, some smiled. Corporal Jord MacAuld was not smiling.

Gunnery Sergeant Coombs moved to the front of the group and shook his head. He was running his hand back through his crew cut as if it would soothe his mind. "Private Patterson, you went down first. Do you have any idea what you did wrong?"

Patterson was obviously embarrassed, her cheeks flushed red as she tried to avoid looking the sergeant in the eye. "I think I engaged the enemy at too short a range, Sergeant Coombs."

"Damn right you did," he snapped back. "You were piloting a *Whitworth*, Private. The bulk of your firepower is long-range missiles. You rushed into point-blank range and tried to fire. Those warheads need some range to arm. Short-range missiles don't need that, LRMs do. You were practically dancing with that *Charger*. *Charger*s are all geared for short range. Hell's bells, you could've pounded Corporal Glancy into snail-snot if you'd just kept back. You'd better spend some serious time getting up to speed on 'Mech capabilities and configurations."

Coombs turned slowly in place, then found Harley.

"I don't even know where to begin with you, Rassor. First you abandon your lance-mate, who, I might add, is already heavily damaged. He orders you to not advance, and you rush into the middle of an ambush.

"You then see what is happening to Corporal MacAuld and instead of attempting to save his life, you instead turn on a 'Mech almost twice your mass and try a harebrained stunt like 'Death from Above.' "

Coombs seemed to be waiting for Harley to say something, so he did. "Sergeant Coombs, the attack worked. I realized that I'd screwed up and I assumed I'd be too late to reach Corporal MacAuld before his engagement was finished. Rather than try and flee the battlefield, I decided it was best to take out the *Zeus*."

"Damned arrogant and the only reason the attack worked was that you were either the luckiest bastard to walk the planet or nobody figured that someone would try a stunt like that against those odds."

"Yes, Sergeant," Harley said, though in his heart he wasn't convinced.

"If you hadn't abandoned Corporal MacAuld

in the first place, you wouldn't have ended up with a dead 'Mech. Next time, Rassor, quit trying to be such a hellraiser and cooperate with your lancemate."

Livia Hawke stood in the corridor as the veteran Aces she'd brought with her to Slewis filtered out while Sergeant Coombs continued his debriefing and dress-down of the new recruits. She and Coombs had watched the entire run from the simulator controls, but she knew there was more to what she saw than datafeed readouts and figures.

As Corporal MacAuld came out the door, he gave her a quick salute, which she returned. "Tell me, Corporal, you were out there with Harley Rassor. What do you make of him?"

Jord seemed to search for the right words. "Gunney is right. The boy didn't stick close to me. That ambush was well staged, but if it had been the two of us together we'd have stood a better chance."

"What else?" she asked, noting his initial hesitation.

"Well, sir, what Gunney won't say out loud was that Rassor was right in what he did. He couldn't have helped me. Yeah, he blew it early on by leaving me so far behind, but in reality, taking out that *Zeus* took cast-iron balls and you know it. Any normal rookie would either have run for the hills, hid behind me wetting his pants, or froze. For him to turn and take out a veteran like Jeremy Lewis, that takes some skill. I'll grant you this is a simulator. It tosses you around and it's more like a holovid game than actual combat, but he's got a real gut instinct in combat. He thinks fast on his feet."

"Bottom line it for me," she said firmly.

Corporal MacAuld rubbed his brow. "Either he's the luckiest kid to step into that simulator in a long time, or he's got a natural feel for a 'Mech that's rare. Either way, I'd be willing to fight alongside of him."

Hawke nodded and gave MacAuld leave to continue on his way. A chill ran up her spine and she stood alone in the metallic hallway, letting the light gravity hold her in place. What MacAuld said left her shaken. Somebody had asked her about Benjamin Rassor just after he'd first joined Able's Aces, and she used almost exactly the same words to describe him.

13

DropShip General Gordon
Inbound, Gillfillan's Gold
Rim Collection
The Periphery
31 March 3059

Livia Hawke sat in her office aboard the *General Gordon* studying the report on the datascreen for what seemed like the thousandth time. She'd ordered a heavy training regime for her raw recruits, and by all indications they were making progress. The fact that everything had gone without a hitch thus far wasn't enough to assume anything more, and Hawke knew it.

Eight days ago the *General Gordon* and the trader DropShips in their charge had docked onto the spine of the merchant JumpShip as scheduled, then jumped out for Gillfillan's Gold. Now the three DropShips were on a burn toward the planet. A lot could still go wrong, and she wasn't about to let her guard down now. Birdsong Ridge had taught Hawke that even a "milk run" could turn deadly.

In two days' time they'd be on the ground. She looked forward to it, because Gillfillan's Gold was the only home she had these days. But until the traders had finished their business here and were safely on their way once more, however, she would remain vigilant.

"King" Morrison had struck all over the Rim Collection by now, but he had yet to attack Gillfillan's Gold. Major Able figured it was just a matter of time. If Morrison was trying to put the fear of god into the Council of Planets and throw doubt on the Aces' ability to defend their worlds, there wouldn't be a better place to do it. Gill's Gold wasn't just the site of the Acer command base. It was home to the Rim Collection government as well.

The problem was that a single planet was a massive undertaking to defend, let alone trying to protect six of them. Major Able had spread the Aces' three battalions thin trying to protect the most vital areas of the Rim Collection. She put those thoughts out of her mind for the moment, and returned to studying her reports. Gunney Coombs had been pressing the new recruits to their limits and beyond. Calisthenics, hand-to-hand and gunnery drills, and hours on the simulators filled their waking hours. She had insisted on a tight schedule with little leisure time. They were all good militia troops, but now they would be on the front lines. She knew from experience that some militia troopers simply couldn't cut it, and it was best to weed them out now rather than later.

This group was doing well so far, and it disturbed her to see Harley Rassor's name at the top of the rankings. He'd started out rough, almost reckless in his actions. But he'd adapted quickly to different 'Mechs in drills and had shown an aptitude for working well in a unit, despite his initial run in the sim. Rassor's ratings in 'Mech piloting and gunnery were a good ten percent above his peers. In hand-to-hand combat, he was topped by only one other soldier. More important, he'd proved that he could learn from his mistakes, which was one of the most important skills a MechWarrior could have.

There was more. He had some of the same physical traits and mannerisms of his brother. That shouldn't surprise her, but it nagged at her constantly. It was as if Ben's shadow were following her, always there reminding her of Birdsong Ridge. She saw Benjamin's face every time she looked at Harley's. It was like a constant reproach for the way Ben had died.

There was something more that wasn't like Ben, though. Harley Rassor hated her. It was obvious in his behavior, which erred just this side of insubordination. It was the reason she'd ordered him to her office today. They needed to talk, clear the air. Major Able had ordered her not to discuss the events at Birdsong Ridge, but she would have to see just how far she could stretch that command.

There was a knock at the door. "Enter," she said firmly, rising to her feet.

Harley Rassor came in and closed the door, then snapped to attention. "Private Harley Rassor reporting as ordered, sir!"

"At ease, Private," she said, gesturing to the chair opposite her desk. "Please sit."

Harley took a seat and sat as rigidly as if he were still at attention. This wasn't going to be easy. She slowly lowered herself into her own chair, again seeing the image of Benjamin staring back at her from Harley's face.

"Private Rassor, you have done remarkably well since your arrival here. Top of the list in terms of combat competencies. Congratulations."

"Thank you, sir," he said stiffly, looking above or beyond or anywhere else but at her.

Hawke clasped her hands and set them on the desk before her, composing herself. "Private Rassor," she said with some formality, "I've called you here to see if we could resolve some of our problems."

"No problems, sir." His tone was clipped, correct.

"Private Rassor," she began again, choosing her words with care, "ever since you came on with the Aces I've sensed your hostility. I think we both know why."

A slight flush rose on Harley's cheeks. "I don't know what you mean, sir."

"You brother Benjamin served under me."

"Yes, sir."

"He died under my command."

"Yes, sir. He did, sir."

"And you blame me for his death."

This time there was a pause, slight, but noticeable. "I don't know, sir." Some of the stubbornness was gone from his voice, but not much.

A part of Livia Hawke wanted to tell Harley just how much she'd loved Benjamin. She wanted to tell him that her nights were a living hell where she would wake up drenched in sweat, wondering if she had indeed caused his death. She wanted to tell him that she too had suffered a wrenching loss.

But she could not. She was an officer. He was a subordinate under her command. To speak of such things with him would be inappropriate. She had crossed that line with his brother and now she was paying a heavy price.

"To be honest, Private, I also have questioned my own actions at Birdsong Ridge. I went back and reviewed every scrap of data from the battle, everything we knew, everything we saw, everything we heard, everything that happened. I was looking for something, anything, I might have done to change the outcome. I didn't find it. Knowing only what I knew that day, I couldn't have done anything differently." It had taken some time, but Major Able had been right.

"I guess we'll both have to be thankful you aren't making that choice again," he said coldly.

She ignored the sarcasm. "When I saw that you were posted to the Aces, I tried to have you removed from the roster, Harley. Your father apparently has some pull with Major Able."

"My father was the one who wanted me to join up."

"Why?" Hadn't their family lost enough, she wondered.

"The truth means a lot to us. I'm here to find out what really happened to Benjamin."

"I was there."

"Yes, sir. I know that. You were the only survivor."

There it was, the unspoken accusation. "Private, are you saying I had something to do with the ambush that killed your brother?" She already knew the answer to that. It was the way Major Able wanted it, but it hurt all the worse knowing that Ben's brother accused her too. Her own burden of guilt was heavy enough.

"No, sir," he returned coolly. "I'm saying that you alone survived the ambush. Nothing more, nothing less. There are others who think you may have set your own company up, that you led them to the slaughter."

"Do you believe that talk, Private?"

Harley gave a slight shrug. "To be honest, Lieutenant, I'm not sure. I've been raised to find out the truth for myself before making up my mind. The truth is all that matters to me. It's all that my family demands."

"If you're looking to assign blame, then I *am* responsible for Benjamin's death. I was in command of the company. I gave the orders that day."

"And my brother died."

"If I told you that I did not deliberately order them into an ambush, would you believe me, Private?" She leaned forward to rest her elbows on the desk.

"You can say whatever pleases you, sir. As I just told you, the truth is all that matters to me."

Hawke saw that she was up against a brick wall. She wasn't sure just what kind of MechWarrior Harley would make, but she had to define the rules for him. To do anything less was to invite rebuke.

"Very well, Private Rassor. You're carrying around some baggage. You don't trust me and you don't like me. I can handle that. Many good soldiers have fought under my leadership who hated my guts. But they didn't make it so obvious. If you hate me, hate me on your private time. When I am present, you will treat me with the respect my rank demands. That means you will look at me when I speak to you, and there will be a whole lot less attitude."

Harley nodded slowly once. "Yes, sir. Respect. Yes, sir."

She stood up, still looking at him. "Your brother trusted me in ways you will never understand, Private. That was between us. Over time, you will have to learn to do the same. I'm your commanding officer, but I know I can't order you to do this. It's something you'll have to work out all by yourself if you intend to serve under me."

"If you say so, sir," Harley said, also standing as he snapped a fast salute.

Hawke dismissed him, but was less than satisfied with the way things went.

Ten hours later she stepped onto the bridge of the *General Gordon,* cupping a mug of coffee in her hands. The call had come from Tagar Edelstein, the ship's captain. Gunney Coombs was there, too, rubbing the sleep from his eyes. It was late, very late. That meant the news was something that couldn't wait.

Captain Edelstein had been commanding the *General Gordon* ever since his father retired twenty years ago. In fact, an Edelstein had been in command of the ship since the day its hull had been laid down some centuries before. This Edelstein was somewhat somber and phlegmatic, but Major Able trusted him and that was enough for Hawke. He also managed to keep the centuries-old ship operational, which was more than she had seen of other DropShip captains in her career.

"Captain, I assume you had a good reason for rolling us out of our cribs?" she said.

"Sorry about the hour, but it's standard operating procedure for something like this."

"What is it, Captain?"

"Twenty minutes ago we lost contact with the primary communications satellite that relays signals to inbound ships. We switched to the backup satellite, and bounced our signal off of that. It was good for five minutes, then it disappeared."

"Satellites go down all of the time," Coombs said.

"Yes. But we ran some long-range photo scans. The satellites are gone."

Hawke understood instantly. "Satellites don't just disappear."

Coombs frowned with concern. "We've got company," he said.

Edelstein nodded. "For a mere mechanical failure, I would have let you sleep. With both of them gone, the only thing that makes sense is that someone took them out."

"How far out are we?" Hawke asked.

"Forty-three hours," the captain said. "If you want a faster re-entry, I can reduce our counterburn cycle. It will add some gees onto the last few hours, but will also get us there a few hours sooner."

Hawke nodded. "Then let's do it."

"What about the traders?" Coombs asked.

"Best to keep them close to us in case there's trouble. They land when and where we do and we give them the protection they need. What's our combat readiness, Gunney?"

" 'Mechs are at full readiness. The problem is that Glancy has come down with a bad case of the Slewis runs. She can barely walk, let alone pilot a 'Mech. Even if she quit running to the head right now, she'll still be down for a few more days fighting this off."

"Who do you recommend, Gunney? You've worked with these recruits."

"They're all green, sir. But if you're going to take one, Rassor would be my pick."

She'd known, of course, who he'd recommend. "Relay the information to the traders, Sergeant. Keep it routine. These merchants tend to get edgy if they think they're most likely dropping into a hot LZ instead of the marketplace. Contact Rassor and tell him and the rest of the lance to report to my office at 0700. We've got a battle to plan."

14

DropShip **General Gordon**
Zenith Jump Point, Gillfillan's Gold
Rim Collection
The Periphery
2 April 3059

Harley stared at the holographic display showing the hellish terrain surrounding the spaceport and Rectortown, the city closest to it on Gillfillan's Gold. Both sat in the bowl of a huge crater three kilometers in diameter that was encircled by mountains with dangerous passes, some filled with stagnant pools of water blackened by the industrial waste runoff from centuries past, others dry and barren of life. Small forests dotted the rocky hillsides. It was a slice of hell, yet it was home to Able's Aces and the struggling Rim Collection government.

The surrounding mountains, low plateaus, and tight passes were difficult terrain that could probably be navigated in vehicles, but the going would be slow in anything but a BattleMech, and even that wouldn't be much faster. About two hours away was Maroo, the capital of Gillfillan's Gold and the seat of the Rim Collection's Ruling Council.

For the last two days Livia Hawke and her lance of recruits had been gathered to plan a battle. Communication with the planet's surface and the Aces' base was open, but it was mostly filled with static, indicating that someone was attempting to jam the signal at the source.

Soon they'd be on the ground. Despite all the planning and study of the terrain, Harley was as nervous as before a big hunt, especially since this time the prey might be hunting him as well.

Lieutenant Hawke was speaking to them now. Harley saw Jord MacAuld hanging on her every word, as was Sergeant Jeremy Lewis. Jill Sutcliffe, on the other hand, looked diffident, perhaps because they'd gone over the plan so many times. It was true that by now they'd covered almost every variation and version of how the battle might unfold, if it did at all. Gunney Coombs was there, too, and his look of weariness showed that he, too, was probably fighting the battle in his sleep.

What they knew was that the someone had sabotaged the communications satellites and was jamming the signals from the Able's Aces headquarters. It was surmised that an unknown force of unknown size had dropped on Gillfillan's Gold, most likely to attack and seize the traders' precious cargo. The Aces' command base was about an hour away from the spaceport, located in the hills between the planetary capital of Maroo and Rectortown.

Harley's thought was to leave the trader ships in orbit while Hawke's lance linked up with the Aces on the ground. But that was his opinion from the cockpit of a single 'Mech. When he'd suggested it, Hawke had cut him off quickly. If the raiders had aerospace fighters, they'd be able to strike at the ships in orbit, she said. The merchant Drop-Ships were armed, but not capable of defending themselves for very long, if at all.

The *General Gordon*'s fighter bay carried a single *Lucifer*. That meant the ground defense would consist only of a full lance of four BattleMechs and an additional 'Mech that was being shuttled back to the Aces' base. Five 'Mechs, and a platoon of heavily armed infantry under the command of Gunney Coombs. Sergeant Davis Gilbert would pilot the lone *Lucifer* fighter. He'd drop at the same time as the ship, providing combat air patrol support.

Hawke's plan was elegant if not simple. The *General Gordon* would touch down a few minutes before the three trader DropShips. She would then deploy her small force to secure the landing zone for the traders. Depending on what her force encountered, they would expand their secure area to include all of Rectortown. Hawke told them that Major Able had run a secret land-line communication system from the Aces' base to a small office at the spaceport. Once the LZ was air-tight, they would establish communications with the rest of the Aces and formulate a plan from there.

Harley was surprised to be here at all, but Gunney had ordered him to take command of Corporal Glancy's *Sentinel*, saying she was too ill to take her place in Hawke's lance. He'd logged some sim combat with it, but this would be his first time in the cockpit. More than that, if it came to a battle, this would be his first time in a real fight at the controls of a BattleMech.

Harley's thoughts kept circling around his meeting two days ago with the lieutenant. It had been tense, and he'd resented her probing. He couldn't trust her after what had happened to Ben, but now she was his commanding officer, as she had been Ben's. He had to obey her, follow her orders, even though he suspected she was a traitor.

He brought his mind back to the present, where Hawke was using her laser baton to indicate a point at the bottom of the crater. "The path to the backup communications center is fairly tight going. Gunney, you and your infantry are going to have to do the lion's share of the work. Sutcliffe will escort you to provide some cover fire if the enemy is still there."

Jill Sutcliffe was shaking her head in doubt. "Sir, I have no problem with the plan," she said, "but should we risk it so soon after landing? For all we know, the bad guys have already disabled the land-lines to the base."

Hawke shook her head. "Major Able used his own people to run the fiber-optic line, so the locals don't know a thing about it. It was put in place for just this kind of situation."

Listening to those words, Harley felt a knot in his stomach. If there was a traitor in the ranks of the Aces, that person might well know about the secret communications system. If so, the enemy would have the same information. Then he gave himself a mental shake. He had to stop thinking that way or he'd start seeing daggers in every shadow.

As if to underscore that thought, the dull tone of the klaxon suddenly began to sound and the yellow light over the door lit up, casting a saffron glow over the room. Harley's heart began to pound.

Hawke spoke louder over the noise. "That's the signal, folks. We are commencing landing burn sequence. Suit up and let's get ready to rock."

The room galvanized into motion. The Mech-Warriors present trotted down the narrow hall to the ready room outside the 'Mech bay. The techs were there to help them strip off their ground gear and slip into their cooling vests. Harley dressed down to standard cockpit wear: shorts and tank top, a pistol belt and holster, and his vest. The neurohelmet would go on once he got inside his 'Mech. Oddly silent, they all suited up except for Gunney Coombs, who opened a locker and pulled out a menacing assault rifle that looked older than Harley—maybe even older than Da.

Harley was fourth in line as they proceeded into the 'Mech bay, with no time to pause and admire the 'Mech he'd be piloting. The *Sentinel* had been painted with the jagged black and white striping used for urban warfare. Black and white were also the Able's Aces unit colors, which Harley thought was good luck. An ace of spades was painted on the *Sentinel*'s left shoulder. Armed only with an Ultra autocannon, a small laser, and a small short-range missile pack, the *Sentinel* was a light 'Mech that depended more on dodging shots than armored protection.

Harley climbed up the gantry to the cockpit and climbed in, sealing the hatch behind him. It seemed smaller than a simulator cockpit, much smaller. He tried to ignore the confined feeling, but it was hard. Born and raised in the countryside around Thorpe, he had spent much of his life out of doors and in the open. Now his whole world was only as wide as he could reach out and touch with his fingers.

He carefully went through the 'Mech's pre-heat sequence, bringing the fusion reactor on line and throttling it up in less than a minute. The cockpit lights flickered to life, as did the primary and secondary displays. The *Sentinel* had been around for a couple of centuries and must have been patched together hundreds of times to have lasted this long. Harley wondered if he was worthy of it.

The DropShip rocked slightly, reminding him to tighten his safety harness. Then he adjusted the neurohelmet and tested the gyro controls. The neurohelmet read the neurofeedback from his own brain, translating his sense of balance to that of the BattleMech.

Suddenly his commline crackled to life. "Fireball Five, this is Fireball Leader," came Lieutenant Hawke's voice.

"This is Fireball Five Leader. I read your five-by-five," Harley said, assuming it was a standard communication system check.

"Rassor, this is your first combat drop. It's probably not the best time to tell you this, but the first time Benjamin dropped it was against a party of raiders on All Dawn. He was so wound up he forgot to detach the restraint system holding his BattleMech in the DropShip. He ripped it out and got KP detail for a week for the damage to the ship." She chuckled slightly in relaying the story.

Harley smiled at the memory of Ben, always so eager for action. "I'll try and avoid damaging the ship when we land."

"Good," she said, switching to a broad-band channel. "This is Fireball Leader to all units. Stand by for landing in fifteen."

Harley braced for the landing, which came as an oddly subtle "thud" that echoed even in his cockpit. The massive bay door opened, flooding his cockpit with the yellow-orange light of the sun of Gillfillan's Gold. Ahead were the walls of the crater and the broad tarmac of the landing zone. He toggled the restraint system release and throttled the *Sentinel*'s reactor to full power. In a dozen steps he was down the ramp and standing on the surface of the planet.

The buildings around the spaceport were of dull stucco construction, unremarkable and seemingly out of place beside the BattleMechs that fanned out from the *General Gordon*. He saw the figures of some civilians at the far edges of the landing zone, and his long-range sensors picked up nothing other than the transponders identifying the other Acer 'Mechs.

"This is Fireball Leader to all units," said Hawke. "Execute the second phase now."

Harley moved to the west edge of the spaceport. Switching to short-range sensors, he hoped to pick up some sign of an enemy, but got nothing. Reaching the small support shacks and fueling trucks, he swept them to make sure no enemy 'Mechs were using the buildings for cover. Still nothing.

His heart hammered in his chest as he checked the settings on his sensors.

"This is Fireball Six," came the voice of aero-pilot Gilbert in the earpiece of Harley's neuro-helmet. "Lieutenant, I've crisscrossed Rectortown twice. No sign of the bad guys."

One by one the members of the lance checked in, all with the same report. No sign of any enemy raiders. After several long minutes, the voice of Gunney Coombs came on. "Lieutenant, we've secured the comm center. I am relaying Major Able on the broad-band channel now."

There was a snap, then a firm male voice sounded over the commline. "Lieutenant Hawke," Major Able said, "sit rep."

"Yes, sir," Hawke replied. "We have secured Rectortown and are holding there. The trader DropShips should be landing in a few minutes. We assumed the worse when we saw that the relay satellites were down and we couldn't get through to you."

"Good move. I'm using communications protocol Charlie," he said, though Harley was not familiar with the phrase. "We have a raider force on-planet. Estimates are that it's a reinforced company, perhaps two companies. They arrived a few days ago, knocked out communications, and have been jamming our transmissions and generally harassing us. When we go after them, they fade away into the hills, only to come back and take sniping attacks at us. I've sent Black's Company out in pursuit, but thus far the enemy simply fades away."

"How many 'Mechs can you confirm, sir?" Hawke asked.

"We've seen just one company that we can confirm."

Harley knew that meant probably double that number of enemy forces were there, just not yet seen.

"Identity of the raiders?" Hawke asked.

"Morrison's Extractors, of course," said Major Able. The words hit Harley hard. The same pirates who had killed his brother, the ones who'd shot the weapons that took Ben's life. This was a chance for revenge, not just for him, but for Da and Jolee as well.

"And Lieutenant, you need to make sure your folks are up to speed on Clan tech. I went out against these folks when they first landed and I tangled with a Clan *Mad Cat*."

The information was disturbing. Clan technology was far superior to anything in the Inner Sphere, not to mention the older tech found in the Periphery. The idea of a pirate like Morrison having access to Clan 'Mechs was something to drop the Aces' morale. "Sir, are you sure?"

"Rat-bastard took me down. A Clan *Timber Wolf*—a *Mad Cat* by our battle computer's warbook. I couldn't believe it. I have no idea where Hopper Morrison got his hands on it, but we all know how deadly is its firepower. My own 'Mech is still in the repair bay from trying to fight it."

"Sir, I have the trader DropShips on approach as we speak," Hawke said. "Do you want me to have them divert to orbit or land?"

"Diverting into orbit might place them at risk of fighter attack. Even worse, it would damage us politically and financially if the trader ships aren't able to conduct their business. You're going to have to land them and provide them cover while they trade with the locals. Don't let them dawdle, though. If this is Morrison, chances are he's here to steal their booty.

"There are four platoons of militia in Rectortown. I haven't been able to reach them because they don't know about this land-line. Assume command of them and do what you can to secure the area. I'd like to send you help, if only a couple of 'Mechs, but it's too risky. We're going to remain here in the base. You're on your own. Able out."

"Yes, sir," Hawke said. "All right, Fireballs, you heard it from the Major himself. Those merchants are on their way down, and our job is to secure the area. I want every building around this spaceport vacated and secured. Jord, you and Lewis will stay here in town along with the infantry and militia. The rest of you will deploy on the upper rim of the crater. Check the area. Monitor and plant sensors at all the approach points. The rim of the crater gives a high-ground position that would let a 'Mech with the right armaments hit the ship and the spaceport. We've got to hold that high ground in case any of Morrison's people show up.

"Keep crispy out there, people. These raiders didn't show up just to have a cold beer. They came to steal, plunder, and raise hell. I've faced these boys before, and the last time cost me dear. I have a score to settle with the Extractors. But this is more than personal. We're going to teach them that no one tangles with Able's Aces."

=== 15 ===

Rectortown
Gillfillan's Gold, Rim Collection
The Periphery
4 April 3059

The past few days had been oddly quiet for Harley and the rest of the Acer and militia forces on the ground. When he heard that Judith Glancy was feeling better, he kept expecting an order to relinquish the *Sentinel* to her, but it never came. Maybe it was because he'd been patrolling his quadrant of the crater rim for two days, and was now familiar with the lay of the land.

Corporal Glancy was an experienced Mech-Warrior, but it would take time for her to catch up and learn the terrain and to identify the passes most susceptible to incursion. Hawke probably didn't want to risk Glancy not getting up to speed fast enough. Harley really didn't care one way or the other. Whatever his current posting and assignment, he had joined the Aces to track down the truth of happened to Benjamin. What Livia Hawke thought of him, one way or another, didn't matter.

Down in the crater that housed Rectortown, the traders had set up shop on the spaceport tarmac. The locals, despite the heavy security, had showed up in large numbers and were busy trading, dealing, and negotiating in the shadows of the Drop-Ships. Cargo-haulers arrived to drop off goods and carry others away. The market and the trading continued on into the night because Hawke had ordered them to cut their visit short because of the danger of an attack by the Extractors. The traders didn't complain. They said they would make even more profit if their time was short because the locals wouldn't be able to stall as long on deals.

Harley had always believed that the militia was a valuable part of planetary defense before he'd joined the Aces. That was before he knew what it was to command a 'Mech. Militia troops were armed with rifles and rocket launchers, but they wouldn't last longer than a few seconds against a raiding party of 'Mechs.

Gunnery Sergeant Coombs and his platoon of Acers infantry were groundpounders too, but they were trained and equipped to take on Battle-Mechs. The grapple rods they carried allowed them to scale a 'Mech, and their weapons were heavier and more deadly. Their man-pack PPCs and lasers were capable of eating up 'Mech armor.

In a few hours the merchants would begin loading their ships and then depart. The *General Gordon* would escort them safely to the jump point. If all went as planned, Harley would, in a few hours, be able to sleep somewhere other than the command couch of the *Sentinel*, which had been his home for the last two days.

He was adjusting his long-range sensors as he'd done so many times already on this watch when a glimmer through his viewport caught his eye. It was a flash of light, small, but out of the ordinary. It came from the opposite side of the crater, where Jord was posted. At first Harley thought it might be a flash of lightning, but there were few clouds in the sky.

"Fireball Five to Fireball Two," he barked into his neurohelmet microphone. There was no response on the commline, except for a snapping, a popping, "—ert. . .epeat—enemy . . ." Then the message broke up.

Harley throttled up the *Sentinel*'s Pitban 240 fusion reactor and switched to the company's broadband signal. "Fireball Five to Fireball Leader. Red, Red, Red." That was the signal announcing enemy engagement.

"Where are you, Rassor?" came back Hawke's voice.

"It's not me, it's Jord," Harley said. "Someone's jamming his signal, and it looks like weapons fire in his quadrant."

Hawke quickly took command. "Five and Four, hold your positions on the rim. This could be a diversion. Coombs, your people remain on the ground with the militia to keep the spaceport secure. Have the traders start loading up now. All other units, converge on Fireball Two's coordinates."

Harley saw a cloud of smoke rise from where

Jord MacAuld was posted, a sure sign of weapons fire. He was in a fight, but help was on the way.

A tense four minutes passed as Hawke and the others maneuvered through the passes up to the crater's lip. As Harley monitored the battle, the tempo seemed to pick up. His long-range sensors reported faint signals as the enemy 'Mechs moved among the rock formations, every so often coming into clear range.

Seeing a flash of PPC fire, and an errant missile salvo stir dust and throw smoke into the air, Harley considered ignoring his orders. He was of no use at all here. He should be over there, helping Jord. For a fleeting moment he remembered his first time in the simulator when he'd abandoned MacAuld and rushed in on his own.

No, he had orders and the Lieutenant might be right; this whole thing could be some sort of diversion. That was when his sensors flashed bright blue lights at him.

Over the last few days he and the others in the unit had set up remote sensors to monitor the passes and approaches. Something had just tripped one of his sensors in a pass not far from his position.

"Fireball Leader, this is Five," he called. "I have motion on outer marker eight. Bad guys are at the back door."

Livia Hawke's voice was tense in reply. "Understood, Five. We're engaged here. Four, move in to support Five while we clean up here."

Jeremy Lewis responded quickly. "On it, sir," he said, switching to a channel where he and Harley could talk without distracting the others. "I'm two minutes from your twenty. You wanna hold until I'm there, Rassor?"

Harley brought up the short-range sensor sweeps on his primary display. He was no longer alone. Four, possibly more, BattleMechs were starting to move, but not on him. They were heading toward the crater rim and the city/spaceport below. His battle computer was already dumping down data on the 'Mechs and attempting to identify them. One thing was for sure. The odds were against him.

"I can't wait. Tell Gunney that company may be heading his way. I'm going to move in and see if I can distract them."

He took the *Sentinel* quickly along the narrow roadway that ran along the crater top and emerged in a small clearing, filled with thin scrub brush, boulders of every size and shape, and Extractor BattleMechs. His head's up display rang out with multiple targets, and Harley wasted no time swinging into action.

Two of the 'Mechs stood near the crater's downslope. The lead 'Mech, a *Dragon*, was only partially visible, having begun its descent. Other enemy 'Mechs had also started down toward the spaceport and city below, and Harley understood that he was coming up on their rear-guard. A *Trebuchet* was facing away from him when he emerged into the clearing. Its thin rear armor beckoned him to open up with his weapons.

He began firing his short-range missiles and autocannon. One missile missed its mark, plowing into a rock formation past the pirate 'Mech. The other buried itself into the armor plating of the *Trebuchet*'s center torso, ripping open a nasty hole. The autocannon rounds were more accurate, stitching up the butt and back of the *Trebuchet*, flaying armor wildly with each impact. A wave of heat washed over his cockpit as Harley saw that he had stripped the rear of the raider clean.

The *Trebuchet* MechWarrior fought to keep from losing his balance on the crater rim. He half-turned his 'Mech and torso-twisted the rest of the way to bring his weapons to bear.

Harley rushed forward. The *Trebuchet*'s primary weapons were two racks of long-range missiles, fifteen each. If Harley could get close enough, they would be useless, lacking enough time to arm. He was counting on the fact that the raider pilot would instinctively try to use those weapons first, and he was right. Thirty missiles swarmed toward his *Sentinel*.

More than half of them hit as he charged his foe at a full run, but Harley had closed the necessary distance. He braced himself for the impact a milli-second after they fired, but the warheads flew about randomly, like fireworks, their propellant still burning. They danced madly in the air, scattering around the clearing.

Harley's heat was still high, but he knew he'd have to risk another attack. The *Trebuchet* out-massed and outgunned him. In a battle of attrition, he knew that time was running out. The *Dragon* that was almost out of his field of vision had stopped, most likely to join in to repulse the sudden attack at their rear flank.

Harley didn't waste time with his small laser, but instead used the joystick to sweep his target-ing reticle onto the head of the *Trebuchet*. He fired his missile rack first, followed swiftly by another barrage from his Ultra autocannon.

The short-range missiles dug into the right arm

of the *Trebuchet*, mangling armor plate in clouds of gray smoke. The autocannon hit the upper right torso and traced a line of blackened and blasted armor right up to the 'Mech's cockpit head. The larger BattleMech listed slightly under the staccato fire, tipping back slightly, most likely from the MechWarrior being tossed about in the cockpit by the deafening impact of artillery rounds.

Harley was determined to blast the 'Mech's rear, which was nearly stripped clean after his initial assault. Another good set of hits and he might possibly down the *Trebuchet* before the *Dragon* joined in the fray. He continued his charge, wishing his heat sinks could also pick up the pace, and came within forty meters of the *Trebuchet*. As he moved across its field of vision, the pirate 'Mech fired a blast from one of its medium lasers, almost hitting Harley mid-stride. He crossed in front of the 'Mech as if he were making for its soft rear.

Then he stopped his run and began to back up.

The *Trebuchet* MechWarrior had to know that his rear armor had all of the consistency of toilet paper. Harley was counting on the MechWarrior trying to protect that rear. Again, he guessed right. The *Trebuchet* torso-twisted once more to where the *Sentinel* should have been if Harley hadn't stopped and reversed. By backing up and turning slightly, he had tricked the pirate into giving him what he desired, a point-blank rear shot at a 'Mech that was almost standing perfectly still.

He couldn't miss.

He didn't.

His small laser sliced out part of the center and right rear torso, burning away the myomer bundles that were a BattleMech's muscles. The short-range missiles seemed to disappear into the hole in the armor from his earlier attack, only to explode from within. Black smoke and crimson flames shot from the hole.

Due to the heat buildup in his 'Mech, he held off for a full second before firing his Ultra autocannon, then sent a steady stream of shells into the guts of the *Trebuchet*. Each round exploded deeper and deeper into the heart of the battle machine, mangling internal structure and important subsystems. He saw arcs from electrical discharge snap from within the hole and a bright yellow roaring flame that told him he'd struck the fusion reactor or at least its shielding.

Through the heat that was cooking him in his cockpit, he watched the *Trebuchet* start to quake like a man in a seizure. An internal explosion, albeit a small one, seemed to take the life from the 'Mech. It went limp and crashed down over the rim of the crater toward Rectortown, down toward the *Dragon* that was now retracing its steps back up.

Harley's eyes darted to his heat monitor, which was spiking from his running and attacks. He didn't waste time. He turned slightly and began to move across the image of the rising *Dragon* that was pursuing him. Somewhere, moving down toward the spaceport were the other two Extractor BattleMechs. But for now, Harley had his own problems.

He felt no arrogance about the death of the *Trebuchet*. He'd only downed it because he'd surprised it from behind and had maintained the initiative in the engagement. The same wouldn't happen with the *Dragon*. Its MechWarrior knew Harley was there, and at sixty tons, he had such a sheer advantage over Harley that it was only a matter of time. The *Dragon* kept to a slow walk, letting Harley get some distance before he would unleash his deadly wall of long-range missiles. First, he let go with his standard autocannon and medium lasers.

One laser shot missed by less than a meter from the cockpit. The other dug into the *Sentinel*'s right leg, slicing through the armor plating. The autocannon fire hit his left torso, mauling most of its armor. Another hit there and he would start to die just the way his victim had.

He dodged his 'Mech behind a tall rock outcropping that blocked the line of sight and continued to pull back.

"Sergeant Lewis, I could use some support here," he said into his neurohelmet mike. There was no response, and Harley didn't wait for any. As he moved the *Sentinel* to bank around another mound of boulders, he took another blast from the *Dragon*'s autocannon, this time hitting his right arm just below the elbow actuator. Though it only damaged armor plating, Harley knew that time was running out.

His sensors blared a warning that another 'Mech was near, then Harley looked out and saw the form of a *Hermes II*. "Is this a private party or can anyone join?" Lewis' voice said in Harley's earpiece.

"Call it, Sergeant," Harley managed to stammer.

"I'll get his attention on the right. You move to his left flank," Lewis said. The *Hermes II* was an older model 'Mech but still packed a lot of firepower. It swept past his *Sentinel* and moved out, blazing away at an unseen target with its auto-cannon and laser.

Harley backtracked his steps and came back to find Jeremy Lewis and the *Dragon* squaring off like two sumo wrestlers, blazing away at deadly close ranges. Harley throttled his *Sentinel* forward into a trot and switched all of his weapons to the same target interlock circuit.

Despite the damage the *Dragon* had sustained, Harley knew his weapons would not tip the balance. It would take something more, something dramatic to tip the scales of the battle. Great victories require great risks, Ben had always said. Now Harley understood all too well.

He broke into a charging run, not moving to flank the *Dragon,* but to take it down. Harley lined up the Extractor 'Mech in the view of his cockpit and throttled the *Sentinel* forward with every ounce of power the reactor could muster. The *Dragon* warrior was so occupied with Lewis that he never saw Harley until it was too late. Harley triggered his weapons in a final salvo a full second before the collision took place.

In his mind he saw the flicker of light from his missile barrage just before the *Dragon*'s torso filled his cockpit view. The impact was staggering, and he felt his body strain hard against the command couch's restraint straps. The blood rushed to his face, and his cheeks burned hotter than the air in the cockpit as he struggled to control his 'Mech. Even the feedback from his own brain to the gyro system wasn't enough. The *Sentinel* staggered and fell backward, again throwing Harley around in the cockpit.

The damage indicator on his secondary display

was not painting a pretty picture. Much of his torso armor was gone, but his weapons were still intact. Thus far he hadn't suffered any internal damage, but it wouldn't be long. He only hoped the *Dragon* was suffering from similar damage, enough for Lewis to finish him off. Otherwise his ordeal would be even worse.

Working the foot pedals and joystick controls like a dervish, Harley rocked the *Sentinel* up and saw the results of his charge. The *Dragon* was lying on its side as Lewis pumped laser and autocannon fire into it. It was blackened from the damage, and its armor and myomer were so badly burned from Lewis' assault that it barely looked like the 'Mech Harley had slammed into a minute before.

The *Dragon* shook violently as its missile ammunition started to explode internally, ripping the 'Mech apart. The MechWarrior attempted to eject, but the angle of the fallen *Dragon* was not good. The ejection seat blew clear of the head, but instead of rising straight up into the air like it was supposed to, it was launched at an angle, straight into a rock formation. The parachute opened anticlimactically as the smashed MechWarrior and seat tumbled down the rock face, leaving a red-brown smear where the pilot had been crushed.

"Sit rep," Lewis snapped.

Harley rechecked his systems. "I'm operational, but my armor is mangled."

"That was one hell of a move, Rassor. That *Dragon* topped you off by twenty tons, but you got him off his feet and that was enough for me to finish him."

"Sergeant Lewis," came a third voice over the

comm system, a voice Harley had never heard before. "If you and Glancy are done, there are 'Mechs moving against the spaceport and a lot of scared civilians."

Lewis responded quickly. "It's not Glancy, Major. It's one of the recruits, Private Harley Rassor."

Harley turned his battered *Sentinel* around and saw the form of a ferocious ninety-five-ton *Banshee* standing a hundred meters away. The Aces' unit insignia and a large red number "one" were painted on its brown and gray camouflage pattern. Harley knew who it was without needing to be told.

"Rassor, eh? That was one hell of a move, kid. I take it you took out that *Trebuchet* I came across, too."

"Yes, sir," he said.

"Well, your brother was a good man, and it looks like you're cut from the same cloth. Welcome to the Aces. I'm Major Jerry Able."

The Major didn't wait for Harley to answer. "Form up behind me," he said. "We've got some mopping up to do."

16

Rectortown, Gillfillan's Gold
Rim Collection
The Periphery
4 April 3059

The spaceport was in a state of pure chaos as Harley trailed Major Able's *Banshee* to the scene. Smoke rose into the air from some burning cargo containers on the tarmac, and civilians seemed to be running in every direction. From the cockpit of his battered *Sentinel* Harley could see at least a lance of four 'Mechs moving among the citizens, firing wildly at cargo haulers, pallets of goods, and apparently other BattleMechs at the far end of the spaceport.

"Provide cover for those noncombatants," Able ordered over the commline. "Drive the pirates out of the city."

The raider 'Mechs were weaving among the panicked civilians to make it hard to shoot at them without risk to civilian lives. BattleMechs were massive machines that could run at speeds of up to sixty kph or more, but doing so without stepping on innocent people in this situation would be impossible. Though the crowd was rapidly breaking up in flight, it was still a problem that Harley had no experience dealing with.

His mind raced with the adrenaline rush of combat. Though this was his first real battle, his fingers and feet moved to operate his 'Mech controls and weapons more by reflex than conscious thought. He couldn't help thinking of Ben and that these were the pirates who'd killed him. This was a chance to right the wrong done to his family. It wouldn't be just revenge to destroy these pirates, it was justice.

He saw Lieutenant Hawke's *Orion*, seemingly undamaged, blazing away with its autocannon and large laser. Her target was one Harley had never seen close up before. Painted a dull green, it was a Clan *Timber Wolf*, the one the Inner Sphere had named a *Mad Cat*. The pinnacle of 'Mech technology, it shrugged off her attack as if it were more a noisy nuisance than a viable threat.

Harley didn't wait around the see the counterattack. His *Sentinel*'s armor was almost totally gone, and tangling with a deadly monster like the *Timber Wolf* was not very high on his agenda. He spotted a more tempting victim, an older model *Crab* that was drawing fire from Jill Sutcliffe's *Panther*. Aptly named, the 'Mech was oblong-shaped and squatted closer to the ground, with pincerlike weapons at the end of its arms. From above, the *Crab* looked like a giant mutated crayfish.

From Harley's point of view, it looked more like a target.

Sutcliffe's *Panther* fired its deadly PPC, unleashing a bolt of charged particles that tore into the *Crab*'s torso. One armor plate was so badly damaged that it flew almost fifty meters in the air before clanging down onto the tarmac. The *Crab* tottered slightly, and just as it reached the apex of its list, reeling from the damage Sutcliffe had inflicted, Harley opened up with a blast from his Ultra autocannon.

The stream of shells seemed to link the two 'Mechs across the space between, if only for a millisecond. The shells slammed into the left torso of the Extractor, blowing even more armor away. The *Crab* MechWarrior staggered a step back, stunned by the arrival of a new threat, and was most likely trying to assess the situation.

In the distance Harley saw a *Crockett* and the *Timber Wolf* fending off attacks by Major Able and Lieutenant Hawke. There were other 'Mechs in the distance, but they were moving away rather than toward the battle site, which was fine with Harley.

The *Crab* brought one of its large lasers around to bear on Sutcliffe's *Panther* and fired. The brilliant beam hit her left leg, frying off most of its armor plating with a popping sound that Harley could hear even inside his cockpit. The *Crab* MechWarrior needed to be distracted. Harley juked to his right and brought his short-range missiles on line, letting go a paired salvo.

One missile missed its mark, continuing into the side of a nearby building and blasting part of the outer wall away in a cloud of dust and brown smoke. The other dug into the midsection of the *Crab*, cratering even more of the few remaining armor plates there.

It was enough to get the pirate's attention. The *Crab* turned to face Harley and suddenly found itself bathed in an azure blast from Sutcliffe's *Panther*. The barrage hit the damaged left torso, plowing past the scraps of remaining armor and digging deep into the *Crab*'s internal structure. The 'Mech spun and dropped hard, and Harley turned to find another target.

The one he found was the *Timber Wolf*. Its firepower didn't make it a target Harley relished, but he had no choice but to take it on. The *Timber Wolf* was raining a deadly barrage of long-range missiles at Major Able's *Banshee*. Harley thought the force of the blast must have destroyed the *Banshee*, which was now obscured by a cloud of smoke. Then, through the smoke, Harley saw the *Banshee* lumber into motion, battered, charred in many places, yet still functional.

At seventy-five tons the *Timber Wolf* was a 'Mech to strike fear in any warrior. Forged with technology that only his brother Ben could have dreamed of, the *Timber Wolf* could tangle with the larger *Banshee* and bat it about like a toy. Ben had told him all about the wonders of Clan technology, of weapons with greater range, less heat, and more kick. Now Harley found himself facing that same deadly technology at the controls of an already battered 'Mech that had been in service for centuries.

Remembering what he'd done with the *Trebuchet*, he brought his *Sentinel* to a full run and darted across the *Timber Wolf*'s forward field of fire. Speed was an ally regardless of technological differences. He ran in a direction away from Major Able's *Banshee*, hoping the pirate would be more interested in the larger, more deadly foe.

In the background he saw Hawke's *Orion* riddle the pirate *Crockett* to the point that the 'Mech was in the process of turning and running. Fire from shoulder-launched anti-'Mech missiles spilled out from several buildings as the *Crockett* passed, evidence that Gunney Coombs and his men were still active and in the fight as well.

The running kept Harley's heat levels high, but he ignored them. The *Timber Wolf* was formidable, but it had the same weak rear armor as most 'Mechs, and he hoped to reach it. He felt the massive feet of the *Sentinel* slide slightly on the tarmac surface, and he compensated as much as possible as he arced toward the rear of the *Timber Wolf*. He lined up his Ultra autocannon and pressed the trigger on the target interlock the very instant he heard the tone of weapons lock.

The stream of shells hit the boxy weapons pod arm of the *Timber Wolf*, rending some of its armor protection, but not hitting the thinly protected rear torso Harley had hoped to blast. As the Major's *Banshee* advanced, Harley felt his stomach tighten as the *Timber Wolf* pivoted its torso faster than he had ever seen or imagined a 'Mech capable of doing. Its weapons pods seemed to find him, and then he saw the crimson burn from two large lasers sweeping in his direction. One missed, the other hit his left leg with such tremendous force that he lost control of the *Sentinel*, dropping and sliding across the tarmac with a grinding sound that sent a chill down his spine.

The 'Mech's knee actuator was gone. Without control of joint movement, the task of righting the BattleMech at all became tricky. Harley began trying immediately, rolling the 'Mech on its side and pushing with its arm extended. It took effort, but eventually the 'Mech was back on its feet, though he didn't know how reliable the left leg was. He took a step, dragging the damaged limb like a wounded animal, but he was operational.

Part of him expected to take another savaging from the *Timber Wolf*, but his sensors and eyes told him the other 'Mech had bugged out. In the distance, he could see it and three other Extractor BattleMechs climbing up the crater wall on a worn trail, leaving Rectortown, fleeing into the mountains.

He glanced over to where his sensors told him Able's Aces were gathering. The Major's *Banshee* had lost over a third of its armor and was almost totally blackened from the attack. Jord's *Black Knight* was badly mauled and so was Sutcliffe's *Panther,* one of its arms hanging almost as limp as Harley's leg. Hawke's *Orion* had some damage, but seemed to have been spared the brunt of the fighting, at least from what Harley could see.

"Fireball Leader," he said on his channel to Lieutenant Hawke, "request permission to pursue."

Her voice was stern. "Rassor, you should have been on the broad-band channel. Major Able has ordered us to stand down and secure the spaceport."

Harley wanted to protest. These were the people who had killed Benjamin. Letting them go seemed wrong, criminal. He glanced down at his damage display, where the red and yellow lights told just how battered the *Sentinel* was. Pursuit, all on his own, would be certain death, even if he could catch up with the pirates—which was doubtful.

The next hour passed quickly as the repair crews and militia moved in and began the cleanup effort. The Aces had taken relatively minor damage. Jeremy Lewis' *Hermes II* had been downed by the *Timber Wolf* in a matter of seconds of engagement at the spaceport proper. Lewis had survived but been injured while punching out of his cockpit. Five of the pirates had been dropped, though none had been as fortunate as Lewis. All were either dead or dying by the time they were recovered. The Aces infantry lost eight men, and the militia even more.

Harley stood at the foot of his *Sentinel* and surveyed the damage to the towering machine. Gone was most of the camouflage paint, either scraped clean or burned off by weapons fire. The knee actuator was totally exposed and looked like a human's broken knee bone, only this one dripped a black ooze from the wound. He was surprised at how much damage the 'Mech had taken, as well as how suddenly weak he felt.

A sound on the tarmac behind him made him turn to see who it was. Approaching him were Lieutenant Hawke and another man, who by his rank insignia alone could only be Major Jerry Able. Harley managed a quick salute, which the Major returned.

"Not too shabby for your first time in a shooting battle," Hawke said. "From the initial reports I got from the Major and from Sergeant Lewis, it sounds like you handled yourself admirably."

"I did what I had to sir," Harley said, embarrassed by the praise.

"I wanted to formally introduce you to Major Able," she said, gesturing to the Major at her side. "Major, this is Private Harley Rassor."

The major shook Harley's hand firmly. "You did a good job up there. Your father and brother would be proud." The mention of his father and Ben seemed to add to the weight Harley felt on his tired shoulders.

"Your brother was a good MechWarrior, Private Rassor, and this unit will take some time to recover from his loss. You and your family have my sympathies."

"Thank you, sir. I was surprised to see you after hearing your communication that you wouldn't be able to send any units."

The major smiled and cast a knowing glance at Lieutenant Hawke. She answered for him. "The communications code the major used in his message indicated that he assumed the land-line communications had been compromised. So everything he said was essentially a lie to throw off whoever might be listening in. In the end it was a pretty good move."

"So there is a traitor in the unit," Harley said, more to himself than his commanding officers.

Able nodded once and slowly. "There's a rat somewhere. Lieutenant Hershorn of our intel unit is double-checking everything, but this is twice we've been outfoxed. This time, however, we were able to turn the tables on them."

"Did they get away?"

Able nodded again. "Their DropShips were spotted by Gilbert's *Lucifer* heading toward the jump point. They left, but they did their damage," he said, waving his arm at the debris and burned pallets of goods left behind by the attack. "Odd, though. Hopper Morrison is playing a much deadlier game than he has in the past."

"How do you mean, sir," Hawke asked.

"First off, he hit us here on Gillfillan's Gold, which he hasn't risked doing before. He's getting bold now that he's got a mole in the unit who can tell him where we'll be and when. When I stepped up our timetable, only eight other Acers knew your arrival date, yet the pirates were waiting. They also knew how to tap our back up communication system."

Able crossed his arms and looked in the direction the enemy 'Mechs had fled. "And second, this was not a standard pirate raid," he said.

After all he'd just been through, Harley felt free enough to say he didn't understand.

"When 'King' Hopper Morrison raids, he comes to steal," Able began. "But none of those pirate 'Mechs were equipped with cargo nets. That tells me that they had something else on their minds besides stealing." Cargo nets were needed because transport space on a BattleMech was virtually nonexistent. Able shook his head. "No, Morrison was raiding here to scare the locals, to put a scare into the Rim government. I'll give him this much, he's starting to show some imagination. At least now he's demonstrating some strategy."

Harley heard more footsteps approaching, and turned to see Corporal Judith Glancy standing a few meters away, staring up at her 'Mech. Her eyes followed the damage down to where Harley stood at the foot of the 'Mech, and she came to stand in front of him, hands on her hips.

"Private, what in the name of hell have you done to my baby?" As if to emphasize her point, a thick blob of green coolant dripped from the damaged heat sink in the torso and spilled onto the tarmac, spattering Harley's bare legs.

"He saved some lives, Corporal," Major Able said, smiling broadly. "And he pounded the bejesus out of some of the men and women who killed his brother."

17

Able's Aces Command Post
Gillfillan's Gold, Rim Collection
The Periphery
12 April 3059

Harley stepped into the office and snapped a fast salute that was curtly returned by the officer waiting for him there. He was a lieutenant by rank, which in Able's Aces carried a lot of weight. Harley had received the summons to report to Lieutenant Hershorn's office in the Aces' command center. He assumed that the man sitting at the desk was Hershorn.

Harley accepted the lieutenant's offer to take a seat. The officer was lanky, mustached, and with the wrinkles that came from much time spent out of doors. There was a hint of cologne in the air, which Harley found unpleasant. "You've made quite a first impression in the Aces, Private," the man said. From where he sat, Harley could now make out the "Hershorn" name plate on the lieutenant's uniform.

Harley shrugged slightly. "I did my duty, sir. Nothing out of the ordinary."

Hershorn shook his head. "I'm not just referring to your action in the Battle of Rectortown, Private. It's rather out of the ordinary for a new member of the unit to request classified intelligence data or battlerom readouts from an engagement. Especially without the consent of his commanding officer."

It had been a week or so since Harley's first bittersweet taste of battle, but he hadn't forgotten the reason he'd joined the Aces. Lieutenant Hershorn was the Able's Aces intelligence officer, responsible for maintaining internal security and providing intelligence data to Major Able and the battalion/company commanders. Learning where the data from the Birdsong Ridge engagement was stored and who was in charge of it hadn't been too much of a problem. But Harley had been a long time waiting for permission to meet with the lieutenant.

"I was unaware that I needed the permission of Lieutenant Hawke, sir."

Hershorn cocked one eyebrow. "Your need to know regarding that engagement is limited. For me to release the information you require usually requires the permission of your CO."

"Sir, my brother—"

"—was a highly valued member of this unit," Hershorn said, opening a file on his desk, glancing inside, then closing it again. "I am well aware of your connection to the Aces. I know that your brother died in the fighting on Caldarium. I reviewed the after-action report and was on the relief mission that recovered our dead."

"Then you know why I asked for the data."

"Revenge?"

"I want the truth about what happened to Benjamin. I want to know how the ambush was set, who had access to the mission operation parameters."

"You speak as if you suspect someone in the unit, Private."

Harley paused, fearing he may have said too much, too fast. This was, after all, the man in charge of intelligence. If anyone suspected a traitor, it would be him. "I'm not sure what I suspect. I haven't seen the data. I will say this, my family and I find it suspicious that my brother and virtually his whole unit were wiped out."

Hershorn tapped his fingers on the table in thought. "The concerns of you and your family do not warrant a violation of standing orders regarding intelligence material. Why not simply ask Lieutenant Hawke for permission to access the files?"

Harley wasn't sure of what to say next, then decided that only the truth would do. "I'm uncomfortable asking her, sir."

"Understandably so." Hershorn seemed to hesitate, as if Harley were touching on his own thoughts. "Private, I knew Ben. He wasn't an officer, but some of us don't stand on formality. Ben was my good friend. He was also a good Mech-Warrior. Very good. I was disturbed at the way he died, what happened to him on Caldarium."

Hershorn slid a file folder across the desktop

toward Harley. "This is a report that addresses the questions you raise."

Harley reached over slowly and drew the file to him. He started to open it and stopped. "This is against regulations, isn't it?"

"Technically no. It's against regulations for me as the Intelligence Officer to release this material to you. I'm not releasing it to you. That *would* be a breach of protocol. That file was on my desk and you happened to come across it. You were flipping through it, but it never left this office. And the material in that file . . . well, let's just say that it was not properly marked as classified material. It must have been an oversight on my part. Since we had a meeting here, there was nothing out of the ordinary. Do we have an understanding, Private?"

With those words, Lieutenant Hershorn turned his chair around, rose, and walked to his one small window and stared out through the blinds.

Harley watched him for a moment, then opened the file and began to read. It wasn't thick, a report of only three pages. The document was labeled "Intelligence Summary" and had been prepared by Lieutenant Weldon Hershorn. The conclusion was the same one Harley had come to: The ambush of The Hawke's Talons on Caldarium was the result of an intelligence leak to the enemy. The source of the leak was unknown, but relatively few people had access to mission orders. Major Able and Captain Max Chou, First Battalion Commanding Officer. Livia Hawke, her direct reports, who were all dead, and an assorted list of comm officers.

Reviews of all transmissions and communications logs showed no communications with

Hopper Morrison, but the security breach had to have been accomplished in a short period of time. From the time Able ordered the mission to the time his troops were slaughtered on Birdsong Ridge was a matter of two months. It would have taken some time for Morrison to get his troops in position to ambush.

The list of primary suspects was very short. One was a comm officer who Harley had never heard of who had a cousin in Morrison's Extractors. The other was Lieutenant Livia Hawke.

Harley didn't know how long he sat there staring at the pages. Finally, he closed the file folder silently and set it back on the desk. The words he'd just read were not proof, but they took him a step further down the path toward the truth. And now he thought he could glimpse where he was going and even make out the figure at the end of that path. Lieutenant Livia Hawke.

"Sir, thank you," Harley said, rising to his feet.

"I have no idea what you're thanking me for, Private." Hershorn returned, taking back the file and returning it to the safety of his desk drawer. "But there is one more thing you and I need to discuss."

"Sir?"

Hershorn did not return to his seat but crossed his arms as he faced Harley. "As I said, I was on the team that led the relief and rescue on Birdsong Ridge. I recovered the remains of your brother. Because we didn't arrive until several days later, a proper burial was not possible, so we had his remains cremated. We were going to forward these on to your family on the next transit flight to

Slewis. If you wish, I could include a message from you to your family."

Harley felt a little shaken by these words, but he kept his outward composure. "Yes sir, thank you. I'd like to send a message to my Da and my sister."

"We'll be sending the remains back this week. Just drop off your letter before then and I'll make sure it goes with them to Slewis."

Jord MacAuld jogged three steps to catch up with Harley. On Harley's left side, Bixby Finch did the same. The three of them had become fast friends over the last week. Bix was a tow-headed farmer who had come in as a recruit from Waypoint in the same group as Harley had. He and Harley had so much in common that they seemed to become good friends right off the bat. As for Jord, he and Harley had bonded ever since he'd seen Harley in action at Rectortown.

"So, Hellraiser, how'd it go with Spooky?" MacAuld asked.

"Spooky?" Harley chose to ignore the nickname he himself had picked up during the recent battle. He suspected that one of his two friends was responsible for tagging him with the moniker, and hoped that ignoring it would eventually kill it. Thus far, though, that had not been the case.

"That's the name the guys on the flight line have for Lieutenant Hershorn."

"Spooky because he's in the intelligence business?" Bixby asked.

Jord shrugged. "Sort of. He was a MechWarrior for a few years. They say he was really kinda odd. He doesn't have a lot of friends in the unit and keeps to himself. I hear he mumbles to himself a lot, kinda out there."

"Well, he seemed pretty nice to me," Harley said.

"Did you find out what happened to your brother?" Jord pressed.

"Yes and no. I learned that it's possible we've got a traitor in the unit."

"Most of us have already figured that out," Jord said. "I'm just shocked you think it's Lieutenant Hawke." Jord had not been attached to Hawke's company until it was rebuilt. He continued to insist she couldn't be the one, but that didn't change Harley's mind.

"She was the sole survivor," Harley said, as the trio continued walking along. "And in the last battle, her 'Mech came through the fight with barely any damage while everyone else got all chewed up."

Jord frowned slightly and shook his head. "You're saying you think she's guilty because she had the luck to survive an ambush and because she's a good MechWarrior? You're going to have to do a little better than that, Hellraiser."

Bixby jumped in before Harley could launch his rebuttal. "I'm new to the unit and all, but the scuttlebutt running through the ranks is that she's a little miffed about Chou getting promoted to Captain. It's a rumor, but maybe it was enough for her to decide to turn against Major Able."

Jord again shook his head. "Sorry, but I've been in the Aces for a while now. What you got a hold of is a rumor based on nothing. Chou was already in command of First Battalion when Hawke enlisted. He's always been her direct commanding officer, though Major Able takes a very hands-on approach with all the company commanders. Besides, if there was a problem between them, Chou himself would have been here on Gillfillan's Gold rather than training militia grunts on All Dawn. I'm afraid, Bix, that as a rookie, you need to develop some better rumor-mill contacts."

"What do you say we run down to the city and see if the new holovid has arrived?" Bix said, though he couldn't hide his dislike at being called a rookie. Harley had felt the same way, but thanks to the battle at Rectortown the unit veterans didn't rag him as much.

Bixby was hooked on the Immortal Warrior series, which took a long time to reach the Rim Collection. Most of the episodes of the holoseries had been made years before in the Inner Sphere and were only now making their way out to the Periphery.

"You guys go on ahead," Harley said. "We'll meet up later."

"You're not just going to mope around the barracks, are you?" Jord asked.

"No. I've got to write a letter to my father."

"Dear Da," Harley wrote, "I'm sorry it won't be me bringing Ben's remains back to Slewis, but I haven't accumulated enough leave time yet. When they told me about it, I got permission to send this note home with Ben.

"I'm sure you know how much I miss you and Jolee and how sorry I am not to be there with you when this sad package arrives. I am well, Da, and fought in my first battle as soon as we arrived here on Gillfillan's Gold. We fought the same raiders that killed Ben, and I killed one of them with more honor than they showed him. I met Major Able after the fight and he spoke highly of you.

"Don't worry, though. I wasn't injured in the fight and am doing well here in the Aces. I've even made some friends.

"I haven't forgotten why you sent me and have been trying to find out the truth about Ben's death. I have an idea who might have been the one who betrayed his unit, and it might be someone who was close to Ben. I can't prove it yet, but when I do, I'll make sure justice is done.

"I also wanted to tell you something Ben and I used to promise each other. As kids, we often climbed Baldman's Hill and sat there talking in the shade of that big tree up there. You know which one I mean. We decided that when we died, we wanted to be buried at the top of that hill, overlooking the valley. We promised never to forget our vow.

"We can't really bury Ben. The pirates that murdered him left his body to rot, which is another sin that they will atone for. I'm asking that you and Jolee go up there and scatter Ben's ashes onto the hill and down into the valley, and think of me and Ben and when we were all together in better times.

"I send my love to both you and Jolee, and hope that one day soon I'll be able to tell you I've fulfilled what I came here to do. Your son, Harley."

Able's Aces Command Post
Gillfillan's Gold, Rim Collection
The Periphery
16 April 3059

Major Jerry Able stared through the holographic map of the six worlds of the Rim Collection to where the other two officers stood. The dim dots of light from the holographic stars speckled their faces and arms.

Captain Maxwell Chou, commander of First Battalion, had arrived secretly the day before on a personnel transport. He was slight of build, with features showing sharp intelligence, one of the traits for which Jerry Able valued his old friend. With the three companies of First Battalion spread out over three of the six Rim Collection worlds, Max Chou needed to be a smart commander as well as a superb administrator.

The other officer present was Lieutenant Livia

Hawke, who Able had seen much more of in recent months. She stood at ease, but it looked like she'd regained some of the edge she'd lost at Birdsong Ridge. He hoped it would be enough. Able was about to ask a great deal from both of them.

"Max, I appreciate you taking time from your training duties," Able began.

Chou gave his impeccable smile. "Gladly, Major, though I was surprised that the orders did not come through the standard channels." The message had been transmitted and then hand-delivered with the greatest secrecy.

"It was necessary," Able said, deactivating the holographic display. "As you both know, we've been hit twice in the last few months. On Caldarium we lost virtually a full company of 'Mechs and aerospace fighter support. And now we've been attacked here on Gillfillan's Gold. The only good news is that our losses in the last strike were light and we kicked the pirates' butts."

" 'King' Hopper Morrison," Chou said coldly.

Able nodded. "The same. Until now Morrison has always attacked to steal and plunder, like the good little pirate he is. But these recent two strikes have been more strategic."

Chou nodded without command, waiting for Able to explain further.

"At Birdsong Ridge his goal was to destroy a company of 'Mechs, plain and simple. Oh, he ran a raid, but it was more a diversion. His real intent was to hurt us and hurt us bad. In one fell swoop he knocked out a third of First Battalion. That's not typical pirate behavior. If anything, pirates usually try to avoid a general engagement."

Able frowned as he thought about all that had

happened of late. "And when Morrison's band showed up here it wasn't to rob the merchants like he's done before. They made no attempt to steal the cargo. No, he came down to hurt us and to stir up the local population, to put the fear of god into them."

Captain Chou smoothed his dark goatee in thought. "If I didn't know better, I'd say Morrison is branching out. He's starting to look at a bigger game."

Able leaned on the table and held the eyes first of Chou, then of Hawke. "He aims at crippling the Rim Collection to the point where he can take the whole shooting match."

Hawke was obviously startled. "Sir?" she said.

"By weakening us he scares the Council of Planets. We did beat him back during the raid on our base, but he knew we would. He still got what he wanted, which was to make the locals think they aren't safe enough with us. If he destabilizes the situation enough, Able's Aces could lose its contract with the Rim Collection.

"President Moroney has already been accused of using us as his own private army here on Gillfillan's Gold. The other planetary representatives are saying that while they suffer from Morrison's raids, on Gillfillan's Gold we drive off the pirates."

Chou nodded. "It makes it look like we can't do our job."

"Will they try and hire other mercs?" Hawke asked.

Able knew the issue had already been raised in the Council of Planets several times, usually after one of Morrison's raids. Each time the motion was voted down, but the margin of votes was getting tighter.

"Oh, Hopper Morrison would love that," Able said sarcastically. "Classic divide and conquer. Each world would press to have its own mercenary force. There'd be no shared resources or ability to coordinate our efforts. Without a central command structure, each planet would be a free-for-all for whoever was there.

"Morrison could play each planet off against the rest, each mercenary leader against the others. Knowing him, he might even persuade some of the mercenaries to join him. A lot of the merc units out here in the Periphery are only in it for themselves. Some might sell out their employers to set up their own piece of a private kingdom. No matter how you slice it, a decentralized military apparatus would be easy pickings for someone like him.

"Morrison might even be able to intimidate individual planets or the entire Rim Collection into paying him protection to end the raids. Aside from the Aces, the Extractors are the only military presence of any size out in this part of the Periphery. That's another way he could get control."

The Rim Collection was a young government, still somewhat wobbly, learning to walk before it could run. Now it was in jeopardy. It wouldn't take much for Chou and Hawke to realize that both their livelihoods and their homes were at risk. Chou had a family on All Dawn. The last thing he would want was for "law and order" to be in the hands of a ruthless pirate like Hopper Morrison.

"There's more," Able went on, "and it's the

hardest part of all of this. In both the last two raids, a traitor turned over vital information that permitted Morrison's Extractors to pull off their attacks. It's the only explanation for how the pirates seem to be more prepared with each strike."

Chou was shaking his head in disbelief. "Are you sure, Major?"

"Positive. On Birdsong Ridge they knew exactly where Lieutenant Hawke intended to deploy. At Rectortown, they knew we'd pushed up the timetable of our arrival. If anything, we may have been more than one leak, but I'm willing to bet it was one primary source for now."

Livia's expression was grave. "Any idea who, Major?"

"Actually, I'm almost positive," Able said. "And it's going to be you, Livia." He pointed a finger at her. "You are on restricted duty for three more days performing non-combat related assignments. After that you'll have to leave Gillfillan's Gold. You are exiled until I say otherwise, Lieutenant Hawke."

President James Moroney, leader of the Rim Collection, looked more like the professor he'd once been than a politician. His receding hairline, wire-frame glasses, and seeming frailty gave him the air of a timid, bookish man. In his case, looks were deceiving.

Jerry Able knew that Moroney had been kicked out of the Inner Sphere for stirring up dissent, which was how he'd ended up out here in the Periphery. In a very short time, the former professor had mobilized the leaders of six independent worlds and persuaded them to form a confederation. They were now known as the Rim Collection and hoped to go from being backwaters of the Periphery to become a true state to be reckoned with. That dream was now at risk.

"Jerry," Moroney said, "I've always been straight with you. This plan of yours is full of risks."

"I understand your reservations, Mister President," Jerry Able said. "This is a turning point for both of us. You brought me in to defend your nation. We did that, and we raised and trained militia on each of the six Rim planets. Morrison's Extractors are a real threat to all you've accomplished so far. I believe this is a plan that will eliminate the danger they pose."

Moroney took off his glasses and rubbed his eyes before speaking. "There are others in the Council who might turn your plan to their own advantage."

Able knew that was true. Councilman Roberts, the representative from Otisberg, was the outspoken leader of Moroney's opposition and he'd managed to win more support of late.

"You're right, Mr. President, but I think you can sell it to them. Tell them how bad we've been hurt both militarily and financially. All I'm asking for is a few months' time, three months—four tops— and when I'm done, the Rim Collection will be more secure than ever."

Moroney took off his glasses and methodically began polishing the lenses with a handkerchief. Able knew it was a ploy to buy himself a few moments of thought, enough to weigh the alternatives, consider the risks, and look down the undefined roadway to the future.

"Which worlds would be left undefended by your troops?" Moroney asked finally, slipping the wire frames of his glasses back around each ear.

"Gillfillan's Gold, All Dawn, Waypoint . . ." Able said. He paused, then softly, ". . . and Otisberg."

Moroney winced at that, knowing what it would take to convince Roberts to accept such a condition. "Does it have to be Otisberg too?"

Able nodded. "I'm afraid so, sir. But they won't be totally defenseless. We'll move out eighty percent of our force, and the other twenty percent will remain behind. Weakest of the worlds will be Gillfillan's Gold."

"Jerry, history is my specialty. I studied it my whole life before coming here, and since then I've lived what I studied. I agree with you that this little government we've cobbled together is at a crucial turning point in its history. I've seen it coming, but I never dreamed it would be like this." He looked past Jerry Able as he templed his fingers in thought.

"Morrison's Extractors are a viable threat. You're right about their recent raids. They've upped the ante, and are making it a new game. They want to break us or take us. Either way, they win. And you may not be the only one who has a traitor in his ranks."

Able nodded. That someone in the Rim Collection might be working with Hopper Morrison was a real possibility. He suspected it too, but didn't have the resources to prove it yet.

"Mister President, I think I've found a way to

deal with my internal security problem," he said.
"If all goes as planned, we should be able to disable any security leaks of yours as well."

"I hope you're right, Jerry. If not, a lot of people
will suffer."

Jerry Able knew it was a risk they would have to
take. "I am right, sir. I just need you to buy me
some time with the other council members."

Moroney let out a long sigh of resignation.
"Well, then, all that's left is for me to do my part."

The Council Chamber of the Rim Collection
was a relatively small room, befitting the young
government it housed. A semicircular ring of
desks faced a central podium where the President
stood. The room was dark, windowless, and the
gleaming wormwood furnishings gave it a regal,
yet forbidding air of formality and power.

Each of the six Rim Collection worlds sent a
single elected representative to the Council. From
his podium, President Moroney looked around at
their faces, one at a time. It wasn't hard to read
their expressions, and he knew well enough which
ones were friends and which enemies. Now he
had to do something he hadn't needed to do in a
long time; he had to control them.

"The next order of business is a security issue
under article three of our charter," he said, citing
the confidentiality rule. By law, no member of the
council could speak outside these walls about the
matter they were about to discuss.

"Yesterday I received a report from Major Able
regarding the recent raids against our worlds. In
both cases, his unit suffered considerable damage.
As such, he has invoked a clause in our contract

with Able's Aces. One that I am sorry to inform you of at this time."

Councilman Roberts spoke up from his seat, his arms crossed defiantly. "What clause are you talking about, Mister President?"

"Major Able is pulling two of his three battalions out of the Rim Collection. He has negotiated a short-term contract with the Lyran Alliance and will be leaving for a five-month operation."

The announcement went off like a bomb. Everyone began to protest at once. "He can't do this, Mister President. The Rim Collection will be left defenseless against these pirates," said Councilwoman Warner.

"According to our legally binding contract with the Aces, Major Able *can* do this for upwards of six months. Considering how behind we are in our payments to him, I fully understand both your apprehension and his predicament. Able assures me that the goal of this undertaking is to raise enough funds to fully refit and expand his units to better defend us when he returns. He will leave some of Third Battalion behind, and we still have our planetary militias to defend us."

"When he returns?" spat Roberts, leaning forward on his polished desktop. "We won't be here when he returns. Morrison will mangle us but good. The time has come for us to approve my motion to hire additional mercenary units."

The other five representatives again began talking at once, and it sounded like a vote, if taken, would favor Roberts.

"Esteemed Councilman," Moroney said, "I appreciate your desire to bring in additional forces, but I must point out that the proposition requires a majority vote and my signature, which I am not prepared to provide."

"Sure," Roberts countered, running his hand over the few hairs left on his balding head. "You've been using the Aces like your own private army. I notice that during the strike on Gillfillan's Gold, your losses were minimal. Unlike the last time Otisberg and Caldarium were hit."

Moroney smiled in a deliberate manner, maintaining his calm. "Your allegation is completely false, Councilman. For you to even hint that I have misused the power of my office is inflammatory and carries the risk of censure. What proof do you offer for this wild accusation?"

Roberts backed down, but his eyes were hard. "I apologize, Mister President," he said, his tone subdued. "I am simply concerned for the safety of the people that I represent."

It was obvious to Moroney that the debate was far from over. "You would be mistaken if you believe for a moment that I am any less worried about our people than you, Councilman," Moroney spoke as if he'd taken offense, though most of it was for show. "However, Morrison's Extractors are mere pirates. If we beef up our militia forces and tighten security, I think we can weather this tiny storm."

"And there I disagree," Roberts countered. "I propose that each world be allowed to hire additional mercenary forces to bolster our militias. My people will demand it."

Moroney had been waiting for the discussion to reach this point. He had planned on it. Jerry Able had asked for only three months, maybe four, and

Moroney had promised to give it to him. They'd come too far together to part ways now.

"Councilman Roberts, esteemed leaders of the Rim Collection, I share your concerns. However, we are also bound by the terms of our contract. I would agree to support the proposition that we enter into only short-term arrangements with other mercenary forces. That allows us to fully honor the terms of our contract with Able's Aces and still maintain a strong defense. Both sides win."

"Who do you have in mind, Mister President?" asked Councilman Warner. "How many trustworthy mercenaries can we find who are close enough to even get here in time to do us any good?"

"We will recruit through legitimate channels, namely the Mercenary Review Board on Outreach. All contracts would be signed by me as President, per our charter. That way none of us risk a member planet attempting to raise a private army, as Councilman Roberts points out. Furthermore, upon the return of Able's Aces, all interim contracts terminate."

Roberts was clearly thrown off stride by Moroney's sudden shift. From the look on his face, his mind seemed to be scrambling to find any flaw in the logic. "You would be willing to allow us to hire mercenaries with such agreements?"

"You have my word, and will have my signature on such an article, with the provisions I have indicated."

Councilman Randel of Slewis spoke up, "I am no expert in travel times, but Outreach is in the Inner Sphere. It will take a long time to get someone there and back with a mercenary unit."

Moroney did not waver. "If we are doing this to

protect ourselves legitimately, then we do negotiations and recruitment through legitimate sources only. If that means a trip to Outreach or to a world with a Class A HPG to contact Outreach, so be it."

"It will take time," Randel added.

"Yes, it will," Moroney returned, but he was smiling inwardly. He'd bought Jerry Able his time. Now it was up to Able to pull off his end of the bargain. If not, neither one of them could predict how things might end up from there.

Within two hours of heated debate President Moroney was signing the article as he proposed, and Councilman Roberts was gloating over having his way.

19

Able's Aces Command Post
Gillfillan's Gold, Rim Collection
The Periphery
16 April 3059

From the journal of Harley Rassor:

So much has happened in the last few days it's hard to know where to begin. We're going to be leaving the Periphery for a while, and off time has been in short supply between all the drilling and sim runs.

Bigger than that for me is that my suspicions regarding Lt. Hawke have been mostly confirmed. Two things have helped set my mind on that. The first is that Major Able announced that she was being relieved of duties effective tomorrow. Jord heard she was being sent off-planet to one of the Aces' other bases. Bix said he thinks she's being drummed out of the unit. All I know is that the Major has removed her from command of

our company and has made Gunney Coombs a
Brevet-Lieutenant. It's only temporary, though.

I don't want to read too much into this but after
the information Lieutenant Hershorn showed me,
it seems like removing her from front-line duty
shows they don't want her in a position where she
can leak intelligence. Maybe the Major and Lt.
Hershorn simply don't have the evidence they
need to prove she's the traitor, so sending her off
somewhere is the best they can do right now.

She came out and gave us all a good speech
about how much she enjoyed serving as our CO
and how she hopes we will give Lt. Coombs the
same degree of support. It was a pretty short cere-
mony, but it sure sounded like she was leaving for
good. I'm not sure how I feel about that. If she was
the one who sold out Ben and the others, why
should she just walk away alive? But now that I'm
part of the Aces, I'm also glad she won't be able to
hurt us again if she's the one who gave away se-
crets in the past.

I decided to do some more investigating on my
own, and I followed Hawke to Rectortown last
night. She went to three bars, looking for someone. It was easy to keep to the shadows so she
wouldn't see me in those seedy joints. They reminded me of Brent's Bar back home. Dark places
for dark people and dark thoughts. That was in
one of the poems in the book Da gave me.

I wasn't too worried about her seeing me anyway. I was off duty and what I do with my time is
my own business. Besides, I doubt she'd say anything, being an officer and not encouraged to frat-
ernize with us noncoms, but I didn't want to take
the chance anyway. She's up to something and I'm

going to prove it. If she knew I was following her, it would just muddy things up.

She met with some pretty shady characters in two of the places. I asked some questions afterward, but the patrons were pretty tight-lipped. I finally got a waitress to tell me that one of the men she talked to is Klaus Freeman, a "pirate." I think the locals use that phrase to describe anyone who doesn't have an obvious means of support, so it's hard to know. Another guy at the bar said that he was a JumpShip captain who lost his ship a few years ago. In places like that, it's hard to say who is telling the truth.

If this guy was a pirate, though, it adds to the long list of things pointing to Hawke as the traitor. But until I know for sure, it would be reckless for me to act. I know that's what Da would say if he were here.

I'll never forget how I felt when I saw her *Orion* out on the tarmac with barely a scratch while the rest of us were beaten black and blue. Either she's one hot MechWarrior, or they simply didn't shoot at her. Jord told me her 'Mech was totally destroyed on Birdsong Ridge and that she barely escaped with her life. Maybe that's just the way she wanted it to look. She could have punched out and then they fried her 'Mech afterward. Since Lieutenant Hershorn wouldn't give me access to the recovered battleroms, I have no way of proving it one way or another, at least not so far.

Guilty people shouldn't get away with their crimes. Da once told me that time was the greatest leveler of justice. That one way or another, the guilty would always pay. I know I don't want to wait years for time to play judge on her if she's guilty. Justice should be swift. Anything else just doesn't seem fair.

Apart from that, I got assigned a permanent BattleMech. It's an *Enforcer*! A medium weight 'Mech. Ben would've been pleased, just like I am. Most of the new recruits got either lights or mediums. I checked her out both in the bay and on the training course. She's old—a real antique—but she's mine. With an autocannon and a large and small laser, she packs quite a punch. She's got jump jets, too, which they say can be handy in a pinch.

I came back from lunch today and found that someone had painted "Hellraiser" on my cockpit hatch. I assume it was Bix did it, but he says not. It looks like I'm not going to be able to shake that nickname any time soon, but I'm not making a case out of it. A lot of the veterans have nicknames painted on their cockpits, too.

We got pulled out this afternoon for a formation, the entire company. What Major Able had to say kind of bothered me and still does. He told us he'd accepted a short-term contract for the unit with the Lyran Alliance and that we'd be shipping out in the next month or so for a half a year. I signed up to fight for the Rim Collection, not to go off and fight for some other government. Bix and Jord told me they feel the same, but no one is saying so out loud. Major Able is popular with all of us and no one wants to go against what he thinks is best for the unit.

Bix says it's all about money. The Aces are a mercenary unit. From some rumor Bix has heard, the Aces haven't been paid regular by the government. With the raids and the losses we've taken from Morrison's Extractors, they say the major was forced to look for a way to generate revenue elsewhere.

Until I joined the Aces, I'd never left my home-world. Now I'm going to leave the Rim Collection altogether and even the Periphery and go all the way to the Inner Sphere. Ben would've loved such a chance. It was all he talked about in the last few years, all the new weapons and 'Mechs and other military ware they were coming out with. Me, I don't care much for any of that stuff. I didn't sign up to kill people but to find out the truth about what happened to Ben so Da and Jolee and me could see some kind of justice done.

I did kill someone in the fighting at Rectortown, but I did it defending the Rim Collection. I'm not like "King" Morrison and his band, killing people just to make money. There's a difference between murder and defending yourself and your people. Besides, the warrior I killed was a member of the pirates who killed my brother.

They've been keeping me busy lately. Not just me but all the new recruits. First Company is start-ing to come together real well. Jord got a replace-ment 'Mech. The damage to his *Black Knight* will take some time to repair, so they gave him a fairly beat-up *Victor*. He's assigned to Fireball Lance under Sergeant Coombs. So's Jill Sutcliffe and Jeremy Lewis.

I'm in Bishop Lance. Bix says it's named after the chess piece, but it sounds too religious to me. My "official" designation is Bishop Two. Bix and his *Vindicator* was Bishop Three. The fourth MechWarrior is a woman named Dabney Fox who pilots a *Hatchetman*. From what I've seen on the simulators and on the test fields, she's good with a 'Mech but not with people. Whenever I've tried to talk with her, she barely answers, then walks away.

Our Clash Lance has Gilbert's *Lucifer*, two tanks, and a platoon of jump infantry. They were originally Gunney Coombs' troopers, so those infantrymen are no slouches. Most ground-pounders are intimidated by 'Mechs. These guys eat Battle-Mechs for dessert. They're kind of hard to get to know too, and keep to themselves tighter than a pack of bandi rats in heat.

Despite being busy with all the drilling and other work, I miss home. I haven't been able to hunt here. Those were some of my best times back on Slewis, out in the forest with my bow and in my leathers. I did a lot of my thinking that way, with only the sounds of the wind and the trees and the forest life around me. Back home, I was alone a lot. I didn't even have to think about it. Now I eat, work, and sleep surrounded by other people eating, working, and sleeping just a few steps away.

I better stop now. We've got a night combat drill on a training field none of us have run before. I've never fought at night. I wonder what it will be like?

20

"What are you waiting for, Rassor?" asked Brevet-Lieutenant Gunney Coombs, chomping down on his cigar so that it raised slightly. "An engraved invitation? Why don't you just make your bet, boy?"

Harley looked at the cards and then at the other members of Coombs' Company gathered around the table. A thin haze of smoke hung in the air, along with the smell of sweat and of the beer they'd all been enjoying. He was having fun, the most fun he'd allowed himself since joining the Aces, since the death of Ben.

The game was new to him, and he won several hands right off the bat. He stayed in the game, but then his luck seemed to turn.

"Well?" Coombs grumbled again.

"I'm thinking, sir," Harley said, staring at the cards of his hand.

"Cut that 'sir' crap, Private. They can pin lieutenant's bars on my shoulders, but I'm still a sergeant at heart." Coombs wasn't much at home with his new rank as commander of First Company. He knew the promotion was only temporary, but he still couldn't seem to get used to it. Maybe that was why tonight he violated the regulation against officers fraternizing with non-coms, or maybe it was because he thought it didn't apply to their final night on Gillfillan's Gold.

"Thinking?" he scoffed. "Is that what you call sitting and staring at those cards?"

Harley studied his hand one last time and realized that logic was about to be damned. "I think you're bluffing," he told Coombs.

"And what about me?" asked Jill Sutcliffe, the only other member of his lance still in the game. Bix had folded without even waiting to see what he might get dealt next. Jord had held out through two rounds of betting, then he too had folded.

Harley looked at her. "You aren't bluffing, Jill. You simply don't have monkey-dung in your hand." He turned back to Gunney. "I call your raise."

Coombs smiled, his cigar tipping upward at an even sharper angle. "I like your style, boy. Let's see what you've got."

Harley spread his cards out on the table with what he tried to make a flourish. "Two pair, threes and jacks."

Jill tossed her cards onto the table, not even bothering to flip them up. "It's bad enough I didn't have zip in my hand, but now some wet-behind-the-ears-private knew it just by looking at my face. What's this planet coming to?"

Coombs shook his head. "Don't lose the faith, Jill-girl. This private is contributing to my retirement." He showed his hand. "Two pairs as well, tens and aces." With a sweep of his massive forearm, he pulled the chips over to the pile already sitting at his place, chuckling to himself. "Aces were always kind to me."

Harley stared at the cards in disbelief, then back at Gunney. "How'd you do that?"

Jord laughed once loudly. "It's easy, Harley. He set you up."

Harley looked quickly around the room and saw that everyone, save Bixby, was smirking or outright laughing out loud. He turned back to Gunney Coombs and saw that he too was chuckling. "Is that true?" he demanded.

"You didn't really think you were that lucky for the first hour, did you?" Coombs chided. "I just wanted you to get overconfident and feel a little more free with that first payroll wad of C-bills."

Harley felt his anger boil, which didn't happen very often. He stood up and was about to stomp out of the room when Coombs also stood and laid his beefy hand on Harley's shoulder.

"Don't get all torqued off, Rassor. This is a little initiation we do in First Company. It was your turn, that's all."

Harley was still angry, but the way Gunney's hand rested on his shoulder reminded him of Da. That calmed him down right away and suddenly he couldn't help giving a chuckle of his own.

Coombs blew a stream of cigar smoke up into

the air. "Why don't the rest of you kids play the next couple of hands," he said. "I want to take this private outside and have a little chat with him."

Coombs motioned to the door and Harley followed him out into the cool night air. He drew a long breath of the fresh, clean air, knowing that tomorrow they would be leaving this world. After that, they'd be breathing DropShip air for a long time until they got to where they were going in the Lyran Alliance.

Coombs sucked on the cigar, its tip glowing dull orange and yellow in the night. "It was a night just like this," he said, staring up at the stars in the perfectly clear sky.

"Just like this," Coombs said, waving his cigar toward the sky. "We did the same thing to your brother Ben. Same initiation you just went through. He had almost the same look on his face when he realized what was going on. Seems like he caught on a little faster, but he was older, too. That night, we came out to this same spot to talk."

"They say he was a pretty good MechWarrior," Harley said, also looking up at the stars, wondering which one was the sun of his faraway home on Slewis.

"He was," Gunney said. "But he was no saint, Harley. I don't mean this as any disrespect, but Ben had a bit of the hellion in him. You do too, I've seen it. The difference is you've got more control. Ben, he let that hellion guide him. I damn near busted his testicles on more than one occasion. He didn't run with a good crowd, either, other than the Lieutenant."

Harley was caught off guard. "You mean Lieutenant Hawke?" He hoped that there was some

other Lieutenant that Gunney was referencing . . .
any other Lieutenant.

Coombs nodded. "I know you didn't know, and
nobody ever said anything to you. Ben and Livia
Hawke were a number, but we don't gossip about
other people's private lives in the Aces."

The words hit Harley like a brick wall. It just
wasn't possible. "You're joking, right?"

Coombs blew another slow stream of smoke
into the night. "No joke, Harley. Ben was doing
the sheet-dance with the lieutenant for some time.
Most of the rank and file knew only by rumor. I
saw them out together once."

"But regulations . . ."

Coombs snorted, holding back a laugh. "Hell,
Rassor, if regulations had all that power, we
wouldn't even be having this talk."

Harley felt dazed, barely knew what he was
feeling. Over the last month he'd started to come
to grips with the loss of his brother. He'd also
spent almost every hour of his free time trying to
find out the truth about what really happened at
Birdsong Ridge, or to find someone who had even
a shred of a clue about who had set up Ben and the
others who died there.

He still hated Lieutenant Hawke, but he'd
thought about her less now that she'd been
drummed out of command of First Company.
Still, he'd felt cheated by her transfer, because it
made it harder to learn the whole truth about her.
Now he didn't know what to think or feel or say.
Livia Hawke and Ben. Together?

"Why?" he demanded. "Why are you telling
me this?"

Coombs held his cigar out in front of him and

rolled it in his fingers as he studied it for a moment. "Because you aren't your brother. You've been keeping Ben alive with this manhunt of yours and it's time for you to move on. Living in the past has killed more than one MechWarrior. You've got some serious potential. Your company rankings are higher even than some of the veteran Acers. But you're fighting a battle you can't win, a battle with the past."

"Gunney, Ben was my brother. I can't just forget him."

"That's not what I'm saying, Rassor. I'm telling you that you need to use the same control you've got in the cockpit on your feelings about Ben. I've heard how you think Hawke had something to do with his death. That she betrayed us."

Harley felt like Gunney was trying to put him on the defensive, which confused him. "That's right" he said. "Everything points to her as a traitor. I've seen some of the reports, talked to people. Who else could've done this . . . could've betrayed the Aces?"

Coombs shook his head. "You've talked to some people, done a little digging. But I've got something you don't have. I knew Ben Rassor and I know Livia Hawke. She couldn't have led her own company to the slaughter anymore than she could cut off an arm or a leg. Even if her own life depended on it, she'd never sacrifice her command. Especially if her lover was among them."

Harley shook his head, feeling like Gunney's words only pulled tighter the knot around his heart. "What you're telling me is that I'm no closer to the truth, to the justice my Da sent me to find, than when I got here."

"No, Private Rassor," Gunney said, turning to Harley. "What I've told you is that you know who *didn't* betray the Aces. That narrows down your hunt by great leaps in this universe."

"So what do I do now?" Harley asked.

"You get on with your life. Ben would never have obsessed over your death this way. He wasn't big on ties to other people. You, you make friends, even good friends. You'll eventually find out the truth, as soon as you stop looking for it."

Harley felt more confused than ever, but again something about Gunney reminded him of the way Da used to talk to him. "Thanks, Gunney," he said finally.

"Think of it as friendly advice from someone who happens to hold a crapper-load of rank on you. And now I'd recommend you get back to the barracks and get your gear together. We head out for the jump point tomorrow, and you and the others better be crispy about it. You don't want to make your lieutenant look bad, do you?"

21

DropShip General Gordon
Outbound, Gillfillan's Gold
Rim Collection
The Periphery
19 May 3059

The yellow warning light went dim over their heads as the *General Gordon* roared upward out of the atmosphere of Gillfillan's Gold. The ship arced into low orbit, and Harley's stomach seemed to roll to one side as he fought back the odd sensation of light gravity. Wondering if he'd ever get used to space flight, he wiped the beads of sweat off his brow and drew a long, steady breath trying to control that last wave of nausea.

The three Aces' *Union Class* DropShips had lifted off at the same time from Gillfillan's Gold, taking with them most of the Aces' headquarters. They were going to need its infrastructure to carry out the new contract in the Lyran Alliance, but it had been a few years since the mercenary unit had mobilized its HQ.

Technicians, support personnel, comm operators, and other personnel crowded onto the DropShips for transit to the system jump point, where they would link up with the JumpShip that would start them on the journey to their new employ. Harley had even caught a glimpse of Lieutenant Hershorn, the officer in charge of intelligence, just prior to takeoff.

He hit the center release pad on his harness and pulled the straps over his head. Bix looked almost as bad as Harley felt, white as a sheet, his teeshirt wet with sweat around the collar. Though he looked like he was about to see his breakfast again, Bixby Finch managed to give Harley a weak thumbs up. Both now knew to get up slowly, accustomed to the weightlessness. Harley reached down and adjusted the straps on his deck shoes, which had enough of a magnetic hold to keep attached to the deck plating rather than floating around the room. Then they made their way with the others to the hatchway.

Three hours later, they all stood in front of their BattleMechs in the cavernous 'Mech bay, each with a required checklist to walk through. Most of the procedures involved checking over their equipment and their restraints. Harley looked up at his *Enforcer* with pride. Four months ago, he'd never have dreamed he'd be piloting a 'Mech for a living. Ben was always the one to dream of working with the faster, more deadly 'Mechs. Now Harley was filling his dead brother's shoes.

He climbed the gantry alongside the 'Mech, checking along the way to make sure various hatches were secured. All around him was the sound of metal clanging as the rest of First Company did the same.

He saw a handful of technicians gathered around Judith Glancy's *Sentinel* as she barked out comments to the techs climbing over the 'Mech. The replacement armor plates still bore the dull gray of undercoat, and she was overseeing work on the knee actuator maintenance. Harley respected that 'Mech. In it, he had proven himself for the sake of both his father and Ben.

His *Enforcer*'s green and brown striped camouflage pattern also showed some minor pockmarks from previous fights, but the 'Mech was all in one piece. When he reached the cockpit, he noticed that someone had added a demonic head with a sinister grin to the name "Hellraiser" painted in red next to the hatch. Harley couldn't help but laugh, knowing that the culprit had to be either Bixby or Jord—or both.

Inside the cockpit he settled into the command seat and thought about how many times it must have been replaced in this 'Mech's long lifetime. The current one looked like it had seen at least three decades of use. It had a musty smell, too, but Harley liked the way his body fit into it, like it had been molded just for him.

He ran through the checklist to make sure the *Enforcer* was in good working order. This was purely precautionary, but he'd listened to enough warnings during training about reactors and gyros going off-line during lift-off, leaving a Mech-Warrior stranded when he needed the systems later on. Better to be safe than sorry.

His body gained a sensation of weight as he settled into the seat. He knew it was common to have some gravity under you during acceleration to the jump point while the massive fusion engines gave thrust to the ship. But for the ship to get a small surge of gravity in another direction meant that it was changing directions. Harley knew that was something out of the ordinary. Not necessarily something wrong, just out of place.

He felt for a moment like he was back hunting in the woods on Slewis, where he could become hyperaware of the animals, the trees, the air, everything. Any disturbance would light up his senses. Now it was happening again, but in a very different setting.

He pushed back the sensation, but couldn't help the hairs standing up on the back of his neck. Returning to the checklist, Harley continued to run through the systems checks and power relay verifications. He could see very little of the deck from the *Enforcer*'s cockpit, but from time to time he glanced out, still wondering about the *General Gordon*'s sudden change of course.

When he'd gone through the whole list, he climbed out of the cockpit and started down the ladder rungs along the body of his 'Mech to the deck far below. As he reached the bay floor, he heard a deep, echoing metallic "thud" that seemed to quake the ship slightly. Jord was walking toward him but seemed not even to notice the sound as he came up.

"What was that?" Harley asked.

Jord shrugged. "It happens now and then. We've either retrieved or launched a fighter from the bay. Then again, it might be a shuttlecraft. The major has several of them and is known to shuffle between ships in transit. They make that noise from time to time." He pointed to the far end of the bay toward the ship's fighter bay.

Harley felt the slight acceleration gravity suddenly stop as the ship slowed. He would have drifted if not for the thin magnetic soles of his deck shoes. Something wasn't right. He could feel it. His heart began to pump faster, though he seemed to be the only one concerned about what was happening.

From the fighter bay he saw several infantrymen emerge from the airlock. As the iris valve cycled open, Harley recognized the first one instantly as Major Able dressed in a faded gray flight suit. He moved with a speed that belied his age.

Behind him was Livia Hawke.

The hairs on Harley's neck tingled even more, and he felt his face get hot at the sight of her. This wasn't possible. Hawke had been exiled by Major Able, now here she was, walking across the deck as if she were still in command. She too wore a gray combat jumpsuit, which displayed her rank insignia.

Harley and Jord watched as Coombs went over to meet the pair. The three talked for a few moments, nodding their heads at one another. Gunney even showed a thin smile as they spoke.

Then he barked out orders to the pair of infantry guards at the hatch, and they in turn passed on the order to several others. Major Able walked to the ship's intercom system and spoke into it, most likely to the bridge.

"It looks like the Hawke is returning to the

roost," Jord commented as Bixby came over to join his friends.

"I thought she'd been sent away," Bix said.

"I was right, wasn't I? I told you it was all a mistake," Jord replied confidently. "I told you Hawke was on the level."

In a matter of moments the entire infantry platoon of First Company was moving through the ship, jogging across its various corridors. Harley watched, stunned at the sudden flurry of activity. "Is this normal?" he asked the more experienced MacAuld.

Jord shook his head. "Something's going on."

The officers turned toward the troops scattered across the deck. Most of First Company was here, with the exception of the infantry, which was making its way through the zero-gravity of the ship like a pack of rats on the move. Able motioned for those in the bay to draw closer. Even the technicians, who usually ignored what the MechWarriors and ground-pounders were doing, stopped working and drifted down from their gantries to get within listening distance.

"I apologize for the deception I've had to carry out against you," Major Able began. He smiled slightly, but his tone was serious. "I'm afraid it was necessary.

"Some of you may have noticed that we've started to decelerate and are no longer on course to the jump point. Instead, we are diverting to the Bhide Asteroid Belt to rendezvous with the rest of Aces."

Harley remembered hearing about the asteroid belt during the briefing on the Gillfillan's Gold system, but he hadn't paid it much attention. Now all that seemed like years ago rather than a mere few weeks. The thought of all of Able's Aces being together at one time seemed exciting, yet extraordinary. His watched Livia Hawke, who stood with her arms behind her back at parade rest, also listening to the major.

"Up until now, everyone except for President Moroney and a very few officers has believed we are on a standard burn to the jump point, on our way to the Lyran Alliance. Well, folks, there is no contract with the Lyran Alliance. We staged the whole thing to trick Morrison's Extractors into action. Chances are they'll show up here like they did before, via a pirate jump point. They'll think Gillfillan's Gold is defenseless. They'll be wrong.

"Dead wrong.

"Once they arrive we will burn in for a combat drop right on top of them. Once we've beaten them here, I've got a few other surprises for Hopper Morrison." He glanced over at Lieutenant Hawke, who gave him a knowing nod and a smile in return. Then the major resumed addressing his people.

"We had to keep this secret because, as many of you have suspected, there is a traitor in our ranks. We're using this ruse to flush him out. That's why I had to let Lieutenant Hawke take the fall. She agreed to it, though it was painful for her. As far as anyone would know, we had ferreted out our traitor while the real traitor would be bringing Morrison to Gillfillan's Gold based on false information."

For the first time since she had arrived, Hawke seemed to catch Harley's eye among the crowd. He couldn't be sure, but the thought left him feeling embarrassed, ashamed, and foolish, all at the same time.

"Lieutenant Hawke is not a traitor, but has helped us stage this little operation. Effective immediately, she will reassume command of First Company. Gunney, please resume your rank of Gunnery Sergeant in command of the infantry platoon."

Gunney responded by tearing off the lieutenant's bar insignia from his uniform, and tossing them to the deck where they bounced and floated back up into the air, spinning slightly in the null gravity.

"No problem here, sir. I don't think those bars matched my uniforms anyway." Then Gunney looked over at Hawke. "I'm sure glad to have you back running the unit so I can get back to my old job."

Major Able nodded to Hawke and she stepped forward, letting her gaze sweep the faces of First Company. "Like the major said, we're sorry for having deceived you, but this operation is critical. Hopper Morrison and his Extractors have done a lot of damage to both the Aces and the Rim Collection of late. Everything they've done has been aimed at crippling our government and military.

"Now all that changes. From here on we go on the offensive. We will seize and hold the initiative and we will make the Extractors pay for what they've done."

Harley saw many of the Aces around him nodding approval as they listened, and he found himself nodding too. But if Hawke wasn't the traitor, then who had led Ben and the others to their deaths? A ripple of panic swept his mind as he tried to think about who'd had the opportunity, the means, to do what he'd believed Hawke had done.

The answer wasn't long in coming, but at first Harley didn't realize what it was. First he heard the hatch of the fighter bays hissing shut and sealing. Several infantry troopers leapt to the door and tried to key in the override on the lock, but it blared a dull red light and abort signal. Suddenly Harley felt a deep rumble, the unmistakable sound of a fighter launch. Flashing red lights went off on the deck and a warning klaxon sounded, echoing across the 'Mech bay.

"Damn!" Able cursed as people began to rush about. Harley pushed forward, the scramble of people bringing him closer to Hawke.

"What's going on?" he yelled to her as Able and Coombs raced over to the ship's intercom.

"Lieutenant Hershorn," she spat back. "That bloody slippery rat bastard just stole our shuttle."

Harley thought about the mustached, balding man who had helped him—helped him believe Hawke was the scum who had set up the death of his brother. The whole thing hit him at once.

Her expression was bitter. "He's the traitor, Rassor. He sold us out twice."

By now Major Able was back. "I don't know how he got past our infantry. He must have decided to bug out when he realized we weren't heading for the jump point. Shifty sleaze-pucker, isn't he?"

"Can't we shoot him down?" Harley asked. The weapons in the DropShip turrets would make quick work of the shuttle.

"Negative," the major said. "He's got a head

start on us and has slightly more thrust. Captain Edelstein is pretty smart, though. He started jamming as soon as he realized it wasn't an authorized launch. We can hang tight on his tail, pace him, jam his communication channels, but he's not going to be in weapons range until we're on our way back to the planet.

"I want all security codes changed," he told Hawke. "But for what it's worth, the captain just told me he picked up the signature of a ship exiting jump at the pirate point the Extractors used last time they were here. It looks like Hershorn's got some buddies."

Pirate jump points were tricky "holes" in the gravity wells within star systems. They were risky to use, but they permitted a JumpShip to arrive much closer to the target planet than at the standard jump points.

"The other Aces?" Hawke asked.

"Captain Chou has the rest of the task force heading in-system from the asteroid belt. If initial calculations are correct, we'll be dropping on-planet about an hour and a half after they do, less if we push the engines. Imagine their surprise when they find out that Gillfillan's Gold is not abandoned at all, but that most of the regiment is in the system."

Hawke looked from the major to Harley, and there was fire in her eyes when spoken. "Good. Private Rassor and I have a personal matter to settle with Spooky."

Major Able put his hand on her shoulder. "Let's take him alive if possible. We don't want this to become a vendetta. Remember, you two aren't the only ones who want to see this bastard get what he deserves. We want justice, but I don't want anyone to die just trying to keep him alive either. Either way, Hershorn goes down and hard . . . Got it?"

Down and hard, Harley told himself. Down and hard.

22

DropShip **General Gordon**
Inbound, Gillfillan's Gold
Rim Collection
The Periphery
19 May 3059

The tactical operations room of the *General Gordon* was stuffy with a mix of sweat, excitement, anticipation, and tension. The dull light and drab gray walls seemed an odd contrast to the heightened emotions of those gathered there. Lit up on the holographic display was the blue globe of Gillfillan's Gold and the three large dots of green light representing the DropShips of Able's Aces. They were the points of light farthest away from the planet, but they were closing in, creeping closer.

Also showing on the display were two pulsating red dots. Separated from the green lights by only a few centimeters on the holographic display, the real distance was measured in hundreds of kilometers. The red dots, the DropShips of Morrison's Extractors, were approaching the atmosphere of the planet. Between the two sets of dots hovering in the air was a flickering yellow one.

This was the shuttlecraft stolen by Lieutenant Hershorn. Harley stared at that point of light, thinking about how Hershorn had betrayed the Aces. The thought brought a wash of grief and anger for the fact that Hershorn was the one who'd killed Ben.

Da had sent him to Able's Aces to learn the truth, and now it seemed that he had. All that remained was to bring the traitor to justice. He remembered the night he, Da, and the other men had extracted their own justice against the trader reps on Slewis. He vowed silently that Hershorn wouldn't get it that easy or quickly . . .

Harley brought his mind back to the moment at hand. What he didn't understand about Major Able's plan was why the Aces hadn't simply scrambled their fighters and sent them out after the shuttlecraft. The K-61 shuttle was slower than most of the unit's light fighters and had no weapons to speak of. Dabney Fox of his lance raised the question just as Harley was about to voice it.

Hawke reminded them that the Major wanted Hershorn taken alive, if possible. There was another reason, too, she said. Weapons fire might attract the sensors of the Extractors' DropShips, and that would give away the whole plan.

Hawke turned back to the images glowing on the display, then looked down at the data screen built into the control table. She touched the control studs, and multicolored figures and data began streaming across the screen. The light from the display table made her face almost sinister in the shadows as she read.

"We are tracking two DropShips, both *Union* Class. We can assume a total of two companies of Extractors." She looked around at the members of her restored First Company. "As most of you know, the Extractors are outfitted with some lostech BattleMechs and vehicles they found. We've got some of the same gear ourselves, which could offset the advantage that would give them. The real threat is that Clan *Timber Wolf* we spotted. Keep your eyes sharp. Watch slugging it out with them at long ranges. They may have some of the extended-range technology that we don't."

Harley had heard the same rumors as everyone else in the Rim Collection about the lostech King Hopper Morrison had gotten his hands on. If the stories were true, he had stumbled onto a cache of BattleMechs and gear left behind several hundred years ago by General Aleksandr Kerensky and the Star League army when they had left the Inner Sphere forever, vanishing into deep space beyond the Periphery. This stockpile of 'Mechs and vehicles were the means by which he'd bolstered his small band of marauders in recent years, turning them into the dangerous band of pirates they had become.

"Have we got a projection on their drop zone?" asked Jill Sutcliffe.

Hawke pressed several tabs on the holotable's control pad. On the blue globe of Gillfillan's Gold, a light began to flash near Rectortown, just south of the Aces command post. "It looks like they won't be landing at the spaceport or the capital, which is good news. Hershorn must've planned this pretty good. They're burning on a direct course to the flat plateau of our old southern firing range. From there, using the river, they can strike at the capital and be inaccessible from the spaceport."

"We know that terrain," Jeremy Lewis said. "We know it real well. Aren't they taking a big risk landing there?"

"We've been jamming communications from the shuttle Hershorn heisted from us, and we're still out of their scanner range. Unless they were expecting us to be burning in on their asses, I seriously doubt they even know we're on our way in too. They think they're landing on a planet defended by nothing more than a handful of local militia."

"They're in for a surprise," Jord said, with a grin.

Hawke smiled and nodded. "You've got that right, Corporal." She tapped the studs on the control panel again, and the large holographic planet suddenly collapsed, and the view zoomed in on the projected drop zone. The image spun in the air and became a three-dimensional display of the area that might become their battleground.

Small clusters of trees lay to the east and west of the area. They were more like scrubby cedars, none more than five meters high, hardly enough to hide a BattleMech, but enough to impair movement and deflect some of a missile barrage. To the north, in the direction of the Aces' now abandoned base, was a series of steep hills and box canyons, which would make for deadly fire zones. Near the southern edge of the battle zone was a small marsh, with swamps to the south of it. Harley remembered the spot from some of the training exercises they'd run. His 'Mech had gotten bogged down in there, and the memory of it was still fresh.

In the center of the image was a four-kilometer-long plateau. Barren except for some scrub brush, it was the only area where a DropShip could easily land and debark troops. Harley remembered that it was a short but steep rise up from the plains to the plateau. The terrain was rugged, and climbing to the top would be hard going. Once up there, it was wide open and a flat run.

Hawke's tactical summary continued. "They'll have, at best, two companies. We're coming in with three. Our window of surprise will end about the time they debark and their DropShips' sensors pick us up on final burn. By then, our little back-stabber will also have tipped them off that we're ruining their party. Keep in mind that we need to catch them before they reload and depart. We do this right, and they'll be on the ground, spread out and deploying, when we hit them."

Using a laser pointer, she called their attention to the northern edge of the display. "We will execute a combat drop on the northern edge of the plateau, Second Company will take the east, Third Company the west. We will converge on them from three sides."

"What's the objective of the hit, Lieutenant?" Sergeant Lewis asked.

"Plain and simple, Jeremy. We're here to crush them. Major Able wants us to inflict as much damage as possible and, if possible, keep them from debarking any of their troops. We've got a total of six fighters with our three companies, and that should make it tricky if their DropShips try to lift off."

Gunney Coombs looked at the display, shaking his head in thought. "There's more to this than what we're seeing here, Lieutenant, no insult intended." He pondered the display for a few seconds more. "We're hitting them with First Battalion. Almost an entire Extractors regiment was mustering out there in that asteroid belt when we were heading that way. What about that?"

Hawke cocked one eyebrow and smiled again. "I don't want to spoil all of Hershorn's fun, but let's just say the Major has invested way too much in the Rim Collection to throw it all away on a piece of living scum like Hopper Morrison. As we speak, Second and much of Third Battalion are on the way to the jump point where we've got Jump-Ships waiting. For obvious security reasons, I can't reveal all of the details, but for now, consider this Counterattack Phase One of our operation."

Then she spent the next few minutes going over the operational details of the combat drop. Harley squeezed in between Sutcliffe and Lewis to see better where they would engage and move.

Having a thirty percent firepower advantage on the Extractors should make for a fast fight. Like the battle at Rectortown, this was Harley's chance to pay back Morrison's people for what they'd taken from him. That alone sent a jolt of adrenaline even beyond what he would normally feel on the verge of battle.

As the meeting broke up, he and the others left to strip down to combat gear and don the bulky cooling vests that would help keep them alive in their sweltering cockpits. Before he could reach the door, he felt a hand on his shoulder from behind. He stopped and turned to see it was Livia Hawke.

"A word with you, Private Rassor," she said as the last of First Company filtered out of the room, shutting the door behind them.

"Yes sir," he said, suppressing a gulp. He had come to hate this woman, believing she had betrayed Ben. Now, in just a few short hours, all of that changed. He wasn't supposed to hate her anymore—he'd learned that she was a friend and not an enemy—but it was still all mixed up in his mind and heart. He felt tongue-tied and embarrassed.

"I know you thought I was the one who killed your brother, Harley. If that's going to be a problem, let me know now, before we do this drop."

Harley felt shame redden his face. He licked his lips as he tried to think what to say. "Permission to speak candidly, sir?"

Lieutenant Hawke crossed her arms and leaned back slightly on her heels. "Permission granted, Private. What's said here, stays here."

He straightened up and looked her directly in the eye. "It's not going to be a problem, Lieutenant. And I apologize for suspecting that you were involved with Ben's death. It's just that, well . . . you were the only survivor of the ambush. Then, when we fought at Rectortown, your 'Mech came out of it with barely a scratch. On top of that Lieutenant Hershorn showed me a document pointing to you as the primary suspect."

She shook her head once. "Hershorn played us all for fools—me, you, even the Major. He was clever in trying to mislead you. From what we've learned, he's been passing intelligence to Hopper Morrison for the last ten months or so. Hopper's only recently started to act on it."

"Then when the Major sent you off like that," Harley said, "it just seemed to solidify it all in my mind."

Hawke shrugged slightly. "That was necessary. The Major wanted to plant the queen-mother of all red herrings for Hershorn. This whole business about the bogus contract with the Lyran Alliance was set up to give Hopper a target he couldn't pass up. It looks like he fell for it too. When the Major sent me away, I worked with selected members of Aces intel, so Spooky wouldn't get wind of what was really going on. It kept him totally out of the loop regarding troop redeployments and the true nature of the mission.

"Captain Chou fed out fake communication traffic to make it seem like we were bugging out for the Lyran Alliance. Major Able sent verigraphed orders, something that couldn't be faked, so we could move the Aces into position without alerting that rat-bastard traitor."

"I feel like a jackass," Harley said.

"Don't," she replied. "Hershorn was just good at his job. He had almost everyone fooled, even the Major for a short time."

"We can't let him get away. Not just for the unit. My family also wants to see that justice is served."

"So do I. I cared for Ben. I'm sure your digging eventually turned up the fact that he and I had a kind of special relationship. I want to see Spooky strapped to the business-end of a PPC just as much as you do."

Harley's embarrassment had faded briefly, but

the thought of the Lieutenant with his brother sent another wave of heat to his cheeks. "I didn't find out about that until after you left. But now I'm glad to know Ben had someone like you in his life. He was always so obsessed with 'Mechs and his ambitions that maybe he shut off the other parts of his life too much. He never even told the rest of the family about you."

Hawke looked saddened by that. "I shouldn't be surprised that he kept it from you and your family. Like you said, he was so obsessed that sometimes I thought he cared more for his tech readouts than he did for me. Other times I knew he did care. Your brother was a complicated man."

"I agree," Harley returned, the thought of Ben in better times bringing a smile. "When we were kids we used to daydream about this kind of fight. Good guys against the bad guys, with the fate of the universe as the stakes. It's too bad he's not here."

She chuckled slightly. "You and I have to do this together, Harley. We've got to take out Spooky, if only to make Ben's death and the deaths of the others in my old company count for something. If Hershorn gets away, their deaths will have been all for nothing."

Harley was silent, thinking about Hershorn's betrayal. "Why?" he burst out suddenly. "Why did Hershorn do it? It doesn't make sense." Knowing the answer wasn't going to make him feel better, nor would it bring back the dead. But a part of him had to know what reason could drive men to such deeds.

"We may never know," Hawke said softly. "Most traitors do it for money. Some do it for promises of power or to get something else they want. I never found out what it was with Spooky. If we capture him, we'll find out."

Harley gave a slow nod of his head. "There's something else I wanted to ask you, sir," he said.

"Call me Livia. When we're alone, you can drop the formality. I gave that privilege to your brother and, after what we've been through, I owe it to you as well."

"Okay, Livia," he said, feeling odd using her given name. "My question is how did you know I was tracking you?"

She smiled. "Harley, I've lived in the Rim Collection my whole life. I was raised on the back streets of a dozen cities and villages. I spotted you at three bars trying to blend in with the locals."

Harley grinned ruefully. "I thought I was a good tracker."

She laughed once. "Sure, in the wild. This time you were on my turf."

"Then you're going to have to teach me how to hunt on your turf, sir—Livia."

"Done. First we take out Spooky. Next we beat the wet-stickies out of Hopper Morrison. We pull that off, and you're going to learn a lot from me. Now then, it's time for Counterattack Phase One." She motioned to the door.

Harley walked through it and into the 'Mech bay. For the first time since he'd learned of what happened to Ben on Birdsong Ridge, he felt truly alive and free of the burden of his brother's death.

23

Rector's Plateau
Gillfillan's Gold, Rim Collection
The Periphery
19 May 3059

Harley strained as his *Enforcer* landed on the hard rock of Rector's plateau with a half-step, half-lurch forward. He killed the jump jets the instant the 'Mech's feet touched the solid ground. Around him, the rest of First Company, once more named The Hawke's Talons, also hit the dirt and began deploying.

Bixby's *Vindicator* almost lost its footing as he landed and staggered forward like a massive drunk. Michael Ling's huge Von Luckner tank kicked up such a huge cloud of dust as it raced forward that it almost obscured the departing Drop-Ship from view. Above Harley, beyond the dust and chaos of the deployment, a roar shook the ground and made his 'Mech quake. It was the *General Gordon* lifting away from the plateau, headed for a small clearing several kilometers away.

Harley's long-range sensors squealed with activity, and the display showed the large targets of the Extractors' DropShips, surrounded by points of light representing nearly two companies. There was another image, too, closer than the enemy 'Mechs, that of a K-61 shuttlecraft.

Harley had an image of chasing it at a run, hoping to catch Hershorn before he could reach his pirate friends. Briefly, he savored the thought of confronting the traitor, a three-story BattleMech bristling with weapons against an unarmed man. That would be cowardly, but even if it weren't, Harley would never break ranks to do it.

"Talons, this is Fireball One," came the crisp voice of Lieutenant Hawke in his neurohelmet's earpiece. "I am painting multiple targets in the Extractors' DZ. Fireball Lance, form on me on the right. Bishop Lance take the left. Clash Lance to the rear and center."

Harley knew that the plan was for Davis Gilbert in his *Lucifer* fighter to provide air support as First Company hit the ground. The weaker Clash Lance in the center would be supported by the heavier BattleMech-equipped lances on the flanks. Anyone pushing the center because it seemed soft would find themselves catching enfilade fire from both sides—all things being equal. Harley had seen enough by now to know that anything could happen in combat, no matter how good the plan.

He inched the throttle of his *Enforcer* forward, bringing its old Nissan 200 fusion reactor roaring to life under the cockpit. Using the foot pedals to navigate the flat rock of the plateau, he veered right to form up near the rest of his lance.

He assumed a position on the far right. On his left was Bix in his *Vindicator*, its right arm/PPC showing a relatively fresh red paint job. Jord had pointed out that the red-flame paint pattern would make the 'Mech stand out and recommended a more traditional camouflage pattern. Bix retorted that camouflage rarely was of use on a three-story BattleMech running at fifty kph. Gunney must have agreed because he hadn't made Bix repaint the PPC barrel while he'd still acting as brevet commander of the company.

Harley switched his Federated autocannon to one target interlock circuit trigger, his large laser to another, and the small laser to the third TIC. As the distance closed, he switched to short-range sensors. The bulbous shapes of the pirate Drop-Ships loomed in the distance above the dust their 'Mechs were kicking up. Harley's sensor display told him that Third Company was just moving into range of the enemy and starting to open fire.

Then his battle computer started to tag and identify the enemy 'Mechs. Racing through the warbook, the computer quickly tagged their shapes and configurations. Harley saw the flag for the familiar *Crab* under one 'Mech. Another was ID'd as a *Mercury*. Still another was flagged as a more contemporary, lower-tech *Javelin*. In all, his warbook tagged a total of twenty-four enemy BattleMechs, fanned out around the base of their DropShips as if they had just debarked, only to learn they were facing a superior force.

At least that much of the plan had worked,

Harley thought. They'd caught them in their skivvies.

Another shape loomed on his tactical display as the warbook flagged it as a threat. It was a *Timber Wolf,* the same 'Mech he'd fought at Rectortown, a battle that now seemed years rather than weeks earlier. The Clan machine was one of the deadliest they would face. Having escaped from it once before, Harley wanted revenge on that pirate 'Mech in particular.

Third Company engaged as planned, but did not advance much further than combat-weapons range. They moved along their assigned flank, keeping the enemy busy while the other two companies stalked forward to join in the fray. Harley's heart pounded and he was wet with sweat even though his *Enforcer* wasn't yet running hot. As they advanced he noticed the shape of the grounded shuttlecraft just as his view was obliterated by a barrage of long-range missiles screaming in his general direction.

The missiles, however, weren't locked onto him, but were targeting Bix in his *Vindicator.* A *Bombardier* had fired the salvo of forty deadly warheads. Most of them slammed into the *Vindicator* with savage fury, stopping Bixby's advance cold. Armor from the 'Mech's chest, arms, and legs was shredded off into the air as Bix tried to regain the momentum of his stride.

"Bix!" Harley shouted into his mike.

The voice that came back was short of breath, almost panting from panic. "That's gonna leave a mark," he stammered, his sense of humor still intact even if his armor wasn't.

"You okay?" Harley asked as he swung his joystick control to sweep his targeting reticle onto the *Bombardier*, which was the closest of the Extractors. He edged his throttle forward to close the distance as the enemy 'Mech stepped back in an attempt to maintain the long distance.

"Let's take him," Bix managed.

On his head's up display Harley saw the targeting reticle flash from red to green, indicating that he was in range. Instantly, his training and instinct took over and he triggered his autocannon, the projectile racing downrange in a millisecond, dead on the boxy *Bombardier*. It hit the 'Mech's right torso, destroying the open missile rack door and blasting most of the armor away there. The 'Mech recoiled under the impact.

The *Bombardier* fired again, this time both of its long-range missile racks targeting Dabney Fox, Bishop Four. Her *Hatchetman*, with its distinctive ax in one hand, jerked at the last minute, abruptly changing the direction of its run. A handful of the missiles streaked past their intended target, the wisp-like rocket-trails hissing past the battle line.

The rest of the missiles plowed into the legs of the *Hatchetman*, mangling armor and nearly sending Fox tumbling onto the hard stone of the plateau. Harley didn't see what happened to her; the *Hatchetman*'s sudden loss of speed dropped it out of his field of vision.

He unleashed his large laser at the same time Lieutenant Hawke triggered her *Orion*'s smaller fifteen-pack long-range missile rack. Likewise, Bix, his gait slowed slightly, fired his red-painted PPC down-range as well, its cerulean blast of man-made lightning following the path of the missiles as they hit.

Harley's large laser had dug into the *Bombardier*'s right torso, doing little more than melting some armor plating in a white, cloud-like blast. Hawke's missiles raked the entire chest and torso of the 'Mech, ripping away more armor. The PPC burst ate the remaining left-chest armor away in a popping explosion as the armor plating expanded on contact with the charged-particle burst, the plates exploding off.

The *Bombardier* staggered backward like a boxer taking a near-death blow. A compatriot *Exterminator* fired its jump jets and landed beside the *Bombardier*, obviously intending to provide support fire.

As Second Company moved into position, they too let go with a fierce fusillade. One of their lasers hit the *Exterminator* just as it was landing, shearing some armor plating from its right leg.

Harley shrugged off the small spike of heat rising in his cockpit and triggered his autocannon just as he heard the metallic snap of a fresh round chambering in the reload cycle. The shell streaked down-range into the already mauled right torso of the *Bombardier*.

The armor that stood between the autocannon round and the internal systems of the Extractor 'Mech was virtually non-existent. The kinetic energy from the explosion as well as the deadly hail of shrapnel ripped inward and upward into the 'Mech. It rocked back and there was flash of internal explosion. Oily black smoke retched out of the *Bombardier* as the long-range missiles stored in the right torso cooked off. The warheads, designed to destroy enemy 'Mechs, wreaked their incredible damage loose on the guts of the Star League-era BattleMech.

Harley's sensors suddenly showed the 'Mech as inactive, yet it was still standing, a stream of black smoke belching outward as the 'Mech died. The battle computer and short-range sensors had detected that its powerful fusion reactor was inactive. Nothing but melted scrap, Harley thought as the *Bombardier* slowly twisted and collapsed in a dead pile on the ground next to the *Exterminator.*

"Splash one," Harley said as he swung his targeting sight on the *Exterminator.* Apparently the pirate 'Mech was a little faster. Its long-range missiles spun in on Harley's *Enforcer* with such accuracy that he barely had time to brace even mentally for the impact.

Most of the missiles dug into his right arm and leg, twisting his 'Mech to the right under the impact. The damage readout showed that his armor hadn't been breached, but some had been eaten away. The *Exterminator* wasted no time, now firing its deadly battery of four medium lasers into Ada Shope's Patton tank. On the far right flank of Clash Lance, the tank's front ablative armor plating buckled, melted, and cratered under the crimson beams of the lasers.

Harley fired his own large laser at the *Exteminator,* but it juked to the right just in time for the shot to go wide. A slow wave of heat rose in his cockpit as a voice came over his neurohelmet earpiece.

"Fireball Leader to Hawke's Talons, slow your pace and spread out. Concentrate on the larger 'Mechs. We'll pummel them from here."

As if to emphasize her point, Hawke's *Orion* fired at the *Exterminator* Harley had targeted, as did Glancy's *Sentinel*. The momentary glimpse of the *Sentinel* made Harley smile briefly. He would always feel a certain affection for that 'Mech, a fact that would drive Judith Glancy up the wall if she knew.

Hawke's missiles plastered the entire front and head of the *Exterminator*, while her autocannon round went wild, flying off into the smoke and dust past the 'Mech. Glancy's lighter autocannon hit the legs of the *Exterminator*, nearly knee-capping it as armor rained down onto the rocks of the plateau. Fox fired a blast from her medium lasers at a running *Hussar*, missing the light 'Mech with one, ripping away at one of its stubby arms with another.

Shots were pouring in on Morrison's Extractors from three different directions at once. For their part, they kept moving, making themselves harder to hit, and giving as good as they took. Able's Aces, however, were laying on the firepower, concentrating on some of the enemy 'Mechs to cripple them.

One of these that was managing to evade such concentrated barrages and ganging attacks was the light green *Timber Wolf*. It fired its extended-range large lasers and long-range missiles with the consummate skill of a trained killer. One salvo blasted into Ling's Von Luckner tank, raking its right side. Its lasers had also virtually crippled Jill Sutcliffe's *Panther*, leaving the 'Mech's legs almost shorn of armor.

Harley figured the *Timber Wolf* pilot could only be "King" Hopper Morrison, or at least one of his key commanders. The Aces would have to take that 'Mech out if they were going to shatter the command integrity of the Extractors. He continued to try to get a target lock on it, but it moved with such speed and ease that Harley couldn't keep it in his sights long enough to do so.

Third Company moved along the flank between the Extractors and their DropShips. Harley couldn't see them through the fog and smoke of the battle, but his sensors showed their movement. He gritted his teeth and locked onto the *Exterminator* but held his fire as the 'Mech suddenly ignited its jump jets, spoiling his shot.

Gunney Coombs and his men rushed forward and secured the shuttlecraft off to Harley's right. Using it as cover, they fired several shoulder-launched SRMs at an injured *Hussar* that drifted into their range. The infantry fire was more accurate than Harley would have given them credit for. As the *Hussar* swung around, he saw that its right arm hung limp at the shoulder joint where the missiles had done their job.

Without warning the Extractor DropShips suddenly roared to life and lifted off on their flaring thrusters. One lifted straight up, obviously heading for orbit. The other two rose some seventy meters into the air, then tipped their rounded shapes toward where Harley and First Company were positioned. They thundered overhead, turrets firing wildly.

Far overhead Harley saw a streak in the sky as the Aces' fighters swept in and fired down at the DropShips, but they did little more than pockmark armor. The ships continued on overhead, then touched down at the edge of the foothills just over the plateau.

A ponderous *Thug* stepped out of the haze of the

pirate position and fired its twin PPCs at Shope's
Patton tank. Both shots hit with such savage force
that they breached the front glacial plate and
punched deep into the tank. The Patton came to a
dead halt, and then three of the hatches suddenly
opened. Dense gray and black smoke billowed out
as the crew clamored to get clear of the vehicle. A
few fell, and even from his distance, Harley could
see that some were badly burned. The PPC fire
had penetrated the interior of the tank, frying and
searing its inner cockpit.

His mind raced to try and figure out what tac-
tics the Extractors were trying to employ. It made
no sense to move their DropShips. They were outgunned, outmassed, and rapidly losing ground.
The noose was closing in around them.

Suddenly he saw the *Timber Wolf* appear next to
the *Thug*. Both 'Mechs charged forward, directly
into the center of First Company's battle line,
where Clash Lance still remained. A badly damaged *Dervish* charged along with them, as did a
pair of *Wyvern*s, both showing signs of some
heavy fighting. The mangled *Hussar* broke into a
full run as well, its great speed putting it at the
front of the formation—a formation charging
headlong into First Company.

The lead *Wyvern* moved swiftly, but the other
one had suffered some damage to a hip actuator
and moved with a distinct limp, its leg flopping
forward with each step as if operating more out of
luck than control.

As if on cue, the Extractors concentrated their
fire on Ling's Von Luckner tank, which had begun
to move backward at the sight of charging 'Mechs,

almost plowing into the smoking dead remains of Shope's Patton.

Harley fired his autocannon into the *Thug,* causing one of its PPCs to discharge in an explosion of the rock in front of the tank as it fell back. The *Thug*'s other PPC, however, found its mark, blasting away armor on the side of the Aces' vehicle as it fought for its survival. The long-range missiles of the *Timber Wolf* turned the gray-green painted turret into a blackened and burned fragment of its former self.

To his credit, Ling and his crew did not panic. They waited and fired their autocannon at the lead Extractor—the *Hussar*—as it charged straight at them. The autocannon, the tank's primary weapon, fired a round commonly known as a " 'Mech-killer," and today it lived up to its reputation.

The *Hussar* took the hit in its forward-mounted cockpit. Its armor couldn't hope to stop even half the force of the blast. The damage was so bad that the 'Mech's head seemed to collapse into its center torso. Harley winced as he watched the 'Mech plow head-first into the rock. The MechWarrior was dead long before his battle machine fell, blasted into bits so tiny it would be hard to gather enough DNA to verify its owner.

"Splash one bad guy," Ling's voice rang out as one of the pirate *Wyvern*s fired its large laser into the already mangled side of the massive Von Luckner. From his angle, Harley could not see the damage, but the smoke and the fact that the Von Luckner had suddenly stopped moving told him the tank was disabled, if not destroyed.

"Clash Four here. I've slipped my tread," Ling called out, wildly firing his long-range missiles at the *Wyvern* in response. Most of the missiles were just in range, and none clustered in any one part of the target to inflict serious damage. "Clash Lance hands off to Bishop and Fireball. Smoke 'em, folks!"

In that instant Harley understood the tactic the Extractors were employing. They were rushing forward and through the weakest point in the Aces' lines, Clash Lance. Behind Clash Lance were the pirate DropShips. The pirates raced past the undefended infantry at the empty K-61 shuttle-craft, ignoring the attacks from their short-range missile and man-pack PPCs. They were intent on plowing through the lines to get to their ships and try and survive the fight.

As if to underscore the logic of the plan, the lead *Wyvern* fired its long-range missile and large lasers into Jeremy Lewis' *Hermes II* as if trying to keep it from reinforcing the center of the line.

"Lieutenant, they're rushing the center," Harley barked into his neurohelmet mike. "We've got to move to support Clash Lance now!"

There was a hiss of static as the *Timber Wolf* loomed closer and closer. Then came the distinctive voice of Livia Hawke in his ears, giving an order he'd never thought to hear—not while they had the pirates desperately attempting to flee before dying.

"This is it, Aces!" she called loud and clear. "We're booking out of here!"

24

Rector's Plateau
Gillfillan's Gold, Rim Collection
The Periphery
19 May 3059

"**A**ces, we're booking out of here!"

Harley couldn't believe what he heard. The voice was obviously Livia Hawke's, yet the command made no sense at all. An order to withdraw? Why? For a crucial moment, he and the rest of Hawke's Talons hesitated and then there was a babble over the commline as everyone seemed to be trying to confirm the order at once.

"Say again, Fireball One," Harley stammered in disbelief.

The moment of distraction couldn't have come at a more opportune time for the Extractors. It happened just as the pirates were crossing through the gap that had been Clash Lance in the spread-out line of First Company. They were plowing through to get behind the Aces, where their DropShips now waited to extract them.

The Extractor *Timber Wolf* was charging full-throttle past Harley like a hurricane wind, its large lasers blazing away at Fireball Lance as it went. One shot missed, while the other brilliant green blast bored into Jord MacAuld's *Victor*, hitting his right leg and devouring the armor plating there. Hawke's *Orion* and Lewis' *Hermes II* both opened fire as it passed, but only a blast from Lewis' small autocannon managed to connect, hitting the *Timber Wolf*'s arm just above the weapons pod and nicking the armor plating there.

Harley twisted in his command seat, using the joystick to bring his targeting reticle on the pirate *Dervish* racing toward the DropShips. Ignoring the moderate risk of heat buildup, he let go with his autocannon and large laser, triggering both target interlocks at the same time. At his side, Bix and Fox both locked on the lumbering *Thug* and gave it a taste of their savage weaponry.

The autocannon round missed the running *Dervish*, but not the laser. It hit the damaged right arm, slicing through the thin, carbon-scarred armor plating and digging deep into the arm. What remained of the *Dervish*'s short-range missile ammo was stored there. The crimson laserfire seared into the ammo housing and feed mechanism, which must have been in the midst of a reload cycle. One warhead went off first, a vibrating blast that shook the arm. A full second later three more rounds cooked off, followed by the remaining ones in a blinding flash of orange and yellow. The arm disappeared instantly in the blast, rocking the *Dervish* in mid-stride as its MechWarrior tried to compensate for the sudden loss of mass and the kinetic force of the explosion.

The comm system crackled to life as Livia Hawke's voice came on line. "Belay that last order. First Company switch to channel Bravo, Lima, Charlie Five."

Harley's fingers flew as he punched in the new channel.

"What happened?" It was the shaky voice of Corporal MacAuld.

"Whoever gave that order was using a recording of my voice. That wasn't me. They knew what frequency we'd be using and used my own voice to throw us off stride," Hawke said. "Fireball Lance, about face and charge. Bishop Lance, oblique right, form up on our flank tight and match our pace."

The *Timber Wolf* had cut easily through the Aces, not even slowing to provide support to its comrades trailing behind. The Clan 'Mech was already putting distance between the remaining two lances of Acer BattleMechs and itself. It left behind the stump-armed *Dervish*, the *Thug*, and the *Wyvern*, all desperately trying to keep up, not wanting to be left behind. What had been two companies worth of Morrison's Extractors had been reduced to this, four 'Mechs, a mere lance. The rest were being polished off by Second and Third Companies.

Harley stabbed his feet down and brought his *Enforcer* around smoothly, bringing him near the rear of the pirates racing to keep up with the lead *Timber Wolf*. The enemy *Thug* was a slow-moving beast of a 'Mech. With its massive arms and hulking profile it looked exactly like its name.

Harley and the rest of his lance wheeled into position on its rear flank at the same time that Fox brought her *Hatchetman* into play. Taking position at his side, Judith Glancy, the lance commander, swept the *Dervish* at maximum range with every one of her ranged weapons.

Harley, too, was preparing to fire, his targeting reticle lighting up and the hum of weapons lock toning in his ear as he saw a salvo of long-range missiles spiral out of the sky, twisting downward and into the back and legs of the *Thug*.

Harley's head snapped out in time to see Davis Gilbert of the battered Clash Lance pull his aerospace fighter up from the strafing run and sweep out across the plateau. The *Thug* turned slightly after the attack, realizing that its dangerously thin rear armor left it vulnerable to another attack.

Harley Rassor felt obliged to fulfill that prophecy.

A ripple of warmth rose in his cockpit as he unleashed the *Enforcer*'s firepower again while running at full speed. The autocannon round missed again, but the scarlet blast from his laser stabbed into the rear armor of the *Thug*'s back, widening one of the holes already ripped open by the *Lucifer*'s strafing run. It dug deep into the spine of the 'Mech, slicing through myomer muscles and leaving a sick green cloud of burned coolant drifting out of the blackened scar it left.

Bishop Four, Dabney Fox's *Hatchetman,* followed Harley's assault three milliseconds later. She fired one of her medium lasers, but the shot went high over the shoulder of the behemoth, just missing the cockpit. The other medium laser dug in where Harley's had, burning even deeper. Her autocannon round slammed into one the *Thug*'s massive arms, mauling the few armor plates left.

In the distance Harley saw the already battered *Dervish* wither under Glancy's assault. It torso-twisted, the stump of one arm whipping torn myomer muscle strands around as it tried to counterattack. Bixby Finch was not as friendly. He joined in from one flank, firing at the same time as Jord on the other.

It was hard to tell who had taken out the enemy 'Mech, given the sheer amount of firepower the Aces had pumped into it. In the end it didn't matter. The *Dervish* spasmed and contorted in what looked like a seizure. Its remaining ammo cooked off in the heat and damage to the other arm. Flames lapped up the sides of the 'Mech in its death throes. The MechWarrior punched out to avoid death, or worse. The cockpit glass blew clear, and on a wisp of white smoke, the ejection seat rose higher and a parachute opened. At the same moment the remains of the *Dervish* fell for the last time, thundering into the rock floor of the plateau.

"Splash," Bix called.

"Like hell," Jord countered. "No offense, rookie, but you get no-joy on that one. That kill was mine."

"You're both buying me a round on *my* kill," Glancy said.

Harley mentally tuned out the conversation and concentrated on business. His target, the *Thug,* was in bad shape. Harley's sensors showed that either he or Fox had inflicted some gyro damage and that the 'Mech's speed had slowed and it seemed to be running hot, signs that its fusion reactor had taken a hit as well. Already piloting a slow 'Mech, the pirate at the controls must have realized how minute was the hope of reaching the DropShips and freedom.

Rather than run, rather than fight, the *Thug* ground to a dead stop, raised its massive arms, then shut down. It was the universal sign of surrender by BattleMechs for centuries. The 'Mech loomed like a mountain of metal as Harley continued his advance and his weapons lock. His thumb hovered over the large laser's firing stud on his joystick.

All he could think of were that these were the pirates who had ambushed and killed Ben. In his mind, they deserved to die. Then a voice began speaking into his earpiece, Livia Hawke speaking to him over a private frequency.

"Don't do it, Harley," she said.

"They killed Ben." Harley continued to advance on the *Thug*, slowing only slightly as the target grew larger both on his HUD and his forward viewscreen.

"He's surrendered and we accept that. If you kill him now, you're no better than him."

Harley tried to push away the words and the truth of them from his mind. He was a hunter, and now a MechWarrior, but he'd never been a coward or a murderer. He also realized that Ben, in the same circumstances, would have fired no matter what she—or anybody—said.

Ben was his brother, but they were different. Only now did Harley realize just how much. Honoring the dead meant respecting the living, that's what Da always said and had tried hard to teach him.

Harley exhaled a long breath and lifted his thumb away from the trigger. "You're right, Lieutenant, but I don't have to like it."

In frustration, he stabbed his right foot down and turned away from the *Thug* and toward the retreating *Wyvern* and *Timber Wolf*. They had already put so much distance between Bishop and Fireball Lance that interception was unlikely. He watched as Gilbert's *Lucifer* made a sweeping pass at the *Timber Wolf*, firing everything he had. The attack left behind a huge cloud of smoke, dust, and explosions, but a still functional and fleeing 'Mech.

Harley slowed his *Enforcer* to a full stop as he realized that pursuit would not be possible. At his side, Bix in his battered *Vindicator* stopped, too.

"Orders, sir?" Bixby called to Corporal Glancy, the Bishop Lance commander.

"Fireball One, call the ball," she returned. In the distance, just off the plateau, Harley saw the flare of the mighty engines of the Extractor DropShips light up and lift the old *Union* Class vessels into the air. Two 'Mechs had managed to get away from the ambush the Aces had staged and were fleeing Gillfillan's Gold.

"Hold up," she said.

Harley wasn't totally convinced, especially after someone had already faked Hawke's voice in the last few minutes. "Say again, Lieutenant?"

"You heard me, Private," she said sternly, then sighed loud enough that everyone could hear it in their helmets. "Two of them got away out of two dozen. I'm not happy about it, but racing under the guns of those DropShips won't buy us anything more. Besides, our fighters are in high-guard position and will inflict plenty of damage for us."

Harley's mind caught up with his racing heart and he took a deep breath. Hawke was right, but that didn't make it any easier to accept. In the distance he watched the flares from the massive fusion drives thrust the DropShips upward into the pale blue skies of Gillfillan's Gold.

Another voice now came over the commline, a deep voice that was unmistakable. It was a general broadcast so that all of First Company heard it. "Fireball One, this is Clash One," said Gunnery Sergeant Coombs. "You'd better get back here pretty quick."

"Sit rep, Gunney," Hawke responded.

"We've secured Lieutenant Hershorn. But we're not going to have him for long. You'd better lock onto my signal and get over here pronto."

Harley jogged on foot the last few meters to join the other Acers of First Company huddled around the remains of a fallen *Lancelot*. Harley caught a whiff of the ozone that still stung in the air, along with the smell of burned fusion engine insulation, the sticky-sweet aroma of fried myomer muscles, and the sooty smell of fiery death. He had smelled the same mix before, after the battle at Rectortown.

The *Lancelot* had been taken down by Second Company, though Harley didn't see any of them in the group. The 'Mech had dropped only a hundred meters from the K-61 shuttlecraft, falling face first onto the hard brown rock of the plateau. Gunney's infantry platoon surrounded the area, providing security for the troops as well as the spot where Harley and the others had parked their 'Mechs. Some of his infantry stood on the remains of an arm or the battered back of the *Lancelot*, their heavy assault rifles ever ready, scanning the area for any possible threat.

From what Harley could tell, the *Lancelot*'s cockpit had suffered severe damage, most likely from an autocannon or missile hit. Most of its infrastructure was caved in, all of it burned badly. As he moved into the small circle, he saw what they were looking at. Lying on the ground, wrapped in a dull gray blanket, was the fallen form of Lieutenant Weldon Hershorn.

"What happened?" Harley asked, his voice almost a whisper.

Gunney Coombs was the nearest to him. "From what we can tell he managed to get himself into a cockpit with one of the pirates. They took a hit to the head that fried the MechWarrior in his seat. Spooky was in the jump seat behind him. It saved him, but not for long."

Now Harley saw what the others saw. Hershorn's hands were blackened to the point that they no longer looked human. His face was also black and cracked, with blood oozing through the wet fissures. Gone was the mustache. Gone was the smell of cologne that Harley remembered, replaced with a baconlike odor that made his stomach pitch.

"He managed to crawl out," Coombs said, "but fell into a puddle of spilled coolant. That stuff is bad enough on skin, let alone on open wounds. He's got all the signs of coolant poisoning."

Harley didn't need to hear more. Everyone knew that the slick green coolant fluid channeled into the heat sinks was toxic. If it got into someone's bloodstream, death was painful and inevitable.

Coombs was shaking his head at the terrible

sight. "The medic has patched him up some, but he's only got a few minutes—if that."

Lieutenant Hawke knelt down next to Hershorn and took his pulse, but from the look on her face, everyone understood that the traitor would soon be dead.

Harley wondered if Hawke was sorry she wasn't the one who did it. At least, that's what he was feeling right now.

"Gunney, hand me the booster," Hawke said, pointing to the medical kit sitting open at the sergeant's feet.

"Sir, if you give him that, he'll be dead a hell of a lot quicker," Gunney said, handing her the syringe.

"I know that. Nothing can save him now. But this way we can at least get some answers, if we're lucky." She bent over Hershorn and gave him a vicious stab with the needle, pumping the red liquid into the man's dying form.

Harley couldn't move or speak, a part of him appalled by what she was doing. Even when hunting, he'd always made sure his kills were clean rather than let the animals suffer. He wanted to speak up now, but he couldn't. Hershorn was responsible for the death of Ben. Harley felt shame at what he was feeling, but for Hershorn to suffer, even for a short time, seemed eerily just.

Hershorn drew in a deep breath and his eyes opened so quickly that Harley thought for a moment he might be faking. The moan he gave left no doubt that he was not. He turned his head just enough to see Hawke bending over him.

Hershorn chuckled, then broke into a sick

laugh. It was the laugh of a dead man, a sound that momentarily unnerved Harley.

"All right, Lieutenant," Hawke said coldly. "Here's the deal. You've got coolant in your body. You know what that'll do to you. I can end it quickly for you. But before I do that, I want some answers." It wasn't a threat. If anything, her voice was almost compassionate.

Hershorn's voice was dry and cracked at first. "You tricked me."

Hawke nodded. "That's right. Now, tell me, Hershorn, is Hopper Morrison planning to hit anywhere else?"

Hershorn coughed once, then was silent for what seemed like an eternity. "Why should I tell you?"

Hawke pulled another syringe out, this one filled with a clear liquid. "Because I know that the poison is eating your body apart. You're on fire. I can end that. Tell me what I need to know." Gone was the hint of compassion of a moment before. Her voice was angry now.

"Most of the Extractors," Hershorn stammered, "are on The Rack. Morrison figured we could . . . take this world with two companies."

"Force strength estimates?"

Hershorn gave her a glaring look as if she were torturing him. "Two battalions."

"Aerospace elements?"

He winced. "Ten fighters . . . total."

"Why?" Her words seemed to hang in the air, suspended.

"Why did I do it?" Hershorn asked, seeming to gain strength from the question. "Why did I turn? I wish it was something as glorious as honor. I didn't"—he coughed, and this time a trickle of blood ran down from the side of his mouth—"do it for honor. Morrison offered me money."

"How did you fake my voice, send that false order?"

"Not false," he stammered, his chest seeming to heave harder. "I knew your command channels. I set them up, remember?" He seemed to spasm for a moment, fighting back the coughing that was killing him. "Not false. I used a copy of your voice from Birdsong Ridge."

Hawke looked shaken by his words, and Harley thought Hershorn wanted to laugh again, but couldn't. Every word, every breath, seemed to drain more of his strength. "Ironic, eh Hawke?" he managed. He smiled, but Harley could see his gums bleeding as his body caved in on itself.

Hawke got to her feet and stood looking over him, the syringe in her hands.

"Morrison will make you pay," Hershorn taunted.

Livia took the syringe and opened it, spilling the contents onto the ground. A look of terror—a look of complete doom swept over what was left of Hershorn's face.

"He's already taken all he's going to from me," she said.

"You promised!" Hershorn croaked loudly, trying to lift his head, but failing miserably.

Hawke kicked at the syringe, sending it out of the circle. "Now you know what it's like to be deceived and have your life wasted for it. You cost me my company and the person I most cared about."

Hershorn's face seemed to cave in. He laughed,

audibly at first, then so weakly that his face contorted with the effort. His eyes closed as he spoke what were to be the final words of his life.

"You don't know, do you?"

25

DropShip General Gordon
Zenith Jump Point, Caldarium
Rim Collection
The Periphery
28 May 3059

From the journal of Harley Rassor:
The only reason I'm taking the time to write here is that all I have is time. Lieutenant Hershorn is dead, but my nerves are on edge, given where we're going and what we plan to do.

The Aces have now left Gillfillan's Gold and jumped out of the system. Clash Lance, with the exception of the infantry, remained on the planet, and we've spent most of our time working with the technicians getting our 'Mechs repaired. Second Company bore the brunt of the fighting, losing a full lance of light 'Mechs at the start. For a bunch of pirates, the Extractors put up some stiff resistance.

A couple of days into the ride to the jump point, I bumped into Jeremy Lewis and he was bragging up how well I'd done. He's stopped using my real name altogether, and just calls me Hellraiser. Then Jord joined in. They kept telling me I fight like a natural.

The truth is I'm no hero or great MechWarrior. When the battle ended I was shaking, just like when I used to hunt saber boar back home. I could have been killed. This isn't a game. People die. I remember the deaths. One in particular.

I keep waking up in the middle of the night remembering Hershorn's laugh. He's paid now for what he did, but it's still getting to me.

I wanted to write Da and Jolee, but I'm not sure what to tell them. Worse, I don't know when I'll ever get a chance to send them a letter. I did write a note and left it in my locker, just in case I don't make it. If I die, I want them to know that the man who betrayed Ben is no longer alive. But until we take our "King" Hopper Morrison, I won't feel that retribution for Ben's death is complete.

Those nightmares bother me. It's not just that Hershorn died so painfully, but there was something in his last words that I can't forget. It was like he knew something we didn't, and he found it funny. I sort of feel that justice was done, but at the same time I think he managed to get away by dying. That might not make sense, but it's what I feel.

Right now, we're in the Caldarium system recharging. I watched the crew deploy the jump sail to collect the solar energy that will recharge the drives and let us jump to the next system. I'd never seen them do it before. It's like a sailboat's, but it's round with a hole in the middle. They really work hard to get it out there and straight. One of the riggers told me that if the sail gets damaged, we could end up not being able to recharge. I never realized how delicate an operation it was. They'll be pulling it back in a few hours, and then we'll jump out.

The Major shuttled over to tell us the plan while we were in the All Dawn system recharging. Even as we were fighting what they're now calling the "Second Battle of Gillfillan's Gold," he was mustering the remaining Aces at the jump point. The Extractors we hammered did manage to get away to their own JumpShips, using an even closer pirate jump point than before. Our fighters did a lot of damage to their DropShips, but the pirates still got off the planet with two of their 'Mechs, including that damn *Timber Wolf*.

We linked up with the rest of the Aces as we traveled. Most jumped with us out of Gillfillan's Gold. Other companies linked up with us at All Dawn. Caldarium is the end of the line for us—the next hops take us into the deep Periphery.

The Major told us that the plan was for us to take the offensive. He had worked it all out with President Moroney weeks ago. They had decided that Morrison's Extractors were a clear and present danger to the survival of the Rim Collection. That was why Moroney agreed to support something that our government has never done, launching a military offensive.

The Major told us that the place to best hurt "King" Hopper Morrison is a nasty little world called The Rack. From what he said, it's an ugly pit, a combination slum and pirate kingdom where Morrison rules and the only law is his word.

Apparently one of his raiding parties ended up on The Rack and were foraging for anything of value when they stumbled onto a buried Star League bunker complete with mothballed Battle-Mechs. Morrison used those 'Mechs to build his little army into a serious threat.

He kept Pain as his commercial base, while his military operates from The Rack. In fact, he's running a slave-based digging operation to see if there's any more Star League tech stored there. They're dredging off the side of a mountain looking for anything else left from the old SLDF complex.

All of us have gone over the scant data on The Rack. Not a nice place. There aren't many flat places to even land a DropShip, if the intel is right. Very jagged rock formation, obsidian, all sorts of metallic and radioactive ore that'll make long-range sensor sweeps almost impossible. They say it's almost always the middle of a rainstorm where we'll be landing, with major thunder and lightning activity. That weather is going to play hell with our aerospace support. Back when there was a Star League they could control the weather on a planet. But that was a long time ago. Nature has a way of always beating the plans of men, just like Da says.

We're going to strike The Rack, the entire regiment. This will be the most BattleMechs I've ever seen in one place at one time. Major Able has told us that we're going to make sure Morrison's Extractors no longer pose a threat. That's a nice way of saying our mission is to destroy the Extractors.

Some of them will still be on Pain, but when we're done on The Rack, we'll have crippled their military capability. Morrison will still have some 'Mechs, but not enough to dare attack the Rim Collection again.

I've changed a lot since joining the Aces. So many things I used to dream about, I now take for granted. Ben and I used to talk about traveling to other worlds, piloting 'Mechs other than that old wreck of a *Commando* in battles to save the universe. That now seems like it was a whole other lifetime ago. Here I am, leaving the Rim Collection to go even deeper into the Periphery, and it all seems so *normal.*

I think I understand why Ben was obsessed with high tech, but in a different way. Working in and around BattleMechs, you gain a perspective about what power is in the universe and how vulnerable people are. We pilot these beasts, we kill each other, all of it using technology. I think sometimes that Ben got so impressed with technology that he forgot the importance of people.

Until now I thought that if the traitor was brought to justice it would lay to rest some of my grief over Ben. But Hershorn's death hasn't done that. It still seems that nothing has been resolved, and that justice hasn't been done.

I'm tired now and need to get some rest, but a part of me is worried that if I go to sleep, I'll wake up in a hot sweat still haunted by Hershorn's laughter.

26

Slice of Hell Hills
The Rack
Deep Periphery
16 June 3059

One of the biggest problems Able's Aces had with The Rack was the lack of a good tactical map of the terrain. Until Hopper Morrison arrived some years back, the planet had been virtually a lost world that no one had thought about for several hundred years. The only reason it even had a name was because Morrison had given it one when he discovered a stash of 'Mechs here.

Obviously, he wasn't handing out any topographical data on the place, and so the Aces tried to piece a map together for themselves. The unit's inbound DropShips had run countless feeds on the planet, constructing a map on the fly even as they approached it from the system's red giant star.

Everyone in the unit got to play at giving names to the planet's various locations in order to easily identify them in combat. Dabney Fox had come up with "Slice of Hell" for these flat-topped hills, and from what Harley could tell he got it right in one.

But neither the maps nor the briefings could have prepared him for what he saw as the Aces deployed from the *General Gordon*, and he began to move his *Enforcer* into position with the rest of Bishop Lance.

It was supposed to be morning, but it was impossible to tell because the blood-red sun of the system was almost totally blocked by dark, water-laden clouds. The light that did get through tinted the cloud formations a sick purple hue. Harley didn't even try to take in the view. The cold, pelting rain that drummed against his cockpit screen made visuals almost impossible. It came in roaring waves, driven by the wind.

Then there was the thunder and lightning. Every minute or so came another crash, either close enough to shake his 'Mech, or far enough away to be a distant rumble. Lightning almost always followed the thunderclaps, jagged white bolts tinged blue. It was so much like a strobe light that it gave Harley a headache. He had to lift his neurohelmet faceplate and rub his brow to try and ease the pain away.

Because of the lack of intel on The Rack's geography and terrain, the battle plan had been drafted on the flight in-system, then relayed between the various units on their DropShips. They had days to go over them and memorize everything their sensors told them about where they would be landing and fighting.

First Battalion was now positioned atop the Slice of Hell hills—more BattleMechs and troopers in one place at one time than Harley had ever seen. Five kilometers away to the planetary west, in a deep, flat-bottomed valley ringed by jagged rock formations, Second Battalion was deployed. It was a place they'd dubbed "The Valley of the Seven Deadly Sins." Third Battalion, which was really nothing more than two companies of 'Mechs, was poised equidistant from the other two companies, forming a triangle to the south.

Rather than spread out against multiple enemy ships, the Aces had all come in on one DropShip, the *General Chamberlain*. As it approached, the pirates scrambled a number of aerospace fighters to try and take it out before the ship could touch down. The *General Chamberlain* took some fairly heavy damage.

The old ship was tougher than it looked, however, and the launch of the Aces' own fighters turned the tables quickly. In the end the Extractors downed two of the Aces' fighters and lost nine of their own. Then the *General Chamberlain* made its way to the small landing strip that constituted the only possible landing zone in the area.

The only source of human life on the planet was a shanty-town set in the middle of an uneven, muddy plain. Running CAP, the Aces' aerospace fighters had swept the area and found a total of two battalions of 'Mechs, most of them from the primary regiment of Morrison's Extractors. There were indications of numerous others there, civilians, perhaps others pirates, and if rumors were accurate, slave labor.

The town was built next to a deep pit surrounded by heavy digging gear and a pumping station to keep the constant rainfall drained so that the workers could perform their work. It had once been a Star League bunker, then lay buried for centuries. After finding a cache of BattleMechs and gear, Morrison had continued the digging in hopes of finding more of the precious Star League technology. It was his source of power, the wellspring of the carnage he'd wrought on the Rim Collection and the neighboring Lyran Alliance.

If intel was accurate, Hopper Morrison fielded a total of two regiments, at least on paper. He also had infantry, some tanks, and the remains of several broken mercenary regiments that the Extractors had absorbed. Some Extractors were always on Pain, but hitting The Rack was going to kneecap Morrison and cripple his ability to mount offensive operations.

The plan was simple. First and Second Battalions would move in from the east and west to engage the Extractors. The odds would be relatively even, though fighting in the wasted terrain wasn't going to be easy for either side. When the pirates were distracted, Third Battalion would move north and hit them with a delayed punch, striking at the 'Mechs and the heavy digging equipment to draw off the enemy and to cripple Morrison's strip-mining operation.

The ultimate goal was to destroy the battalions there. Not hurt. Not intimidate. Destroy.

Destruction of those units would seriously weaken the Extractors. If Hopper decided to retaliate, he would have to leave his two base worlds exposed to other marauding pirate bands in the Periphery. There was little honor among thieves, and any weakening of Hopper's forces would leave him prey to his enemies, or worse, a rebellion from within.

The DropShips' sensor data on the types of 'Mechs present had been inconclusive. Harley had overheard Lieutenant Hawke ask the sensor operators to look for a 'Mech's reactor signature based on data from her battlerom, and he knew what she was looking for—the *Timber Wolf* they had tangled with twice now.

There was no sign of the elusive pale green 'Mech, but that didn't mean it wasn't there. A planet is a big place on which to hide. The 'Mech could be shut down, hidden in a cave, or just not in the area the sensors had swept.

Harley tried to adjust his sensors, but the lightning bursts in the vicinity seemed to play havoc with them. The secondary display would flicker momentarily, then reset itself, each time losing precious time. Despite the interference, he was not picking up any approaching enemy. All that seemed to be on top of the Slice of Hell was First Battalion and the ever-present rattle of the rain pounding his 'Mech canopy.

"Fireball One to all Talons," Lieutenant Hawke's voice rang in his earpiece. "We are on the right flank of the battalion. The rock formations and passes are going to force us to break up. Stay together by lance, and maintain radio contact. There are plenty of tight fields of fire so when the Extractors do show up, we need to concentrate quickly or we'll get plastered."

There were the usual confirmations by the lance leaders over the commline. After confirming for her command, Corporal Glancy then assigned formation orders to Harley and the others. He and Bixby were at the rear while Glancy and Fox took the front.

Harley swung in behind Fox's *Hatchetman*, a burst of lightning showing her dull gray replacement armor plates standing out against the camouflaged ones. Glancy and Fox took position a hundred meters in front of him and Bix as they started down from the hilltop and into the shadowy rock formations.

The lowlands were a series of steep, sharp passageways that turned and twisted tightly. Harley kept his eyes on the constantly flickering short-range sensors, hoping to catch a sign of the enemy before they spotted him. After a kilometer, he was having a hard time keeping Glancy and Fox in his line of sight. As he stepped forward into what he thought was a shallow pool of rainwater, he sank down quickly, then stumbled forward, barely catching his balance.

"You okay over there, Hellraiser?" Bixby called.

"I'm fine. Watch those pools, Bix. Some are deeper than they look."

Glancy's voice broke in. "I suggest the two of you cut the chatter and close up formation."

Harley was moving forward again when he saw a red dot of light appear on his sensor display, only to be lost as lightning struck only fifty meters away, causing the system to reset, for the dozenth time. This time the small red dot did not appear. It was beyond a ridge line that rose in front of them, then spilled out into a long, wide valley at the foot of the hills. The valley offered plenty of wide open spaces for combat.

Climbing the steep rock formations would be difficult if not impossible, but someone there, at the top, holding the high ground, could rain down destruction on those below.

The image of the hills and ridge line sent a chill down Harley's spine, and he wondered if Hawke was thinking the same thing he was. The formation was similar to the tactical displays he'd reviewed for Birdsong Ridge. This was like the place where Ben had died. For a moment Harley wondered if history was going to repeat itself, and if Da would have to send Jolee to learn what had happened to him.

"Bishop Two to Bishop One," he said following the protocol that had been drilled into him since joining the Aces. "I had a contact in our three o'clock position."

"Bishop One acknowledges but cannot confirm," came back Glancy. "Hold up Bishop Lance. Can anyone confirm that reading?"

There was a pause as Harley stopped his *Enforcer* and attempted to pick up the signal again, but was having no luck.

"No joy," came the voice of Dabney Fox over the commline.

"Could've been the storm," Bix said.

There was a slight pause as Corporal Glancy thought about what she knew and what she needed. "Bishop One to Fireball One."

Hawke's voice came through clear. "Go, Bishop One."

"I need a flyby at coordinates zero-three-five-niner-alpha."

"Clash Three, paint us a picture," came the word from Lieutenant Hawke.

Her order was confirmed by Davis Gilbert in his *Lucifer.* Harley saw the fighter appear on his sensors as Gilbert did a fly-by over Bishop Lance. The sleek-nosed fighter swung over the far right flank of the unit toward the area where Harley had picked up the phantom sensor reading. The rocks blocked Harley's line of sight, but he listened intently on the commline, hoping he had been right—or wrong.

"Fireball One, I have multiple bandits, at least a battalion in size. Coordinates at zero-three—" The message cut off with a burst of static.

Harley checked his tactical display and saw the small dot of light representing the *Lucifer* disappear. That was followed by a flashing dot of blue light, indicating that Gilbert had managed to eject safely and was sending out a recovery signal.

His body tensed at the next words he heard. "Hawke's Talons, right flank, stand by to receive the enemy." Hawke spoke as she brought Fireball Lance over behind Harley. Then an Extractor *Guillotine* and a *Flashman* appeared and opened fire.

The *Guillotine* targeted Hawke's *Orion* and let go with its large laser, followed by the mediums. The larger scarlet beam missed, slamming into a wet rock behind Hawke that sent a spray of exploding boulders and debris into the air. The right-arm medium lasers did better, burning and melting plates as they dug deep into her *Orion*'s upper legs. The older model *Orion* shook off the attack, and Hawke opened up with her autocannon and short-range missiles. The *Flashman* slid down a small hillside to the same level as the

Aces and attacked Bixby Finch with a barbarous assault of laserfire.

Harley joined in too. Jerking the joystick around, he dropped the targeting reticle on the heart of the *Guillotine* and fired his autocannon, intending to kill the Extractor. He followed that a full second later with a burst from his large laser, its red beam slicing through the sheets of rain. Harley saw other Extractor BattleMechs entering the fight on both sides of him, but he stayed focused on this enemy, on this part of the overall war unleashing amid the fury of the storm.

Where the shots hit was more of a fluke of bad luck than anything. Half of Hawke's SRMs missed, eating rocks and rainwater rather than armor. The other pair blasted two craters in the lower shin of one of the pirate Mech's legs. Her autocannon round struck the same leg slightly higher, ripping away even more armor plating there.

A heartbeat later Harley's attack came in. His laser only nicked the *Guillotine*'s left arm, but his autocannon fire dug into the same leg Hawke had already brutalized. This time only a shard or two of armor still remained, barely enough to worry about. The shell exploded on the surface, shredding myomer muscle and devouring the 'Mech's knee actuator.

The *Guillotine*'s MechWarrior was caught off guard by the succession of shots all hitting in the same area and the loss of support from the limb whose damage was the equivalent of a shattered knee. It listed forward slightly, firing one of its torso lasers at Hawke wildly, then falling face forward into a shallow pool of rainwater.

"Splash," Harley said through gritted teeth, his head and heart pounding with excitement.

Harley torso-twisted and saw that Bixby's *Vindicator* seemed almost blackened by the beating it had taken from the *Flashman*. The superior firepower of the larger 'Mech had destroyed the *Vindicator*'s left arm, and its torso and legs were black from laser burns. One large scar traced up along the left arm near the flame-painted barrel of his PPC. Bixby wouldn't last long in this fight.

Harley saw his predicament and was determined to see his friend survive. He fired at the *Flashman* with his large laser first, hitting it in the right torso. That got the MechWarrior's attention, the larger BattleMech turning slowly as if to consider its new foe. Bixby used the chance to open up with his medium laser and long-range missiles. One missile slammed into the cockpit canopy while the others ate away at the *Flashman*'s already damaged chest and torso. The medium laser melted away one of the armored plates on the *Flashman*'s arm, leaving it hissing with steam from the cold rain.

He didn't wait to become a new target, opening up with his autocannon so hard that it almost hurt his thumb as he triggered the target interlock. The gun barked, discharging the autocannon round squarely into the cockpit of the *Flashman* as it raised its large lasers and pointed them directly at Harley's *Enforcer*.

Harley's autocannon round exploded inside the *Flashman*'s cockpit as it penetrated the remaining armor there, engulfing the head in an orange ball of fire that rose in a black cloud of smoke into the rain and wind. There was no hope for the pirate

MechWarrior who had been commanding the *Flashman*. The decapitated 'Mech fell to the side, its head hissing as it fell into the rainwater pool.

"I'm hurting over here," Bixby said, sounding like he was gasping for breath in his neurohelmet.

"Fall back behind me," Harley said as he watched a *Cicada* attempt to flank around Lieutenant Hawke and the far right flank. The clearing it was running through was barely one hundred fifty meters of open space with rough terrain of boulders and water. The smaller 'Mech was attempting to get behind them, to find some pathway through the maze of rock formations that would get him to the rear of the Aces.

Dabney Fox leapt into the air on her jump jets, her *Hatchetman* cutting behind Harley and passing just above him as it roared up and over. She dropped a few meters from the *Cicada*, which opened up with its medium lasers, lashing out wildly and hitting more rock than BattleMech.

Harley leveled his large laser and fired, missing as well, but Fox didn't. Her medium lasers exploded armor off the torso of the boxy little 'Mech, and before it could counter or run, she hefted her 'Mech's massive hatchet into the air, then brought it slashing down into the body of the *Cicada*.

The armor plating caved in, the hatchet buried deep into the 'Mech's internal structure. In an instant, Harley saw a flash as its fusion reactor erupted. His cockpit was polarized to deflect the harmful burst of light, but it overpowered his senses. He closed his eyes to clear the dots of light from the blast, and when he opened them again he saw that the *Cicada* was gone, a smoking and steaming ruin of hot metal in the cold rain. The hatchet of Fox's 'Mech was gone, too, as was the 'Mech's forearm, but she had somehow managed to keep her machine upright.

"Splash one light," she said, her breathing heavy over the comm channel.

In the midst of the lightning flashes, Harley saw the outline of a 'Mech moving along the top of the ridge line in front of him. He knew the shape, and knew that it was one of a kind, the only one he had ever seen.

The *Timber Wolf.*

Bixby fired at it from his side, his PPC fire slamming into one of the legs of the massive 'Mech. Hawke moved up alongside his right flank and brought her autocannon to bear on the dull green 'Mech as it fired further down the defile at a member of Fireball Lance who was out of sight. Her shot missed by less than a meter.

Harley let loose with his own autocannon and had better luck, planting the cannon shell into the left torso of the *Timber Wolf.* It struck with such savage fury that the Clan war machine stopped moving away from their position and turned to face where the attack had come from. For a moment, Harley felt as if he were looking right into the eyes of the enemy MechWarrior.

The *Timber Wolf* fired its deadly barrage of long-range missiles in his direction. For a full second all forty of the warheads streaked down from the high ground, coming right at Harley, aimed right at his heart. Instinctively and from fear, both at the same time, he backed up a step and jerked his *Enforcer* to the right to attempt to get out of the way.

It was a futile gesture because the missiles were not coming for him but for Bixby Finch at his side.

They swarmed Bix's already damaged *Vindicator* with so many small explosions that the 'Mech was lost from view as the explosions did their deadly work. Harley watched in awe as his friend's *Vindicator* collapsed in a pile of debris and ruin only a few meters away.

"Bix!" he called.

"Bishop Three respond," Hawke added.

Harley did not wait for Bixby to answer. He adjusted the aim of his targeting reticle on the HUD image of the *Timber Wolf* and triggered his large laser, this time hitting the Clan OmniMech in its left arm just below the boxy long-range missile launcher. The vermilion energy beam melted a long and nasty scar up the arm, destroying armor as it went.

A cough came over his commline. "I'm alive," Bixby said, so dazed he almost sounded drunk. "Barely."

"Hang on, Bix," Harley managed to say as the *Timber Wolf* twisted at the waist toward another 'Mech from Second Company, lashing away with its own extended-range large lasers. At its side a massive 100-ton 'Mech appeared and was pouring fire in the same direction, a *King Crab*. At its maximum range from the ridgetop, it poured down its deadly autocannon fire. An explosion from below shook rocks loose near Harley and told him it had scored a deadly hit on someone he could not see—one of the Aces who, like Bix, was down or worse.

"Forget me, Bishop Two," Bixby managed. "Take out that malfing *T-Wolf*,"

Without warning Harley picked up numerous green dots of light on his secondary display.

Friendly BattleMechs, the long-awaited arrival of Second Battalion. The odds had suddenly shifted.

"Hang on, Talons. I just got word from the Captain that Sheryl Davy's Second Battalion has arrived on our left and is hitting them hard. Bishop One, Glancy, what's left of your lance still has jump jets. Start working your way up to the top of the ridge. I'm going to move along the right flank with Fireball Two and see if we can find a way to the backside. One way or another we will meet you at the top."

Further down the ridge line a furious battle was raging as Second Battalion waded into the Extractors, fighting them for every rock, mound, boulder, and puddle of terrain. Explosions on both sides sounded like the constant roar of The Rack's perpetual thunderstorms. Harley waited for Corporal Glancy to move up on his side, and when she fired her jump jets, he did the same.

His *Enforcer* was far from graceful in its upward flight. It rose with a steady vibration as he used his own neurofeedback to adjust the gyro and keep the BattleMech somewhat steady as it moved. His cockpit was starting to feel like a sauna when he spotted the top of the ridge and saw a level enough area to land. He felt as if he were roasting when he set down on the top.

Glancy landed her *Sentinel* next to him and was quick to pivot to face down the ridge line that they had been firing up for so long. A full three seconds later, what was left of Dabney Fox's *Hatchetman* landed on Harley's right. Up close he could see that the damage from the fighting had left her with a mere shell of the 'Mech she'd been piloting only a short time ago.

Almost two hundred-fifty meters along the top of the rocky ridge was the end of the Extractors' line of battle. The massive *King Crab* was between them and the *Timber Wolf* that had been plaguing him since he'd joined Able's Aces. Glancy's voice was crisp and precise. "Bishop Lance, concentrate your fire on that *King Crab*. Take him down and *then* the *Timber Wolf*."

Glancy must have been reading Harley's mind, knowing that he wanted a piece of the Clan 'Mech. Vengeance had a value to him, but so did following orders when they made sense, and in this case they did.

The trio of 'Mechs aimed what weapons they had left and poured them into the side and rear of the *King Crab*. The shots all hit in the same general area, the long arm and left torso of the Star League-era 'Mech. Harley and Glancy's autocannon shots hit the 'Mech so hard it sagged toward the *Timber Wolf* under the impacts. For an incredibly brief moment it reeled as Harley's large laser sliced up the arm and burned off precious armor. Fox's next autocannon round plowed in where they had already hit, this time burrowing deep and exploding.

Instantly there was another rumble from within the 'Mech as something, most likely some of its own autocannon ammunition, erupted in a series of blasts that rent its arm off totally. Sick green smoke rose into the sheets of rain like some sort of emergency flare.

The *King Crab* turned and its long-range missile hatches popped open. The barrage of missiles streaked in on Bishop Four, bathing her weary *Hatchetman* in an orange ball of fire. It sagged, and Harley saw that what armor was left on its chest was in bits and jagged pieces. Myomer muscles exposed to the cool rains sizzled and steam vented.

"Bishop One, I've lost my reactor. My core has dropped and I'm on backup power," she said furiously.

Harley turned back to the *King Crab* but saw that it was gone. Now nothing was between him and the *Timber Wolf* as it continued to pour an endless barrage of fire down at Second Battalion.

Then, as it had done before, the *Timber Wolf* pivoted in place and charged *away* from the fight, retreating at a full run. From what Harley could tell, it was doing what the *King Crab* had done, saving itself.

"Not this time you don't," Harley said, lighting his jump jets and leaping in response. Glancy's warnings and orders did not reach him as the blood boiled in his brain.

27

Murk Lake
The Rack
Deep Periphery
16 June 3059

"**B**ishop One," Hawke said over the commline, feeling tired, excited, frustrated, and angry all at the same time. In the distance, the fighting had all but stopped. From their position, she and the remains of The Hawke's Talons could see the surrendering battered remnants of what had been the cream of Morrison's Extractors. A few minutes before, the word had gone out on a broad-band cannel that the Extractors were giving up, en masse. Those who didn't surrender had fled into the mire and eerie blackness that was The Rack.

Their morale had shattered upon receiving word that elements of the Aces' Third Battalion had slammed into their small shantytown, freed the imprisoned slave laborers, and begun to destroy Hopper Morrison's expensive digging and dredging gear. "King" Morrison had been leading the attack against Second Battalion, but then he too turned and fled from the battlefield.

Hawke realized with a pang that they had him in their sights—Morrison was the pilot in the *King Crab*! His desertion seemed to leave the rest of his people wondering what they were risking their lives for.

It had taken a full ten minutes for Hawke and Jord to reach the top of the ridge, working their way along a winding trail to join the rest of their company—what was left of it. Somewhere below, Sergeant Coombs and his men were securing prisoners, but up here, the war was still raging.

"Where is Bishop Three?"

Glancy seemed to hesitate, much too long for Hawke's liking. "Hellraiser broke ranks and set off after that *Timber Wolf*," Glancy said finally. "They headed to the east just after we got up here, sir."

"Why didn't you order him to hold his ground?"

"I did, sir. He didn't respond. Maybe his comm system's out . . . He didn't respond."

"Horse-hockey!" spat back Hawke. "Don't feed me a line, Glancy. You hold here. I'm going out after him."

"Sir, I'll come along," Jord said. "I've seen that *Timber Wolf* in action."

"Your leg's in bad shape, Fireball Two," Hawke told him. "Keep your pace up and you're with me."

* * *

The ground leveled slightly, then dipped to form a large bowl with a narrow rock ledge that served as a shoreline. The winds and pelting rain whipped across the water's surface as if it were a cauldron being stirred by mad warlocks. Harley remembered that Dabney Fox had dubbed this body of water Lake Murk when they'd been naming the planet's terrain. Seeing it now, he saw how apt was the name for the almost ink-like waters.

The "shoreline" was where he concentrated his gaze and his sensor sweeps. On one side, deep black waters of a lake of unknown depth. On the other side, a wall of rock rising nearly thirty meters high. And, at the far end of that shore, behind a jutting rock face, a sensor reading from a fusion reactor. The same reactor signal he'd been chasing for kilometers, weaving and winding through what seemed an endless maze of rocks and gray-black canyons.

The *Timber Wolf.*

The same dull green 'Mech Harley had met for the first time on Gillfillan's Gold at Rectortown, where it had fought and fled. He'd faced it again when Major Able had sprung his trap, and once more the 'Mech managed to avoid capture or destruction by plowing straight through the Aces' lines. Now for the third time, it was trying to escape from the battle, to survive to fight another day.

Not this time, Harley vowed silently. The *Timber Wolf* had come to represent all that he and his family had lost. Taking down that 'Mech, or forcing it to surrender would give him some measure of peace that he'd done all he could for Ben's memory. And though the Clan-built BattleMech outweighed him considerably, Harley knew it had also suffered considerable damage. The odds had never been more even.

Unless the *Timber Wolf's* sensors or battle computer were damaged, the enemy MechWarrior knew that Harley was out there too, but he wasn't moving. Harley's secondary display showed at least part of the reason. If his sensors were correct, there was no exit for the *Timber Wolf.* One hundred meters further down, the shore/ledge became too narrow for a BattleMech. The Extractor 'Mech was trapped. There was one way out, and Harley was it.

A part of him wanted to race down and engage, to charge into the 'Mech in a blaze of glory. Instead, he took a long, deep breath. This wasn't the time for impulsive actions. Harley wouldn't hesitate to give his life to take down the *Timber Wolf,* but it would certainly be better to do it without committing suicide.

He toggled the broad-band channel and stared intently down the shore to the rock slab that blocked his line of sight with the *Timber Wolf.*

"I know you know I'm out here," he said. "We both know there's no way out for you. Surrender now and you'll live."

A deep voice, surrounded with static, replied. "Harley, power down your weapons. We don't have to do this." Harley glanced down and saw that the response had come over on a secured channel rather than the broad one he'd used to transmit. Hershorn must have given the pirates the Aces' comm frequencies.

The voice sent a shiver down his back, but

Harley shook off his dread. "How do you know who I am?"

"Harley," the voice said, almost seductively, "you don't have to fire on me to avenge your brother."

"You and your friends killed Ben," Harley said, but he was beginning to sense that something was wrong here.

"No, Harley. Ben isn't dead. You know that. Listen to my voice. I *am* Ben."

With those words the *Timber Wolf* stepped into Harley's line of sight. It had been battered badly. One of the long-range missile racks mounted on its left shoulder was nothing more than scrap, charred and burned beyond salvage. Long scars from laser, autocannon, and PPC fire had turned the green paint job into a sickening burned and cratered mix.

The words hit Harley like one of the lightning bolts that constantly stabbed at The Rack. He knew the voice of his brother, but he couldn't totally make the shift from believing that Ben had died. No one had ever doubted that fact. His entire reason for coming to the Able's Aces was to find out who had killed Ben. Now the truth hit him hard. All that was a lie. Ben was alive.

"Ben?"

"Yes, Harley, it's me."

"How—how is this possible?"

"It's a long story. The bottom line is that I'm not dead. Together, we can get out of here. Morrison has a small *Leopard* Class DropShip hidden away in a cave about thirty klicks from here. We get there, take off, skirt the combat air patrol, and make our way back to Pain." Ben's words almost tumbled over one another, like a criminal on the run, Harley thought.

Harley's whole body tensed. Ben's words were those of a warrior who had changed sides, a traitor. His brother had betrayed the Aces, and because of him good men had died. "Ben, don't you realize what you're saying?"

"Har, it's time you grew up. This is how things work in the *real* universe, little brother. I work for Hopper Morrison."

"And you're a member of the Aces," Harley said, feeling sick as the realization of what his brother had become sank in.

"*Was* a member of the Aces, Har. I know what you're thinking. You want me to come back with you. Well, that's just not going to happen. I'm part of a different unit now."

"You sold out the Aces," Harley said coldly.

"Not just the Aces. What about your family? You sold them out too."

"You were always too melodramatic, brother. It was a business transaction, Har, nothing more, nothing less."

"It was more to those who died at Birdsong Ridge."

"Don't patronize me, little brother. They were MechWarriors. When they climbed into their cockpits, they knew there was a good chance they might get killed in combat. That's reality.

"You're a MechWarrior now too. We've faced off on the battlefield more than once. You've faced death, haven't you? You know what a soldier has to do, what a soldier has to risk. Now, shut off your targeting and tracking system and let's get out of here while we can."

Ben's words cut deep because he was partially right. "It's true what you say, Ben. They knew the risk, but you changed that risk into a certainty when you betrayed them. You sold out your company and now they're all dead. It wasn't just a risk they ran. You had them set up. They never had a chance."

"That's right, Har. They died. Hershorn and I betrayed them. Is that what you want to hear?"

"I'd rather hear that it bothered you. And what about Da and Jolee? You have the blood of a lot of people on your hands, Ben. And you dragged Da and our sister through hell. He pulled in a lot of favors to get me here. I wouldn't *be* in Able's Aces if not for what you did. I came to find out what happened to you, to learn the truth."

Harley felt the anger rising in his blood. He'd always looked up to Ben, tried to go along with his pranks and schemes. He'd wanted his approval, wanted to be his equal. That now seemed a long, long time ago, almost an entire lifetime ago in his mind. In the last few minutes everything had changed.

"Da?" Ben jeered. "You're worried about how Da feels? When did he ever sit and worry about us? He's always played god with our lives, Har, and you know it. He dominated every aspect of what we did. Don't you remember what it was like being raised by him? We could've afforded a better place to live. He had skills that could have made us a lot of money, given us an easier life. Instead he chose to play farmer and raise us to do the same. Maybe that's fine for you and Jolee, but not for me. I want something better. I *deserve* something better."

Harley knew there was some truth in what Ben said about Da, but not enough to justify the things he had done. "He might have been rough on us, Ben, but he taught us to lead our lives without making others pay for our mistakes. You took the lives of others to change yours. I barely remember Ma, but I doubt she'd be proud of what you've done any more than Da would. And before you condemn him totally, remember that Da cared enough for you to send me to find out what happened to you."

"What do you want, Har?" Ben stabbed back. "Do you honestly think I can surrender after what I've done?"

"It's not too late, Ben. Running away isn't going to make this better."

"If you're not coming with me, then get out of my way and let me pass."

Harley wondered for an instant if he should let Ben go, let him flee with his life. The thought only brought back the sick feeling over what Ben had become. This wasn't his brother any longer, but a pirate, a raider, a killer, a traitor. What would he tell Da? What would he tell Jolee?

"I'm afraid I can't do that Ben," Harley said finally, staring at the battered *Timber Wolf*, which seemed more sinister than ever.

"You wouldn't shoot me, Har." The cockiness in Ben's tone reminded him of the days of their youth and how an older brother often lorded it over the younger. "You can't do it."

Harley jogged his joystick, raising the *Enforcer*'s arm-based weapons, leveled squarely at his brother's BattleMech. "You're wrong, Ben. My word and my loyalty aren't for sale. Da sent me to make sure justice was done for what happened to you. If he knew what you've done, he wouldn't any longer consider you his son. And he would want you to pay."

"You were always the slow one," Ben replied, lifting his 'Mech's arms and bringing his deadly duo of large lasers to bear.

Without warning a barrage of autocannon fire followed by the scream of long-range missiles came from behind Harley and slammed into Ben's *Timber Wolf*. The 'Mech staggered back a step as the autocannon round destroyed what armor remained on his right torso. The 'Mech's right arm and head bore the brunt of the exploding warheads. Harley's heart pounded as he watched the destruction of Ben's BattleMech.

A voice came over the commline. "Rassor, back up before he fires!" It was the voice of Livia Hawke. She must have followed him!

"Lieutenant!" he shouted even as a pair of laser beams sliced into the listing *Timber Wolf*. Ben attempted to compensate, but lost his footing on the rain-slick stones and gravel of the ledge along the lake.

"No!" Harley screamed, but it was already too late. The *Timber Wolf* sagged to one side, hovering for a moment over the water, then plummeted into the murky black waters of the lake.

28

Murk Lake
The Rack
Deep Periphery
16 June 3059

"**H**ellraiser, are you all right?" the voice of Jord MacAuld barked over the broad-band channel.

Harley stared in disbelief at the black waters of the lake that had swallowed up his brother and his seventy-five-ton Clan war machine. All that was left now was the slanting rain pounding against the surface of the water.

Was he all right, Jord wanted to know. Harley couldn't say. Would he ever be all right again? Pivoting his 'Mech's torso, he saw the pair of Acer 'Mechs standing on a small rise behind his position. Jord and Livia Hawke.

Harley keyed in the secure channel to Hawke so that Jord couldn't listen in. He still wasn't sure what to say as he opened the commline.

"Lieutenant, that *Timber Wolf*, it was Ben." The words seemed to take a piece of him as they left his lips, like a part of his very soul being torn away.

There was a pause. "Private . . . Harley, it has to be a mistake. I was there when Ben died." Hawke sounded dazed, as if someone had just woken her from a dream.

Harley knew that 'Mechs were designed to operate underwater and even in a complete vacuum, but the *Timber Wolf* had been damaged. Ben could be dead or dying at the bottom of the lake, or he could be still planning to try and escape. Time was short either way.

"No, it was Ben. We were talking on a different frequency. It was him, I tell you. He must have faked his death at Birdsong Ridge."

"My god," Hawke whispered.

"We've got to find him and save him if we can." Harley couldn't let Ben die now, couldn't turn his back and walk away from his own blood. He advanced his *Enforcer* to the spot where Ben had fallen. The murky waters showed nothing, no signs of life at the bottom of the lake.

Hawke jogged her *Orion* down next to him. "I'm scanning the lake bed. That's quite a drop-off, Harley, and jump jets don't work underwater. I think there's a rock ledge we can work our way down to. If these readings are right, he's on that ledge."

"What about Ben?" Harley asked, attempting to adjust his own sensors.

"I'm getting an active reactor signature, but it's a lot deeper. We need to get down there and size up the situation. Follow me." She now retraced her steps to the far end of the lake, where she began to wade in.

Jord's voice cut in. "Do you two mind telling me what you're doing?" His voice sounded worried over the broad-band channel.

"Cover us from the surface," Hawke ordered curtly. Two more steps forward, and then her 'Mech disappeared under the black waters. Harley was right behind her. The water lapped up the sides of his cockpit port, and he double-checked the damage readout on his secondary display to make sure he wasn't losing the integrity of his own BattleMech.

He was almost ten meters underwater when the *Enforcer* seemed to give out a moan, as if struggling under the pressure of the water. The small navigation lights on the front of the 'Mech were enough for him to barely make out the form of Hawke's *Orion* as she continued down the long slope into what seemed like a bottomless lake.

It took a full fifteen minutes for them to reach the ledge. On the right, a sheer rise to the surface of the lake, where they'd just been standing. Down to the left, a plummet toward the real bottom of the lake that, according to the tactical data Harley was getting from his sensors, was much deeper down. They were nearly sixty-five meters below the surface of the lake. Vision was obscured except for their navigation lights, and even those only lit things up a few scant meters before them.

Continuing his descent, Harley now saw the remains of the *Timber Wolf* at the feet of Hawke's 'Mech, barely visible in the dim yellowed lights. There was a glow from within the cockpit of the fallen 'Mech, its cockpit lights providing some of the illumination. The space on the ledge was tight as Harley moved shoulder-to-shoulder with Hawke's *Orion*. He stared down, almost afraid of what he might see.

In the cockpit of the ruined Clan 'Mech he saw his brother sitting in his command seat. The *Timber Wolf* was on its side, resting at an angle. An eerie cloud of green coolant and silt bled into the water around the 'Mech. Air bubbled, bled from the holes and rents in the armor, fighting desperately to reach the surface.

"Harley, switch to laser comm," Hawke said in his earpiece. Underwater radios would prove tricky in this situation. The laser comm system was a line-of-sight tool that would allow for clearer communication.

Harley toggled the control. "Ben, can you read me?" he asked, fearing the answer.

There was a cough, then a voice he never thought to hear again. "I hear you, Harley. Who's that with you, Livia?"

"Ben," she said, then broke off with a kind of sob. Harley could see Ben in the cockpit, moving forward slightly to look up toward hers.

"I'll bet you're surprised to see me," he said, then coughed again.

"You're right about that," she said, back in charge of herself again. "What's your status?"

"The fall finished me off, doll," Ben said. "The gyro housing must be cracked because it's totally off line. I've got reactor power, but I can't seem to get any action in the legs—I think the myomer control circuitry is fried."

There was a pause. "And just to make life

interesting, I seem to have a growing pool of water in my cockpit."

Harley felt his mouth gape open in shock. He knew from his tactical scans that they were deep in bitterly cold water. Ben could blow the hatch, but the cockpit would flood instantly and he would almost surely go into shock. Even if he did maintain his wits enough to clear the cockpit, he'd have the pressure to deal with. The chances of his reaching the surface alive simply did not exist. He could attempt to let the cockpit flood up to where he could open the hatch when the pressure equalized, but that too risked shock and would take far too long. Punching out, activating the cockpit ejection system, would kill him as he plowed into a solid wall of water.

"Well, Har, you used to say I'd end up in over my head one day." Ben laughed humorlessly. "How does it feel?"

"It feels like hell, Ben," Harley said. "I thought I was just starting to accept the fact you were dead, now I'm watching it happen. How do you think I feel?"

"Ben, what happened?" Hawke asked.

There was a pause. "Hopper Morrison made me an offer I couldn't refuse. You know what an addict I am for tech. He stole this OmniMech and promised it to me. All I had to do was give him tactical data on our company, force compositions, comm frequencies, equipment capabilities. He said he'd arrange to fake my death. Then I could work for him directly."

"You betrayed us for a BattleMech?" she said.

"I knew you'd never understand, that's why I didn't try to get you to come with me. You make it sound so bad, like it was a dirty thing. Don't let looks fool you, Livia. This is the most sophisticated piece of battle technology ever fielded."

Harley cut in. "It doesn't look like much now, Ben. I don't think the price was worth it." First the price in the blood of others, and now maybe the price of Ben's own.

"Maybe you're right, Har. But if you want me to cry over my actions, I won't. I made some decisions you don't agree with, but I'm not the heartless bastard you think I am. I spared Livia's life at Birdsong Ridge, that was part of the bargain. And on Gillfillan's Gold, I had the Extractors pull their punches on you and her once Hershorn told me you'd joined the Aces."

Hawke spoke now. "You brought all of this down on us, Ben. Because of you, the Extractors have been blasted to snail snot. Good, bad, or otherwise, a lot of men and women have died because of your actions."

"I love you, Livia," Ben said. "No matter what you think, it's true."

"I used to love Benjamin Rassor," she said. "He died on Birdsong Ridge. I don't know who you are, but by now it's obvious you'll never reach the surface."

Harley had to break in. "Lieutenant, there has to be something that we can do. We can't let him die—again."

"We just don't have the gear and he doesn't have the time," Hawke said, sounding exhausted. Then her voice became bitter. "Whoever you are, *Timber Wolf* pilot, you have my pity."

She turned her *Orion* in place and started back, moving past Harley.

"Lieutenant," he called, then didn't know what else he wanted to say.

"There's nothing that can be done, Harley. He knows that. You know that. I watched Ben Rassor die once before. I can't do that again. I won't. He's your brother. You owe him, even if now he's nothing but a killer. You can stay and do whatever you have to. But I think you know how this is going to end." Then she continued on, moving up through the dark waters.

Harley turned back to his brother's crippled 'Mech. Tipping his *Enforcer* forward, he could see the cockpit lights and the faint outline of Ben inside. He stared blankly at the dying 'Mech and man and wondered what to do. He didn't know how long he stayed there, alone with Ben in the darkness, before his brother spoke again.

"I knew you'd stay, Harley."

"You're my blood, Ben. You're my brother."

"We could've been a great team."

"No, Ben. Your way isn't mine. You know that."

"I guess I do. This can go one of two ways, Har. Eventually, I will drown in here. The water is leaking in pretty steady, and I've got to tell you, it's damn cold. I don't want to drown."

Harley didn't have an answer to that. "Ben, what do I tell Da and Jolee?"

"I don't know anymore. You'll have to decide for yourself. You're your own man now. A few years ago you would've left. But not this time. I really think you would've fired at me."

"I think you're right."

"Well, then, brother, I'm asking you to now. I don't want to freeze or drown here. Remember when we'd go bow hunting on Taylor Ridge? Remember what we had to do when we only wounded the deer? I don't want to drown. You know what you have to do."

Harley understood. "Ben, I loved you," he said. Then his hand went to the trigger button on his joystick. There was a muffled echo as his auto-cannon fired into the cockpit of the *Timber Wolf* at point-blank range.

Harley's *Enforcer* broke the surface, and he saw Livia Hawke's *Orion* standing near Jord's *Victor*. He was surprised to see that the wind-whipped rains had stopped, though the sky was still dark. For The Rack, it was as close to a clear day as you would get. He waded out of the inky waters and stood facing his commanding officer and his good friend.

Jord's voice boomed in his ears. "Are you okay, Hellraiser? What happened down there?"

"I'm all right," Harley said, letting go a long sigh. "The *Timber Wolf* MechWarrior is dead."

"I'm sorry, Harley," Hawke said softly. "You did what was right. You know that, don't you?"

"Yes sir, I did what I had to." The words were an effort, like hefting heavy stones. "I'm sorry too. What do you say we head back and head home?"

"I'd say our job here is done," Hawke agreed. Then she turned her *Orion* and started the long march back to join the rest of Able's Aces.

Epilogue

Able's Aces Command Post
Gillfillan's Gold, Rim Collection
The Periphery
5 August 3059

Personal Communication
From: Corporal Harley Rassor, Able's Ace's,
    First Battalion, First Company
To: David and Jolee Rassor, Porth, Slewis
ComStar Transmission Code: GG2-2121-A-
    55392093-BRAVO DATA ONLY
Able's Aces Clearance Code Charlie One

MESSAGE TEXT AS FOLLOWS
Da and Jolee:
    When you sent me here I came thinking to
right a great wrong. To find out what
happened to Ben, and to make sure that those
responsible got justice. I write you now to tell
you I've learned the truth about what

happened and that I've done as you wished, Da. I made sure justice was done.

Ben was betrayed by a traitor in the unit. It wasn't Lieutenant Hawke, as I thought for a time. I was wrong about her. It was the unit's Intelligence Officer, Lieutenant Weldon Hershorn. He betrayed the Aces. We tracked him down and killed him, and then, as I'm sure you've already heard on the news-vids, we struck at Morrison's Extractors and made them pay for what they did.

Ben's death at Birdsong Ridge has been made right. Now we can all breathe a little easier and go on with our lives.

Major Able promoted me to Corporal for my fighting on Gillfillan's Gold and The Rack and offered me a chance to return home. I did not accept the offer. Da, I know you sent me here for the sake of Ben, but I feel a part of the Aces now. This is my new home. I owe these people something for Ben, to fill the place he once held. That will make me feel that all things are now truly right.

I never thought to become a MechWarrior, but these are good people and I think Ben would have wanted me to fulfill his obligation to the unit. I'm doing this in his memory, and I hope you will understand.

You have my love and my promise that I will come home on leave to see you both as soon as I can.

Signed,
Corporal Harley Rassor

END OF MESSAGE TEXT

Lieutenant Hawke read over the printout Harley handed her, then returned it to him. She leaned back in her chair and looked at the young MechWarrior sitting on the other side of her desk. "This is what you sent your family?"

"Yes," he said. "I thought about it a lot. Telling them the truth about Ben wouldn't bring him back. If anything, it would kill my father, if not in body, then in spirit. I know it's a lie, but all that would be gained from the truth is pain and shame. This way Ben died honorably, and no one else is hurt."

She nodded. "I had the same thought in submitting my after-action report. Anyone who reads that report will learn that neither of us managed to discover the identity of that *Timber Wolf* pilot. I used the words 'unnamed pirate.'" She chuckled slightly at the phrase.

"I appreciate that, Lieutenant."

"I didn't do it for you, Corporal Rassor. It's a lot like what you did for your family. And like what you did for Ben in the end. That wasn't easy for you."

"It was hard, sir. But not as hard as living every day knowing what he'd done to this unit and our people."

"He fooled us all, Harley, not just you, me too."

"I don't know where he changed, where he went bad. But I do know this, I'm going to make right what he did, if it takes my whole life."

Livia Hawke leaned forward, looking into his eyes. "Setting something right that's wrong is a noble cause, Corporal. Just don't let it consume your life."

Harley smiled. "Not consume, Lieutenant, give

meaning to." He rose and saluted before she could give him any more to think about. Besides, he had a busy schedule of drills and simulations ahead of him. And until he made good the deaths of the men and women who had died because of his brother's actions, Able's Aces would remain his home and his mission in life.

About the Author

Blaine Pardoe has been writing for BattleTech® for over thirteen years. He has contributed to over forty books, including the BattleTech® novels *Highlander Gambit*, *Impetus of War*, and *Exodus Road*, and most recently his first *MechWarrior* novel, *Roar of Honor*.

He is also senior manager, in charge of Technology Education Services, at the firm of Ernst & Young LLP in his day job. He is a recognized industry expert, and his articles on technology education often appear in trade journals. He earned his B.A. and M.A. from Central Michigan University.

His book on office politics, *Cubicle Warfare*, was a bestseller and earned him international media recognition as an authority on the workplace. He has authored numerous books on computer games under the Brady imprint. He is also a fan of the American Civil War and has written several articles on the subject as well as having an interesting collection of artifacts.

Blaine Pardoe lives with his family in Amissville, VA, near the mountains in a new house dubbed Desperation Overlook. On those evenings when he is not writing, researching, or playing computer games, you can hear the mournful skirl of his bagpipes in the breeze—much to the chagrin of his neighbors.

For those that wish to reach him personally, he is available at Bpardoe870@aol.com.

Mel Odom is well known to readers of the Shadowrun® line for his popular novels *Preying for Keeps*, *Headhunters*, and *Run Hard, Die Fast.* He is also writing novels for TSR's Forgotten Realms setting, for Sabrina the Teenage Witch, and Alex Mack, and a popular ongoing adventure series. He is an inductee of Oklahoma's Professional Writers' Hall of Fame. He can be reached at denimbyte@aol.com and welcomes comments.

Inner Sphere Designations for Clan 'Mechs

Clan Name	Inner Sphere Name
Adder	Puma
Bane	Kraken
Black Python	Viper
Conjurer	Hellhound
Dire Wolf	Daishi
Executioner	Gladiator
Fire Moth	Dasher
Gargoyle	Man O'War
Glass Spider	Galahad
Hellbringer	Loki
Horned Owl	Peregrine
Howler	Baboon
Ice Ferret	Fenris
Incubus	Vixen
Kit Fox	Uller
Mad Dog	Vulture

Mist Lynx	Koshi
Huntsman	Nobori-nin
Nova	Black Hawk
Stone Rhino	Behemoth
Stormcrow	Ryoken
Summoner	Thor
Timber Wolf	Mad Cat
Vapor Eagle	Goshhawk
Viper	Dragonfly
Warhawk	Masakari

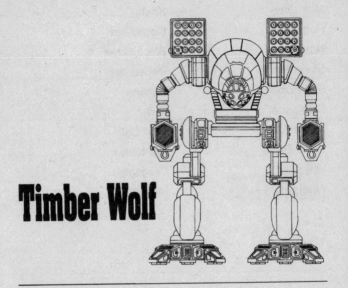

Timber Wolf

Black Knight

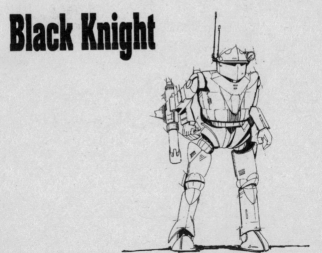

Enforcer

Orion

Hatchetman

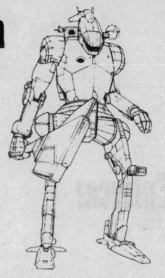

Vindicator

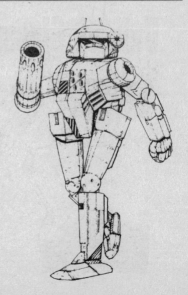

Lucifer Fighter

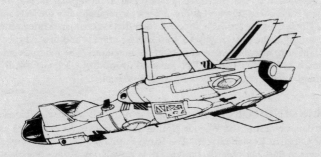

Union-C Class DropShip

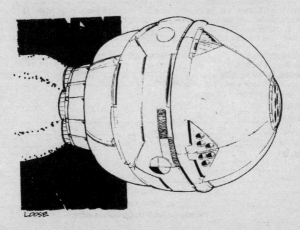

LOOSE